TO HAVE, NOT HOLD!

Carina McEvoy

Published by Carina McEvoy

Text Copyright © 2016 Carina McEvoy

Edited by Deirdre O'Flynn

Cover Illustration & Design © 2016 Fergus Slevin

ISBN: 978-0-9935941-0-6

Also available as an e-book

Hope you enjoy
the Story!
Carina Mc Evoy.

DEDICATION

For all my family and friends who believed in me, even when I didn't
believe in myself!

ACKNOWLEDGMENTS

Thank you to everybody who played a part in making this book a reality! To you Brian, for your constant support and to Anna and Ellie, for such humorous inspiration!

To my wonderful parents and my three beautiful sisters Liz, Miriam and Rebecca, thank you for everything.

Brenda and Amy, thank you for your valuable help.

Thank you to all my amazing friends, for all the encouragement you have all showered upon me during the writing of this book.

Last but definitely not least, thank you so much to the readers of this book, I hope you enjoy it.

xxx

PROLOGUE

If Emma was ever to imagine a prehistoric bar, this would be it. The stink of testosterone alone was enough to overpower the concoction of all the clashing perfumes. The men all resembled cavemen on the hunt for a woman. Presumably to club over the head and carry her rather unromantically back to his cave. The women must have mistaken the dress code for primitive wear. Or *lack* of wear to be more exact! Poor frozen little things mustn't have really got the whole concept of clothes yet. Emma guessed thongs, however, were all in, seeing as there was no obvious visible panty line in sight. This of course, suddenly made her very aware of her own big bum squashing cellulite rather unflatteringly against her black trousers. She'd have worn her own thongs but she hated the way they were swallowed up by her ass cheeks. Then by the end of the night she'd have to go look for them with a tweezers.

Multi-tasking was high on the agenda however she noted. Almost every single girl was amazingly able to flick their hair, pout, smile and sip from a multi-coloured cocktail…complete with erect little finger all at the same time. Their little fingers probably weren't the only erect things in the bar Emma mused to herself, giving the amount of spillage falling out of the majority of the bras in the place.

The gorgeous nude high heel open toe shoes she bought earlier on were now like shoes of sadistic nails. They looked amazing in the shop window and the sales assistant insisted that their intricate pattern and shimmering finish made her legs look extra-long! Surely a shoe with a heel the size of a telephone pole would make anyone's legs look long. She assured her the leather would soften up nicely so that they'd fit like a glove in no time. Emma wasn't really convinced but she had to admit they were absolutely gorgeous and, sure, how much pain could she be in? She'd be sitting all night anyway. But, now, as she stood in the overcrowded bar being knocked around by drunken idiots, she couldn't wait to get home and sling them off. That's if she could even get them off. She was fairly sure her feet had swelled up to twice their size.

She hated this kind of bar, it was really not her scene at all. She wanted to slouch over a drink at the bar and be able to have an actual conversation with Siobhan. She couldn't actually hear a thing because the music was deafening so she just smiled now and again and nodded her head enthusiastically. She didn't want Siobhan to notice that she was actually having about as much fun as someone suffering from arachnophobia at a spider convention!

Siobhan had begged Emma to come up for the night. She wanted to introduce her to Alex. Her gorgeous work colleague. He looked a lot older than Siobhan, Emma guessed by about five or six years, and he had an air of maturity about him. She insisted they were only friends but it was obvious that she fancied the arse off him and he certainly only had eyes for her. They were chatting and laughing so much that they hadn't even noticed that their other colleagues had moved on to another bar leaving Emma feeling like a massive awkward gooseberry.

Her self-confidence was doing its absolute best to do a disappearing act leaving her all on her tod. She had felt great earlier on, as her sleek black trousers and new red top showcased her curvaceous figure perfectly. But then of course, Siobhan sauntered in dressed in a gorgeous little black sleeveless number, exhibiting her skinny frame.

'Well thanks a million!' Emma utter with an instant feeling of deflation.

'What for?' asked Siobhan, puzzled.

'Well, I spent quite a bit of money on this new top and I was feeling….well….. nice….then you appear looking bloody amazing as per usual! Can you not just look crap once so I can feel good?'

'Don't be ridiculous, you look hot!'

'Hardly. Unless it's a pig on a spit you're talking about, I'm sure they're pretty hot!'

'Don't be silly,' Siobhan giggled, 'you have a great figure.'

'Siobhan, I look like an overweight pig…wrapped up *badly* in cling film…with bulges of fat spilling out everywhere!'

'Hardly, you look really sexy in that outfit, I bet you anything the guys will be falling over themselves to chat you up.'

'I've heard the guys would chat up a bag of spuds in this place we're going to, so forgive me if I'm not overly ecstatic at any romantic advances. Plus I'd imagine the only reason they will be falling over will be due to the copious amount of alcohol consumed and nothing to do with my overly expensive top,' Emma moaned, as she pulled a lock of her gorgeous long wavy brown hair behind her ear.

Siobhan could never understand how her best friend couldn't see just how beautiful she actually was. She was an average height and although she carried a few extra pounds she carried it well. In fact Siobhan was sure that other women would only love to have Emma's curvy figure. Her beautiful blue eyes peered out from her round fair skinned face showing a slight vulnerability that only seemed to highlight her beauty even more.

They were on a rare night out together. Before Emma moved home to

Kilfarrig three years previously, they were out every single weekend. They didn't like to admit it but Friday nights were now spent half asleep dribbling in front of some chat show or other. Their friendship however was still as strong as it was when they grew up together in the beautiful coastal town Kilfarrig. After school they hightailed it to the big city together in search of some sort of exposure to a more interesting life. Or night life more to the point. They took pride in their little pokey flat and actually managed to pass all their college exams despite living the high life of cheap vodka and instant noodles! Although in fairness to Siobhan, she actually really put the hours in with the books whereas Emma seemed to be able to glide through her course work effortlessly.

Emma moved home to Kilfarrig when a teaching position opened up in her old school and Siobhan remained on in the city working as a solicitor. Siobhan found it easy to get a job but she found the actual work rather tedious to begin with. Her big break came when she landed a job in O'Callaghan Solicitors. They were well known and it was Siobhan's dream to work for such a high-profile firm. She heard that William, the founder and boss of the firm, only hired the best. So, in a way, it was validation for all the hard work. She came top of the class in most of her exam results and now, all the hard slogging had paid off.

Feeling like a spare wheel, Emma was just about to call it a night when all of a sudden she got a darting pain in her right foot and her big toe felt like it had been completely squashed to the floor. A blond-haired guy turned to her in horror at the realisation that he had just slammed the heel of his size ten shoes right down on her foot.

'Oooouuuucccchhhh, you.......gobsh.........,' Emma threw out a hand to push him away and reached down for her maimed foot with the other. But as she looked up, all she could see was a gorgeous face with piercing blue eyes, attached to a tall muscular body looking down at her in complete dismay.

'Ohhhh, I am so sorry, are you okay?' asked the gorgeous guy while grabbing onto her by the arm. His gorgeous face now distorted with worry.

'Emma, what happened?' Siobhan cried, actually taking her attention away from Alex long enough to show an appropriate amount of concern for her friend.

'It's okay, it's okay, I'm grand,' she insisted, feeling a little embarrassed by all the attention.

'Oh no, is your toe bleeding?' even Alex was all concerned now. 'I'll get you some ice.'

'It's grand, honestly, I'm fine,' she insisted as everybody began examining her foot. She soon felt her face go as red as her big toe.

'No, no, it's bleeding alright. Come over to my table and sit down, I insist, here lean on me, it's just over there.' The hunky guy put his arm around her and dragged her over to his table where a group of lads all looked at her and then her squashed foot.

'Ah now, what did you go and do to the poor girl, Aidan? Can you not just chat her up in the usual manner, do you have to injure her to get her to sit with you?' his friends slagged away but he was too concerned about her toe to notice.

Emma was mortified now, there were big blobs of blood at the top of the nail just creeping out from under her white French tip. Alex came over with some ice wrapped up in a cloth and Aidan, the hunk, took her foot and proceeded to take her shoe off. She nearly died, she was sure that he'd need a crowbar to get it off and, if he did manage to get it off, he'd be greeted with a nasty sweaty foot smell. She moved her foot out of his hand, adamant it was okay, but he wouldn't hear of it. After a few seconds of pulling at the shoe which felt like a few hours to the crimson-faced Emma, he gently applied the ice and told one of his friends to get her a strong drink from the bar.

Siobhan could tell she was feeling uncomfortable with her mangled smelly foot in the hands of a stranger, a rather handsome stranger at that, so she tried to make light of the situation.

'Gosh, Emma, now I know how to get a seat in a crowded bar, you crafty cow,' she laughed and looked up at Alex who was laughing with a little more enthusiasm than someone who was just a colleague. When Emma assured everyone she was not going to die and she was sure her toe would not be acquiring an amputation anytime soon, Siobhan and Alex went back into their own little world with a population of two.

Aidan's friend came back with a round of shots. They clinked glasses and down the hatch they went. She could feel the alcohol gently heat her throat as it slid down. She had almost forgotten about her throbbing big toe in the hands of the hunky Aidan until he took the cloth off, examined said toe, and seemed happy that it wasn't broken.

'I can't apologise enough, I feel terrible, I really do. Is it still really sore?'

He was so cute that Emma hadn't really heard what he had said, she was hypnotised by his blue eyes and extremely black eyelashes. How come some guys are naturally born with eyelashes that women pump mascara on to get the same effect?

When she hadn't said anything for a minute, he looked even more concerned. 'Are you alright?'

'Oh yeah, I'm fine now, honestly. The pain is almost gone!' she lied.

'Oh good, I'm glad, I feel like such an idiot stamping on your poor foot,' he looked at her with a really cheeky grin and found her blushing face endearing. 'I'm Aidan,' he said while holding out his hand to formally introduce himself, 'foot stomper and your personal slave for the rest of the night. Now, what can I get you from the bar?'

The next morning, Emma hobbled into the kitchen nursing a major hangover. 'Oh, my head, I haven't had that much to drink in ages. Have you got something I can take? There's no way I can drive home like this.'

Siobhan was pouring out two cups of coffee and turned to her friend with a smile on her face. 'Well, Aidan did seem to supply rather a lot of alcohol after the foot compression incident. Poor guy was in an awful state. He was lovely though, wasn't he? What does he do again? Oh yeah, a guard, bet you wouldn't mind being cuffed by him eh?'

'Yeah, he was so nice, we talked and talked all night and he was such a gentleman. I can't believe he waited with me till we got a taxi. Then again, he probably thought I'd need the company by the way you and your so-called colleague were wrapped up in each other. So much for you definitely not being into him. What time did he leave anyway?'

Siobhan suddenly seemed overcome with a bout of fictional coughing as Alex came into the kitchen and planted a kiss on her forehead. 'Morning, Emma, how's the toe?'

Even though Siobhan looked a little awkward, Emma could see a glint in her eye. Siobhan gave her a sizzling alka-seltzer and told her to knock it back. It was clear she was trying to ignore the fact that the colleague she swore she wasn't interested in was standing right behind her with a smile painted on his face that made it pretty obvious that they were at it like rabbits all night. Emma wasn't so sure what the big deal was – Siobhan and Alex were hardly the only colleagues in the world to get it on.

'Siobhan's just a little worried about what the boss will say, aren't you, babe?' said Alex casually.

'Sure what the hell does it have to do with him anyway? By the sounds of it, he's a stiff old gobshite anyway, all work and no play. Maybe he could do with a good seeing to himself, isn't that right, Siobhan?' Emma said as she tilted back her head and poured the glass of bubbling solution into her mouth, never noticing Siobhan's face.

'Ah, I don't know what my mam would have to say about that,' chuckled Alex, 'besides, Dad is only happy when he's working.'

Emma coughed and the contents of her mouth sprayed all over them as it dawned on her that he was the boss's son!

The two girls were flaked out on the sofas in the living room a couple of hours later. 'I still can't believe I said that, you could've bloody warned me he was your boss's son.'

'You have to admit, it was hilarious! He thought so too. Isn't he incredible? He hopes to take over the firm someday. He lives and breathes for that place!'

'Oh that's not healthy, Siobhan, people need a work-life balance. If not, we end up so stressed we can be easy targets for heart attacks and other yokes.'

'Nonsense, a bit of hard work never harmed anybody,' Siobhan scolded. 'anyway, tell me more about this Aidan guy. Think you'll meet him again?'

'Oh yeah, for sure, he's incredible!' Emma replied with a dreamy look on her glowing face.

'Awe! You sound totally smitten.'

'I am! In fact, even though I only just met him, I really do think he's the one! I just have this amazing feeling that he's going to be really special.'

'Wow! He really has made an impression on you, hasn't he? Despite trying to manually amputate your big toe.' Siobhan giggled.

'Yes, he has!' Emma responded more seriously. 'I know this may sound a bit weird but I really think I'm gonna spend the rest of my life with him!'

CHAPTER ONE

TEN YEARS LATER...

Emma yawned as she lay back on the grass. She stared up at the clouds in the sky, they were just like little balls of cotton wool floating along through life without a care in the world. They looked extra white against the backdrop of the amazing blue sky. For a late September's day, it was certainly a beautiful one. Although there was a slight breeze, it was a warm one, enveloping her in comfort.

She closed her eyes and concentrated on her other senses. She loved more than anything to hear the sound of the waves creeping up onto the beach. She loved to smell the sea, she'd sometimes just breathe in the unique coastal scent. Feeling comfortable, she continued to ramble on.

'Of course, I'd have to wait to leave my shopping till Saturday afternoon. It was so busy and I had to bring Amy with me. I really thought giving her the Winnie the Pooh ball would keep her satisfied long enough for me to whizz round to get the few bits, I hadn't expected her to aggressively fire it at everybody. And, to top it all off, she was so excited that it was Winnie the Pooh she felt the need shout "Pooh" all over the supermarket!' Emma laughed at the memory of it now.

'And sure then, at the checkout she cunningly manipulated me to buy her some sweets, like as if she needed the sugar to make her any more hyper,' she giggled, looking over at Aidan. He always said he could never get a word in once she started on one of her rants.

Emma continued to tell her nightmare story, determined to get across just how hard shopping with tiny people can be. 'She was grand then for a few minutes so I could throw the few bits from the trolley onto the check out, but then I heard her give out stink to the poor check-out lady. She actually told her she was very greedy for taking her sweets and asked her why she couldn't go and get her own bag seen as she worked in the shop! Mortified I was.' She looked over at Aidan to amplify the 'mortified.'

'So, I gently explained to Amy through gritted teeth that the lady wasn't greedy and she'd get her sweets in a second. But oh no, a full-on tantrum was brewing, her face was going red, and yep you guessed it, she stamped her foot!' Emma said as she looked over at Amy, now busy playing some made up game with the hundred pebbles she insisted on collecting from the beach earlier.

'Naturally, I began to panic. All I could think was, oh no, please don't make a show of me here, in front of all these people. Dread filled my whole body and the two seconds in which the lady was scanning the sweets felt like a lifetime. I wanted to hurl myself across the checkout and scan the bloody sweets myself. I could sense the other mothers looking on at the situation as it was beginning to unfold. I could feel their disapproval of me as a mother. I could hear the 'tut tuts' and in my mind I could see the heads shaking. Of course I didn't actually *see* anyone looking at me but paranoia got the better of me. Just as Amy's incredible hulk was about to emerge fully, I grabbed the sweets out of the lady's hands, expertly yanked them open and shoved about seven of them straight into Amy's mouth. Oh thank Goodness, tantrum averted.' Emma sighed, reliving the stressful experience in her head.

'And then, guess what happened......while she munched away on the chocolate, I had a few moments peace to pack the bags. I was flying it, doing really well, then all I heard was "No no no....that's my pooooool!" I tell you, I grabbed that flippin ball as quick as I could, paid and got the hell out of there.' She took a deep breath after divulging all the nitty gritty of the situation and allowed the stress of it all to melt away.

She loved her Sunday mornings, she always did. She'd rabbit on about all her gossip, her students, any little thing that would have happened to her during the week and Aidan would just lay there and listen, happy enough for her to go on and on. Although sometimes she suspected he had drifted off but he'd always insist he hadn't, yet he couldn't quite remember the last thing she had said.

No news with Siobhan and Alex yet, they're still trying. God love them, it's been almost a year now! She doesn't really talk about it but, sure it must be getting to her. Alex is mad to have kids. He's really cut back on the workload. Can you believe it? She more or less runs things now. It's no bother to her though; she's a real career girl isn't she?' Emma said not waiting for an answer. 'She's worked all her life to get to where she is. It's lovely to see it all pay off for her, nobody deserves it more. But she loves her work, loves being busy. Well, when baby comes, God knows she'll be busy twenty-four seven. I really hope it happens for them soon,' she said as she looked over at Amy. There was no doubt that no matter how crazy Amy drove her, she felt incredibly lucky to have her. She was just so cute. Big blue eyes, the most amazing big pouting lips that many celebrities would pay good money for and light brown hair with gorgeous curls just touching her shoulders. Emma hadn't the heart to cut it yet. She couldn't imagine Amy sitting still long enough to have it cut anyway!

'As for Jack. Don't even ask. He'll never settle down. He's such a ladies man, isn't he?' she asked and again didn't wait for an answer. 'Even though the summer season is over and things have quietened down for him in the pub but he still manages to bring home the ladies. He's a good-looking bloke but, my God, he is one hell of a slut. He's no shame either. He never has any intention of seeing the girl again. How does he get away with it? Honest to God, last night the screaming, "Oh Jack, Jack, yessss, yessss, yeesssss!!!" I felt like banging on the wall myself and screaming, "Oh nooo, Jack, noooo, noooo noooo!" She called out in a far too inappropriate tone for a Sunday morning. 'The Cellar is not doing as good lately. Since August, it's just gone dead. The locals don't seem to be going out anyway. He's fairly worried. Thank God we had a good summer with the weather and it drew in a lot of holidaymakers, that's all I can say. Oh listen to me go on and on again as per usual.'

Amy ran over to Emma with a look of concern plastered on her face.
'Mammmmmy, I need more peggles, I don't have enough.'
'My goodness honey, if we go and get anymore pebbles there'll be no more left on the beach.' Emma giggled. Amy always managed to make Emma smile, she had a wonderful way of just melting her heart. Well, almost always. Emma's heart was fairly melt-resistant at two in the morning.

Amy pointed down to where Aidan lay and smiled. 'Daddy.'
'Yes honey, Daddy is resting, isn't he?'
They spent the next ten minutes tickling and laughing while Aidan was left alone to relax in peace and quiet. Amy soon got bored however and demanded juice.
'Okay, sweetheart, it's about time we went home anyway, Granny and Grandad are coming for dinner.'
She took Amy's hand and looked down at where Aidan lay with that same sadness she always felt when it was time to go. Closing her eyes, she lovingly kissed her index finger and gently placed it on Aidan's headstone. 'I love you forever, sweetheart.'

CHAPTER TWO

'You are an animal Alex O'Callaghan; I can't keep up with you anymore!' Siobhan said as she lay sprawled out on their king size bed. Their royal blue silk sheets abandoned on the floor. She lay with her eyes closed in a total state of bliss feeling energised and relaxed at the same time.

'I aim to please, my dear wife.' Alex replied, lying beside her feeling equally blissful. He turned his head and lovingly admired Siobhan's body with his eyes and there was certainly a hell of a lot to admire.

Sexy and muscular, he turned till he was lying on his side, resting his dark tanned face on his hand. The muscles were protruding from his upper arm as his elbow locked his frame into place securely so he could admire her body that much better from a slight angle. And admire he did, slowly letting his eyes drink in every inch of her as he studied every molecule of her being from the strands of ruffled jet black shoulder length hair that now lay sprawled out on the sheets around her amazingly defined perfect face, with those pouting pink lips sticking out a mile and her amazing cheekbones. He led his eyes down her neck towards her perfectly sized breasts. His eyes wandered further south over her tanned flat and toned stomach, past her hip bones edging out and leading onto her long dark toned legs right down to her professionally painted toenails which exaggerated the slenderness of her feet even more.

'You are absolutely gorgeous do you know that?' he whispered seductively.

Then, without even being conscious of it, his hands reached out to her again. Alex could never admire his wife's body with his eyes alone. As soon as he was finished taking in all of her size ten frame with his eyes, he was ready to do it all over again with this hands and eventually with his body.

Siobhan smiled as she opened her eyes to reveal a stunning green colour surrounding her black pupils now dilated with a newly awakened desire. She turned her head toward Alex with a look of intense satisfaction and complete intention of allowing his body to do all the admiring yet again. Alex smiled knowingly and did just that.

Later on, Siobhan was examining herself in the full-length mirror. Placing her hands on her hips, she stood facing away from the mirror and glanced backwards to see the reflection of the back of her body. She was relatively happy with what she saw. All the exercising and dieting had sculptured her body the way she had always wanted, slim and very toned.

She had to work hard at it though. She spent every morning on her treadmill and also spent time doing all her pilates' moves, keeping her tummy and bum in perfect shape. She was partial to the odd cup of coffee but mostly drank herbal tea which she felt kept the cellulite at bay, that and the numerous laps she'd swim in the pool a couple of nights a week. She looked closely at the fine silver stretch marks on her hip bones and frowned.

'I hate these stretch marks,' she sighed, 'no matter how hard I exercise, how healthy my diet is or how bloody expensive the cream I use is, they just will not fade!'

Alex looked at her from the bed. 'Honey, did you not hear what I said earlier? You are gorgeous! Besides I thought you saw them as your purpose to keep up the exercise, no?' Her mother was a baker for the local coffee shop. She made the most divine cakes and breads and years of tasting banana and walnut muffins, chocolate chip and orange cheesecakes had made Siobhan a very plump girl.

'Ah I know, I just don't want to end up like my parents that's all.' she replied. Both her parents were stout people carrying nicely rounded bellies and meaty cheeks, both above and below the stomach!

'Ah Siobhan, that's just their build, what's this your mother always says…..oh yeah, their big boned!' Alex laughed, defending his parents in law.

'Big bones my ass, it's more to do with fat laden cakes and an all sugar and butter diet,' she said in disgust, 'so unhealthy, besides, I'm proof it's not big bones aren't I?

'Yes you are honey.' Alex said as he got out of bed and headed for the en-suite. He had the fat little girl turn to golf club figure talk so many times now it wasn't really interesting anymore.

'I mean, look at me now, okay I know I could do with losing a couple of pounds but….'

Alex poked his head around the door to interrupt her. 'Eh, where exactly have you got weight to lose Siobhan? You're like…so slim, if you lose anymore I won't be able to see you!' He didn't wait for a reply; he went straight into the shower, tired of all the body nonsense talk.

Siobhan thought about what he had said. She was slim, she'd give herself that. But she always felt she could do with another pound off. She was terrified of becoming that pudgy little girl again. Her parents thought it was great she was bordering on obesity before she was even ten years old! Their mentality was that if she ever got sick sure she'd have a few pounds to spare.

It was really only when she started becoming interested in teen mags and pop bands that she realised she was, well let's just say, a tad chubby.

She didn't look anything like the unnaturally skinny pale and washed out looking girls in the magazines. She never really noticed just how ridiculously flawless they looked however. Images of skeleton models were her idols and her motivation to lose weight! She soon slimmed right down to a skinny little thing. By her final year in school, the memories of a young pudgy girl were long gone, much to the disapproval of her parents who thought she looked sick all the time. She could still remember her father shouting at her every time she ran out the door past him. 'Would you ever put a bit of meat on those bones of yours girl, you look like a flippin' coat hanger!'

Once she went to college, she ate feck all and worked extra hard to tone up and become a mere shadow of her former self. The dizzy spells were a nuisance of a side effect. Her best friend Emma couldn't understand Siobhan's incredible transformation. Emma's idea of tackling any extra pounds was to moan about it while scoffing into a dirty creamy large éclair with plenty of chocolate sauce dribbled generously on top.

Though Emma didn't really have much to complain about. She wasn't stick thin but was more of a normal shape, not too thin or not too big. Plus being an ideal weight never bothered her anyway. Emma seemed to float so easily through life and everything seemed to fall into her lap. Siobhan had to work hard at everything. It took a lot of study, time and commitment to become the brilliant solicitor she was. And she felt like she had done it without much support. Emma sailed through her final school exams and her Bachelor of Education degree without even batting an eyelid. She was one of those people who didn't even need to study. Everything came so easy to her. Her mother was always on the phone to her during her college years asking her how she was getting on, did she need anything, telling her how proud they were of her.

Siobhan couldn't help but feel a little envious at times. Her mother was disappointed she didn't show an interest in following in her baking footsteps. She had dreamed of passing on her recipes and teaching her daughter how to knead bread. But Siobhan had zero interest; instead she slogged her brains out in school to get into a Bachelor of Law degree, while her parents showed little interest in her studies. As long as she was healthy they didn't really care too much about anything else.

After that she worked her arse off as an apprentice to gain admission to the roll of solicitors. It was a long road but she had got there. Emma, of course, walked into a job straight away after finishing her course and went onto a fairly decent salary ladder. Although Siobhan was earning the big money now, she couldn't help but think that Emma had had life much easier, up until Aidan of course. His death was an unbelievably traumatic event in her friend's life. Siobhan had been so worried for her for so long and, truth be told, she still was. Very worried, in fact!

CHAPTER THREE

Siobhan quickly snapped out of her self-examination when Alex came out of the en-suite with a little white towel around his waist, drying his slightly dark but greying hair. He came over, stood behind her and began kissing her neck.

'Just imagine, honey, we could've made a little bit of you and a little bit of me all mixed up together this morning,' he smiled, looking at her in the mirror with his hands covering her stomach.

She smiled back at him, studying his happy face for a few moments, and then walked away and into the en-suite. They had been trying for a baby for ages now but nothing was happening.

'With your looks and brains and with my amazingly positive and charming personality, where can our child go wrong?' Alex called out to her.

Siobhan raised her eyebrows and walked back out to the bedroom.

'Are you saying I don't have a positive and charming personality?'

'Not at all honey, you've a wonderful personality, very charming. You just tend to, you know, look on the more serious side of life. You like to be the serious one taking charge but believe me, I don't mind you exerting your power over me at all!' Alex looked over at her with a cheeky grin.

Siobhan was less than impressed though. Reminiscing about her younger years had actually put her in bad form. 'Yeah, fair enough Alex, I'm fairly serious but I've had to bloody work hard to get where I am. It was alright for you growing up with rich mammy and daddy and being handed your first car and your college fees and then inheriting your daddy's solicitors' firm where you didn't even had to work at getting a good name for yourself. Any son of William O'Callaghan was a sure bet. Besides, you were the serious type not so long ago, you know, till you had your little warning to slow down. You should be very grateful that I'm around and willing to take over so you can play golf all day and swan around with nothing to do.'

'Little warning Siobhan? I had a bloody heart attack! I think at the age of forty-one a full-blown ticker attack is enough for any man to have a little rethink about his life. All work and no play is no good for anyone you know. Anyway, you're exaggerating. I do more than play golf all day, I'll have you know. I love having my odd cuppa coffee and brown scone in Lily's too.' He grinned.

Siobhan zipped up her skinny jeans and rolled her eyes up to heaven. Alex was always messing around these days and sometimes it was hard to have a serious adult conversation with him. He had changed so much from his pre-heart attack days.

'Look I seen what happened my dad, he worked so hard all his life. Too hard! He was hardly ever home. Too busy making sure my sisters and I could have everything we needed and could go to the best schools and that…He didn't just hand over money he picked off a tree Siobhan, he work damn hard for it.'

'I know, I'm sorry, I know how devastated you were when he died.' Siobhan said in a gentle voice.

'Not to mention scared shitless at inheriting the firm! I didn't think I was ready. I just wanted to make him proud.'

Alex was devastated by the loss of his father. Of his siblings, he was by far the closest to him and knew just how hard he worked for the family. Alex understood that his father's distance from his kids was more than made up for in the amount of work he put into ensuring they had a secure life financially. After his father died, he felt the need to really look after them. He worked so hard to be as good as him at the business and to make sure everybody was cared for. Truth was, his father's life assurance pretty much made sure his mother was taken care of for the rest of her days and he had left a little nest egg to each of his children. But for many years, Alex slaved away at the business to make sure he was doing his father proud by following in his footsteps.

He was following in his footsteps alright. The heart attack was a big wake-up call. He had worked hard for years maintaining the business as the success it was when he fully took it over but he was also working hard at digging his own grave. The heart attack was enough to frighten him into changing his ways however. He had sat in the hospital bed for days thinking about what he really wanted from life and where he was headed. A family! That was it, he wanted a family.

And so things changed. He decided to semi-retire from the business and concentrate on getting really fit and healthy instead. He cut down his working hours and only went into the office three days a week. He made sure to be out at closing time and on the road home. He reduced the amount of high-profile clients he usually worked with and reduced his stress levels. But he still wanted to feel he had made his dad proud.

'Of course you made him proud, don't mind me, I'm just being narky!' Siobhan admitted.

'Listen I know how much you've had to take on since I took a step back, but if you want to cut back on some workload too you can, why don't you cut back on the amount of clients you take on.? We can afford to sit back more now and besides we have a great team working for us now too.' Alex said casually.

'Alex, I was more than happy to take over the reins a bit, sure I love it,' she said. Siobhan was still very much into the business although she never really got frazzled or stressed. She loved going out to work and loved being the one to come home to Alex's gourmet meals at night time. He discovered a passion for Asian cuisine and tried out all sorts of healthy dishes on her.

'Ah I know you do, but you'll have to learn to cut back on work someday soon anyway once little baby O'Callaghan arrives!' he said while smiling like a Cheshire cat. All he wanted now was a son or daughter.

Siobhan stood at the sink in her en-suite and looked at her face in the mirror. At thirty-six, she looked good but there was no mistaking the sadness in her eyes. Alex was beginning to mention babies almost every day now. It was a year since his life-altering wake-up call and his decision to start a family and he was beginning to get a bit obsessed with it. She was feeling the pressure big time and felt awful that she hadn't conceived yet. Why wasn't she able to give the man she loved what he wanted most out of life. She knew he'd be a terrific father. They had everything a child would ever need. It would be financially secure, brought into a loving home, and have everything it could ever want. So why couldn't she just get pregnant? She looked at her sad eyes gazing back at her and rubbed her tummy. She had achieved everything in her life she set out to so why was she a complete failure when it came to the most natural thing in the world? She had searched every part of her mind so deeply for answers. But to no avail. She just wasn't cut out for it. The most natural thing a woman could do and yet she couldn't.

She sighed deeply as she opened the cabinet drawer and took out her make-up bag. She waited to make sure Alex wasn't coming in. When she was sure he was in the bedroom getting dressed, she popped a tiny contraceptive pill from its pack into her mouth. She hid the pills carefully away and then looked at herself in the mirror again.

This time she saw deceit in her eyes. And she knew that if he ever found out, it would shatter their marriage completely.

CHAPTER FOUR

The scent of strong black coffee wafted out of the coffee machine in the kitchen and made its way up the staircase and into the bedroom where Adele lay asleep on the bed. Even in her sleep, there was no mistaking the smell of the coffee luring her downstairs for a hangover pick-me-up.

She opened her eyes and looked around the room for the first time. Not at all what she expected, it was spotless for a single guy living on his own. No clothes to be seen anywhere except her own clothes that were thrown on the floor in the heat of passion the previous night.

'Oh no, what time is it?' Adele said out loud as she shot up in the bed and looked over at the locker for the time. Ten forty-seven. 'Sugar!' she muttered. Her friends were going to be less than impressed with her if she didn't get back to the hotel before check-out time.

She had come over to Kilfarrig on a hen party weekend, although hooking up with the bar owner was unexpected. He was the typical tall, dark, and handsome type. With the kind of body you'd read about in a trashy novel. The kind of body Adele certainly didn't mind getting under. But then again the bar had been pretty empty so there wasn't much competition.

She jumped out of bed and dressed herself quickly and followed the coffee smell down the stairs. Jack was standing at the island in the kitchen with a cuppa in his hand, looking gorgeous. He had amazing dark brown eyes and jet black hair that had a slightly curly quiff and a really cute cheeky smile.

The kitchen was as clean and tidy as his bedroom. The whole place had a minimalist feel with as little furnishings as possible, but whatever he did have appeared to be very expensive and tasteful.

'Good morning, I was just about to call you. I thought I'd let you sleep in a little bit first though, seeing as you didn't get much sleep last night,' he said with that cute grin of his.

He got the milk out of the stainless steel American-style fridge which was just as clean inside as the rest of the kitchen. He was an ideal boyfriend actually, thoughtful, tidy, gorgeous and great in bed.

'Ehh, yeah, thanks. I really should get a move on though, I need to get back to the hotel and get showered, dressed, and packed. Our ferry doesn't leave Rosslare till three but the train leaves at 12.40. The gang will be fairly pissed with me if that ferry departs without us.'

'Oh well here, get this coffee down you and then I'll run you back to the hotel.'

Jack was happy that Adele was in a hurry to get going. He always hated the mornings after and the awkward hangers-on waiting for the proposal of a second date or something.

Jack certainly wasn't interested in any second dates. He wasn't even into first dates. A bit of fun on a Saturday night was about all he was interested in. He was never short of ladies wanting to spend time with him. Even though there were still those uncomfortable Sunday mornings when he had to bid farewell to a truly smitten woman in such a way that she knew it had only been a once off. He had put many a love-stricken girl into a taxi and waved her off.

'No, you don't need to drive me to the hotel. Sure I can get a taxi no problem, have you got a number I can call?' Adele was really only being polite now, she secretly hoped he'd insist on driving her back. She was dreading the walk of shame from his front door to the taxi in her extremely short and extremely revealing little black dress. Her high heels were gorgeous and made her legs look endless and sexy but on a Sunday morning, she had to admit they looked a tad tarty. She was also dreading bumping into the next-door neighbour. She had noticed last night that Jack lived in a semi-detached house. It didn't bother her at the time but now with a sober head, she was slightly embarrassed by her rather noisy antics the night before. She was sure the neighbour had heard her screaming with wonderful satisfaction.

'I'll drive you. Honestly, it's no trouble. I have to head into the bar anyway, I want to make sure we're all set for lunch.' Jack knocked back the last of his coffee and grabbed his car keys.

Adele realised he wasn't going to wait around for her to finish her coffee so she gulped down a mouthful, hoping it'd ease her drink induced foggy head but all it did was burn. There was no way she could possibly swallow it. It was scalding the skin off the roof of her mouth. She ran past Jack and spat the coffee out into the pristine clean sink. Wiping her mouth, she looked back at Jack who was standing there with a slightly dismayed look on his face. Ooops, thought Adele, embarrassed that her coffee splatter had dirtied his pristine sink.

He beeped a final goodbye to the latest notch on his bedpost as he drove away from the hotel. Adele waved and then disappeared inside. At least she wasn't going to be the result of them missing the train to the ferry back home, though she thought her pals might still be a little pissed off with her for leaving them last night. After all, she was the bride to be!

A few minutes later, Jack pulled up outside his wine bar. The Cellar was opening at twelve for lunch. Jack had had to let Laura go, much to his disappointment. She was a really conscientious worker and he hated letting her go, but the business was struggling and Jack had noticed it was getting quieter with every passing week.

As soon as the kids went back to school in September, the tourist season was well and truly over. His customer numbers and takings had both taken a nosedive. He even wondered whether opening for lunch would be worth his while at all. If things didn't look up soon, he was going to have to reconsider the entire business. He was lucky he owned his home which he bought outright with the inheritance but he was leasing the building for the bar, and that was being paid for by the money he took in from it. The money coming in was now shaky and so was his future as the proprietor. He was beginning to think that maybe his inheritance money was cursed; maybe he should have told his brother to shove it up his hole after all.

CHAPTER FIVE

'Oh, thank God for morning break! I was longing for a bit of vitamin D.' Tracy beamed while taking in the warmth of the sun.

Emma laughed out loud; Tracy was a good measure of tonic and certainly made supervising the kids at break times interesting. Anyone feeling a bit under the weather should definitely spend at least ten minutes with her to feel better.

'I mean, what is it with Irish weather? You'd swear it had it in for all teachers. Here we are, educating the youth of the land, the future of tomorrow. Teaching little Tommy O'Driscoll that picking his nose and showing the horrified little Amber Sweeney the big green snot on the end of his finger is not classed as nature time. Tommy can you go and get a tissue for that please, good man. Amber doesn't want to see the contents of your nose, don't you not Amber?' Tracy shouted across the yard. 'Honestly, that's just gross, I can actually see that snot from here!' she declared with disgust. 'Anyway as I was saying, we're the force behind tomorrow's great leaders, well okay maybe not Little Jason over there,' she paused to yell across the yard again, 'Jason sweetheart, can you take your foot off Keith's head, you'll break his glasses,' she threw her eyes to heaven before continuing, 'yeah, so we're here dedicated to our jobs, our wonderful children… What Lisa? No, you can show me your new dance move later, now go and play. Honestly you can't have a proper conversation in this yard, can you?'

'Well, in fairness, we are supervising the children!' Emma giggled as she looked around the yard at all the kids laughing and playing happily together. She was ever the diligent one, keeping a close eye on everything going on around her.

'Anyway, as I was trying to say, dare I get to finish, the weather teases us right before our summer holidays.' Tracy began mimicking the day's voice as only Tracy could imagine it and waving her arms around like a mad thing, 'Hello there, I'm a glorious day, I'm going to reach twenty-five degrees and the sun is going to shine all day, I'm going to lead you into a false sense of security so you'll go off and spend all your wages on the latest trend in summer clothes and summery eye shadows and the most beautiful if not a bit pricey but totally hot sexy sandals.' All of a sudden, her face changes completely to resemble a mad woman on Prozac. 'Then, as soon as you get your holidays, bang! Rain, wind, cold, rain, and more rain. But as soon as you go back to work, oh hello here comes the bloody sun again.

Oh, did I say bloody? I'm so sorry, sun, I didn't mean it, I love you, don't disappear,' she cried out with her arms in the air.

Emma couldn't help but smile at the sight of her nutter colleague begging the sun with open outstretched arms to hang around a bit longer.

'You know, not everyone's a complete freak when it comes to the sun Tracy. I can actually imagine you spending your days off peering out at the sky and running out naked to catch a few minutes sunshine. Besides, you're being far too harsh on our weather, we actually had a fantastic August. Myself and Amy enjoyed many a picnic on the beach. You just didn't stay around long enough to see it.'

'Ah yeah, crappy summer and sand sandwiches on freezing beaches with the umbrella just in case it buckets it down or baking beneath the real sun on beautiful white sandy beaches with a cocktail in one hand and a good book in the other...you choose. Anyway, I'm young and hell, you have to take advantage of the two reasons for becoming a teacher in the first place, don't you? Reasons being, one, July and two, August. I mean, come on, why else would we be here?'

'Emm, well, I'd like to think that the children are a pretty good reason, Tracy.' Laughed Emma while tucking her hair behind her ear.

'Ohh, yeah, the children, of course they're important. I'm just saying, why would I hang around? I'm young, beautiful, and not tied down to a boring husband...oh shit Emma, I'm sorry, me and my full-size idiotic gob!'

'Don't be silly, you don't have to watch your full-size idiotic gob for me. I'm perfectly fine and yes, I can see your point. You're young and certainly very beautiful, you should go out and see the world, enjoy yourself before you settle down.'

Tracy was still kicking herself when one of Emma's students, Isabelle, came over. She was adorable and smart beyond her years, even if she was only six. 'Hi Miss, I like your pretty dress today.' Emma's students were always coming over to her, she was idolised in the school and it was no surprise. She was gifted when it came to children. She was so patient and kind and managed to get the best out of all her students without them even realising. She was so encouraging and the students always left her class feeling upbeat, confident and happy. She had always wanted to be a teacher, to follow in her mother's footsteps. She had the same gentle nature her mother possessed all throughout her teaching life and still had to this day. Emma knew she had a way with children, with other people's children anyway. Her own little angel had her rightly wrapped around her little finger and Emma knew it. She often wondered how she could manage a room full of six-year-olds with her eyes shut but at times couldn't manage her own little diva at home!

'Thank you, Isabelle, you're very sweet, did you enjoy your weekend?'

'Oh yeah, it was very good, and daddy and mammy brought us to the park yesterday and we got ice-cream and a bar a chocolate, they were really happy. I think it's because God was good to them,' the little girl smiled innocently.

Emma looked confused. 'Oh, how do you mean Isabelle?'

'Well on Saturday night they were shouting to God for ages, then I heard mammy say, Oh God that was good!'

'Oh, okay, well eh, yeah, that's great, Isabelle. So you enjoyed your chocolate and ice cream anyway, that's great.'

Tracy was sniggering behind Emma's back as she tried to respond to the child's revelations that her parents were enjoying a few prayers at night.

'Miss, was God good to you over the weekend?' Isabelle just finished the sentence when the school bell rang signalling it was time to head back into class and not a minute too soon for Emma.

'Oh dear, there's the bell, love, run along now back into class and I'll be in in a minute.' She let out a deep breath as she watched Isabelle happily skip inside the building.

'Talk about being saved by the bell, but you know, Emma, you are young yourself. You should think about having a little company now and again, maybe go on a date or something.' Tracy was looking extremely sincere and compassionate as she spoke to Emma. She knew Emma was finding it hard to overcome Aidan's death. Even after all this time, Emma was still as devoted to Aidan as she was to him when he was here. She did seem to be a lot happier lately though. Up until recently, she refused to let go at all and even try to move on with her life. She loved him to the very core.

Emma smiled but said nothing; she was beginning to get slightly irritated at the people in her life suddenly deciding it was time for her to move on. Siobhan was especially starting to grate on her nerves. Why couldn't they just let leave her alone when it came to the whole, 'Emma, I'm just worried about you, you need to start living again!' conversation. Truth was, she wasn't alone, she could really feel him around more and more! He was with her, she was sure of it! And it was a wonderful feeling. When he died, a part of her died too. But then Amy came along, what a surprise that was! He had left her a truly miraculous gift. Part of him to live on. And now this too. She always knew she was destined to spend the rest of her life with him and the small matter of him being dead wasn't going to get in the way of her plans at all.

CHAPTER SIX

It was a pretty crap Thursday night for Jack. He sat in the corner of his empty bar and drank a bottle of beer. He knew that drinking the stock wasn't exactly going to help his financial situation but, he figured, what the hell! It was all going so wrong he may as well benefit from owning a pub for as long more as he possibly could.

It had been such a successful pub. Having had a steady trade of weekly and weekend punters. It was one of the best places in the village for bar food. Fresh fish off the boats and a local supply of reliable steaks and poultry made for a mouth-watering menu. He always got in great music on a Saturday night and made sure to have all the sport on in the background on a Sunday afternoon.

Comfy leather bucket chairs, two seater couches and stylish bar stools all governed their own space within in the bar, each style of seating calling out ever so subtly to different styles of customers. And the seats were always filled, as the bar was always busy. What a sense of achievement that was! He made quite a success out of his life all by himself, without his parents and certainly without his arrogant shitty brother. This was all his and he had done it all on his own.

He usually felt unstoppable, like nobody could ever make him feel worthless again, nobody would ever hurt him again. But tonight was entirely different. He was feeling so pessimistic about it all now. Sure, he was used to the bar quietening down a little after the summer season but not to this extent! He had always been able to pull in a fair amount of money every week even without the tourist trade. Now, he had to cancel the bands that were scheduled to play for the month. It was unreal, he had never had to do that before, but the bar was dead, and he couldn't afford to pay for them if he wasn't pulling in the money. There wasn't much competition in the village so the idea of his customers drinking somewhere else wasn't really bothering him! But the downturn in the economy had really caught up with him! Looking around now, he was able to count only five people altogether. Two middle-aged women, one sipping a glass of red wine chatting away while the other was sipping a sparkling water and lime, nodding her head co-operatively every few seconds, looking bored out of her tree. A man sitting on his own, drinking a bottle of beer while studying something on his laptop, porn probably. A young couple who seemed to be totally lost in each other. Too busy gazing into each other's eyes to even drink their drinks. Idiots, Jack said to himself. But deep down, he was jealous. He'd never know what it felt like to sit in a bar gazing into the eyes of someone he loved. He drained the last of his beer and walked back to the bar.

'Steve you might as well head home, there's not much happening here.'

Steven knew it was coming, it was the third night in a row now Jack had let him home early. And the same had happened for the past couple of weeks. It was great the first night but now it was worrying. Steven's girlfriend was seven months pregnant and God knew they needed every penny they could get.

Jack watched Steve head out the door. He knew he was worried but he didn't have any words of encouragement for him. The way things were going, he was going to have to reduce his hours. This was the hard part of running your own place he thought.

He remembered landing in the south east of Spain all those years ago, with a few clothes, a few bob, and very few Spanish words. But he had soon settled in nicely, pulling in a surprisingly nice wage working as a bar tender in an Irish bar. He worked out in the gym during the day and worked hard in the bar at night. The sun agreed with his sallow skin and he became a magnet for the ladies. He quickly learned that being charming tipped well. He picked up the language quite easily and picked up the social life even easier. Although, he could never shake off the disappointment in his father's eyes, the hatred in his brother's eyes and the hurt in his mother's eyes. The feeling of being made to feel less of a man, less of a person always remained with him. Like a sickening ball in his stomach, an anxiousness he couldn't get rid of. His mother passed away within a year of him moving to Spain. She discovered she had cancer and, unfortunately, it was too far gone to treat.

When Jack returned for the funeral, his father turned on him. He told him he was the cancer in the family and the real reason his mother went to an early grave. Jack was devastated and couldn't bring himself to go to the funeral when his father died a year later. He was gobsmacked to realise he'd been left a lot of money in the will. Was it his father's way of letting Jack know he did actually love him? Jack doubted it. He even considered telling Conor to keep the lot but he knew it was his one chance to do something for himself.

He moved to Kilfarrig, bought his home, took out a lease on a building in the town and set up The Cellar. But now that his takings were suffering and money was getting tight he felt that he was going to have to close down the pub for sure. And the very idea of doing so killed him, almost as much as the nauseating memories taunting his mind endlessly. He busied himself with cleaning up for the night and didn't even notice that the place had all but nearly emptied. The only person left was the guy on the laptop. Bottle of beer long drained. Jack stared over at him annoyed.

'The least you could do is buy a bloody bottle of beer!' he muttered to himself, fed up. If he was going to have to pay for the electricity for the lights being on, then the least your man could do was buy another flipping drink!

'What was that?' the man called over from his seat.

'Oh, just talking to myself, not too many in here tonight to converse with as you can see. Don't mind me, you work away there, but I might just close up early if you're nearly done.'

The man packed away his laptop and stood up. He walked over to the bar carrying the empty bottle and sat down on a bar stool. 'Ok, sure I'll just have one more beer, then I'll hit the road. I'll sit here and drink it so, then you can chat to me rather than to yourself, that's the first sign of madness you know!' he laughed.

Jack didn't know whether he was happy to be opening another bottle for the extra few quid or if he was even more pissed off now that he had to stay and listen to whatever shite your man was going to come out with. He planted the bottle in front of him not so delicately. 'So, you seemed to be fairly glued to your laptop there, anything interesting?' Jack smirked, sure your man had been gazing at dirty pictures all night.

'Yeah, I'm looking for work but there doesn't seem to be a lot out there at the moment,' the guy said.

Jack opened up a bottle for himself and took a swig, feeling ashamed for assuming the guy was a creep. 'Oh I know, well the jobs are there but they sure aren't offering the same great wages are they?'

'Yeah, your dead right! I was working away as a marketing consultant, got made redundant a few months back, I really need to get myself sorted out now though, the redundancy money seems to be bleeding profusely,' he laughed, 'the name's Michael by the way,' he said with an outstretched hand.

'I'm Jack,' he said, shaking Michael's hand, 'tell me about it, sure this place used to be hopping with people and now it's sinking big time! Another couple of months like this and I'll be done for sure.'

Michael could hear the surrender in Jack's tone. 'Well, Jack, the way I see it is, the economy is shite, but people still want to live, to enjoy themselves. You know how it is, work, work and more work, everyone living in their own stress bubble. Believe it or not, you're actually in a great place for business. Sure when the recession hit, tonnes of people had to move outside the city and down the country a bit where they could actually afford to rent or buy a house. So I guess you'd a lot of people moving here too.'

Jack nodded in agreement. 'That's for sure, the amount of people who have moved here within the last year is crazy actually.'

'Don't think crazy, think customer, and lots of them. All you need to do is attract them in,' Michael said.

As if it was as easy as that, thought Jack, irritated. 'But how do I do that, people are just not spending, people are just not going out and parting with their hard-earned cash.'

'Like I said a minute ago, people are spending, just a lot more wisely. We all need to get out. What you need to do is come up with other ways to bring the crowd in, offer them a better way to spend their money when they go out, make them feel like they can be wise with their money and have a good night too.'

Michael laughed while Jack joined in too. 'I like the way you say '*make them feel*' like they can be wise with their money.'

'Yeah, well, after a few drinks, Jack, you don't tend to care how wise you are anymore, do you,' he drained the last of his drink and stood up, 'well sure, best of luck with it all anyway, it seems like a great little bar and I hope you get it back up on its feet again.'

Jack drained his own bottle. 'You said you're in marketing, didn't you?' he questioned.

'Yep, a marketing guru I am, a jobless and soon-to-be homeless guru though,' Michael chuckled.

'Well, seeing as you're going to be fishing around in the trash soon then, how about you call in tomorrow and I'll trade some lunch for some ideas of how to save this place?' Suddenly Jack was feeling a little bit more positive about the bar. He had felt motivated by a newfound energy to get up off his ass and try save his bar and his livelihood!

'Sounds good, I'll be around definitely, I'm one of those city boys who couldn't afford the city rents anymore, I'm looking to rent a flat here,' he laughed as he took out his wallet and handed Jack a twenty for the beer.

'Put your money away. I enjoyed the chat and sure, just make sure you come back tomorrow with lots of brilliant ideas to get this place pumping again.'

'No wonder you reckon you're going to be out of business soon. Tip number one you must let punters pay for their drinks!' Michael said with a cheeky smile on his face as he headed towards the door.

CHAPTER SEVEN

It was just past twelve on a beautiful fresh October's day. Siobhan was lost in her thoughts as she drove towards Emma's house along the coast road. She wasn't up that long, which was unusual.

Alex had wanted to enjoy some romantic time between the sheets. She could never fault his tender ways when it came to the bedroom. He had always been romantic but it seemed the more he reduced his stress levels, the more his romantic levels increased. Although lately he was getting more annoyingly mushy every time they had sex. She couldn't even enjoy a five-minute quickie anymore without him feeling her tummy afterwards as if he was magically going to make a baby appear. She was sure it wasn't going to be long before he started to ask her to stand on her head for five minutes after it.

The sight of the graveyard brought her out of her thoughts. She couldn't believe how long it had been now since Aidan's death. Even after all this time, she still found it hard to get used to seeing his grave standing on the little hill. Right beside the little church where he had married his smitten Emma. She had chosen the most beautiful stone surround for the grave and it stood out which made Siobhan think maybe that was a bad thing. His grave was the first one that came into view, it called out to your eyes to glance at it when driving past. She still got the same sadness passing it even though she had passed it so many times now. She honestly couldn't imagine how Emma felt seeing it every day on her way to work or wherever she was going. It was hard enough for herself and Alex to see it. They had all become such good friends all those years ago. Aidan and Alex hit it off so well which made it so easy for the girls. They instantly became double daters.

She smiled to herself as she thought of the first double date they went on. It was certainly a strange one. Aidan dragged the three of them on a kayaking day in Dalkey. Emma was absolutely horrified at the prospect of squeezing into a wetsuit in front of Aidan. The fact that she was the only one that had never kayaked before didn't make her feel any better either. Siobhan laughed at the memory of Emma's face that morning when the instructor handed her a manky wet suit and when she asked where the changing rooms were, he nodded to her car! Priceless. Of course, when Emma realised a swimsuit would have been a much better option to wear under her wetsuit rather than her off white bra and knickers, she really was mortified.

Things turned from bad to worse when they kayaked all the way to the little island just off the coast. Emma and Siobhan were dying for a pee! A one piece wet suit and a full bladder wasn't exactly ideal on a very public island!

But other than the insufferable pain the girls were in from their over exasperated bladders, they actually had great craic! And nothing couldn't remove the smile Emma had plastered on her face when they arrived back to the car park, well, not until she realised she was going to have to try get out of her wetsuit in the back of her car! It vanished pretty quickly alright then.

From that day on they were a foursome. Not a weird type foursome now, just two couples who hung out together. And hang out together they did, a lot!

Siobhan and Alex wasted no time. In less than a year, they were married and had bought a house in Killiney. Alex was on a very good salary and could well afford the mortgage but the wedding present of a considerable down payment helped the newly married couple a great deal. Siobhan always wanted to move home, however, and the couple built their dream home overlooking Kilfarrig Bay three years later.

Emma and Aidan dated for almost two years before they moved in together. He had no hesitation in being the one to move as he had already fallen in love with Kilfarrig. They were living together for almost two years when he proposed. He whisked her off to Paris for her thirtieth birthday and, at the top of the Eiffel Tower, he got down on one knee and asked her to marry him. Of course, she said yes!

They were married just under a year later in the little church on the hill beside the sea. It was such an amazing day. Siobhan and Alex stood by their friends' side as they said 'I do', Alex as the best man and Siobhan as the maid of honour. They watched as the couple pledged their undying love for each other till death do them part. Little did anybody know how quickly death was going to do just that.

Siobhan wondered how Emma was doing as she pulled up outside the house. It was Amy's fourth birthday and she knew that Emma would be feeling very down. It was heart-breaking really! Not only was Aidan not around to see them but he never even knew he was going to be a father.

Siobhan went to Emma's on the pretence of helping her set up for the little party but really it was to supply a shoulder to cry on before the guests came. Amy's first birthday had been very hard on Emma. She didn't even want to recognise the day as an important one in Amy's life. Alex, Siobhan, Jack, and Emma's parents all went to Emma's house and Siobhan brought a cake but Emma showed little interest.

Amy's second one wasn't much better although things were slightly better for her third. Siobhan was surprised though when Emma had said she was having a little family party for Amy this year, but she was sure there was going to be tears at the end of the day. Actually, she was sure Emma was going to open the door in tears.

She had grabbed the pink bike out of the boot and walked up the little pathway to the door. She put the present down, rang the bell, and braced herself for a weepy friend in need. Shoulders at the ready. She was shocked when the door opened to reveal a very smiley Emma waving at her to come in.

Siobhan was confused at the obvious air of happiness radiating from Emma as she followed her to the kitchen. 'Now, tell me honestly, because there's still time. I can run up to Lily's and get a proper cake but what do you think… taa daa!' Emma said as she pointed to a lob-sided half-iced yoke on the table. The only resemblance it had to a birthday cake was the two candles sticking out the top, or was it the side?

'Emm, gosh Emma, that's, that's lovvvelllly,' Siobhan lied.

'Oh really, I'm so glad. I spent all morning at it and, to be honest, I wasn't sure how it was going to turn out, but now looking at it I'm very proud.'

'Really? I mean you should be, it's….it's lovvvellly.' Siobhan had no idea why her 'lovely' was coming out more on the high-pitch side. She also had no idea what was going on with Emma. She looked so vibrant and alive in a gorgeous red dress and was just so darn cheerful. There had to be something wrong!

'Emma, how are you, I mean, you know…. do you want to talk about it or anything before everyone comes and you're overwhelmed with it all?' Siobhan asked quietly. It was almost as if Emma was going to break with the sound of loud words.

'Thanks, Siobhan, you're a great friend, but I feel great today,' Emma put her hand on Siobhan's arm and smiled, 'honestly I do.'

'But, you usually fall apart on days like this. Don't get me wrong, I'm delighted you're feeling great. I'm just worried about you.'

'Honestly, I'm fine, I don't feel alone.'

'Of course you're not alone; you have me, Amy, Jack…' Siobhan was about to carry on listing out everyone in Emma's life when Emma interrupted.

'No, Siobhan, what I mean is I don't feel alone, I feel like he's here with me!' she slowly waved her hand around her. 'Aidan is here, I can feel him here with me, in fact I can feel him all around me, it's such a strong presence, isn't it wonderful!'

Siobhan's mind went into overdrive. She had been really worried about Emma and how she was coping with her husband's untimely death. There was no denying the deep depression she fell into afterwards but Amy's birth seemed to coax her back to life. Amy was in fact a life saver.

But Emma showed no sign of really overcoming the death at all. She refused to put any of his things away and even though she was living without him she wasn't letting go one little bit. She wore his hoody at night and used to spray his aftershave on his pillow. When Siobhan had suggested taking his toothbrush away, she went ballistic. Everyone was so worried about her but in a way it was kind of natural back then. But this was not natural, not at all! Feeling him around and thinking he was here with her was way too freaky. Obviously she was beginning to lose her mind.

Siobhan was struggling to find the right words to say when Amy came flying into the kitchen and up into her arms.

'Sivvvon, Sivvvon, look what Mammy made,' she shouted with great enthusiasm as she pointed over to the cake.

'Yeah, a yummy birthday cake for the birthday girl!' Siobhan said, happy to get her voice pitch just right after what she had just heard.

Amy looked at her as if she was stupid. 'No, not a cake, silly Sivon, it's a lump with candles!'

CHAPTER EIGHT

The oven timer beeped and Emma jumped with anticipation. 'Oh, I wonder how these turned out, banana and chocolate chip muffins, mmmm, smell nice anyway.' The smell of the home baking escaping out of the oven as she opened the door brought back many childhood memories for Siobhan. The smell of the muffins caressed and teased her nose. It was the only thing being teased, however, as she caught sight of the so-called muffins when Emma took them out.

'Ah feck, what the hell are these? They're supposed to be bloody muffins not pancakes!' Emma looked truly disheartened as she viewed the baking disaster in front of her. 'What'll I do now? I only made these and the cake and I can't serve these up. At least the cake was a success. I've a few rice crispy buns in the fridge that Amy helped me make yesterday; I wasn't going to put them out though. Amy was more kind of scoffing them into her mouth as she mixed them and let's just say that the ingredients contain rice crispies that were already half chewed and spat back into the mixing bowl! But better not mention that, okay?'

'Don't worry about it, Emma,' Siobhan replied, horrified, 'you've plenty of food. You went overboard on the sandwiches and vol-au-vents and the salads look amazing.'

'Yeah, I've a lasagne in the microwave ready to reheat too, but I wanted some nice sugary food. I only have the cake now.'

Siobhan looked at the lump on the table again and thought she had better rescue the situation. 'Tell you what, I'll give Alex a buzz and get him to pick up a few sticky buns from Lily's on the way here.'

'Oh would you? I don't have time, Aidan's parents will be here soon and we still have to blow up the balloons. I'll just go get them, back in a second.'

Siobhan dug her phone out of her bag and dialled Alex's number. 'Hi honey, there's been a bit of a disaster on the muffin front. Can you pop in to Lily's and pick up some sticky buns? Thanks, honey, see you soon, love you too.' No sooner had she hung up than Emma came back into the room all smiles.

'Ahhhhh, "love you too, honey." Honest to God, you two. How many years are you married now and you're still carrying on like a newly loved-up couple?' Emma jeered her friend but she really thought that it was so sweet the way they were still so mad about each other almost a decade into their marriage. They were the definition of a solid marriage; nothing could ever come between them.

She handed Siobhan a pack of balloons and ordered her to get blowing and within twenty minutes, the two girls were flat out on the kitchen chairs looking at Amy chase all the balloons around the floor. Siobhan felt her face to make sure it was still intact. 'Oh my Goodness, my jaw and cheeks are aching; I mean they feel like they've been stretched to the last. Oh yeah, they're in pain and out of action now for the rest of the day and night, Alex is not going to be happy with you,' she said with a dirty wink.

'Oh, is that all you can think about, you dirty woman? Anyway, it's no wonder you're not pregnant, I think you're concentrating on the wrong end!' Emma replied in mock disgust.

Siobhan's face fell and Emma instantly regretted her comment. 'Oh Siobhan, I'm so sorry, that was really stupid of me to say, I was only joking, God I can be a right plank sometimes.'

'Don't be silly, it was actually funny. I just, I don't know.' Siobhan looked down at her feet because she couldn't look her friend in the face. She had no idea what Emma would think of her if she ever found out that she was secretly on the pill. Emma loved Alex like a brother and would be furious if she found out he was being lied to and deceived. Siobhan's stomach always turned when Emma brought up the subject of babies and pregnancy, she had always been able to share her most inner and darkest secrets in life but she was too ashamed to share this one.

'No, Siobhan, it was really insensitive of me. So how are things going on that front anyway?' Emma's voice had softened as if this time it was Siobhan who was going to break if she spoke any louder.

Siobhan didn't break, even though her tummy started its automatic turning motion at the sheer mention of pregnancy. 'No nothing yet, let's not talk about this now, Emma. It's Amy's big day, so is there anything else I can do for you?'

She stood up and walked over to the sink and started washing the coffee mugs from the draining board even though they had already been washed.

Emma knew this was a touchy subject; Siobhan was always trying to avoid talking about it. She felt totally blessed to have Amy for a number of reasons. The most important, however, was the fact that she was part of Aidan. When he died, Emma felt so alone. She felt as if part of her had died too except he had left her behind so she had to go on living without him and it was too much to face.

When she found out she was pregnant, she was overjoyed that a part of Aidan was going to live on. That she was going to be sharing her life with his child, his flesh and blood. Although it was hard to accept that he wasn't going to be around and that they had never got to share such happiness, but Amy was her life now and her reason for living. She couldn't imagine a life without her and she couldn't imagine having to wait for her either. It must be so hard to want something so badly and get knocked back month after month. She felt so bad for Siobhan. It was a year now since Alex's heart attack and their big decision to start a family.

It's funny; Emma thought to herself, in their teenage years, both their parents were always warning them how easy it was to get pregnant. In a way, maybe her father was right, because she hadn't exactly been trying for Amy when she found out she was pregnant.

In fact, Emma often wondered if Amy was a gift sent to her by her husband when he died. A sort of Immaculate Conception scenario. To ease the loneliness and pain for the loss of her one true soul mate. In the beginning, she would laugh at herself for thinking such a thing, but now she wasn't so sure that it was such a crazy idea. Aidan seemed to be sending her lots of signs lately to let her know he was around. So, who knows? Maybe he did plant a little seed of love in her tummy from heaven.

Siobhan's parents had scared the shit out of her too but not to the same extent. She wasn't as innocent as Emma when it came to experimenting with the opposite sex. She was always so careful though. Now, it seemed that nature wasn't too co-operative with her! It was a pity, though; Alex had always loved kids. She'd had no doubt that he and Siobhan would be the perfect Godparents for Amy when she came along. Alex doted on her and he made such an effort with her seeing as she didn't have her dad around.

Emma was surprised at how suddenly he came to a decision to start trying for his own baby. For years, there had never been a mention of the patter of tiny feet but, after Alex had had his heart attack, all he could think about was having a baby. She wondered how Siobhan was coping with Alex putting the pressure on so much. She knew Siobhan was trying to put on a brave face for Alex; she had often heard her tell him that it could take months to get pregnant and to be patient. In truth, Emma had no idea how Siobhan was coping. She was keeping her feelings to herself big time. She was glad in a way that Siobhan was insisting that she wasn't going to get stressed out about it, but there was just something about her that made Emma think there was something deeper going on. She felt that her friend was carrying the weight of not getting pregnant heavily on her shoulders and she wished she'd open up and talk about it.

In the coffee shop, Lily was serving a customer when Alex walked in. He went straight up to the cooler to check out all the delicious cream cakes and sticky buns. Lily's was a beautiful hidden gem on the edge of the town, the last stop on the way to the beach. Its prime location was only part of its success, however. The food was amazing and Lily and her husband were so charming that people were happy to go back.

The coffee shop itself was a charming little place. A small space with only six tables, it had a gorgeous garden out the back which was a favourite during the summer months. Inside, the décor had a real farmhouse feel, with wooden tables and chairs, black wrought iron fixtures, a solid wooden floor, and red-brick effect walls with oil paintings of majestic leafy trees standing proudly in woodland. Gorgeous in winter.

'Hiya Alex love, are you not going to little Amy's birthday party today?' she said as she came over to him. She was particularly fond of Alex; she had got to know him really well in the past year. He dropped in almost every week for a cup of tea and his wholemeal healthy bread with her homemade marmalade.

'Hi Lil, yeah I'm on my way to Emma's now. Siobhan rang me and asked me to pick up a few buns, apparently Emma didn't have much success on the baking front.' Alex rubbed his hands together as his eyes were glued to all the delicious looking cream cakes behind the cooler glass.

'Oh poor Emma, she is amazing at the auld lasagnes but she never had any success at the baking'. Lily had a sad look on her face as if not being able to throw together a few cakes was the end of the world. 'Isn't it funny though Alex, wouldn't you think that a primary school teacher would be great at the auld baking?'

'Ah Lil, you know not everyone has buns like yours.' Alex grinned.

'Oh Alex, you little brat, only Sean can get his hands on my buns, but if you want I can get you some of my lovely jam doughnuts and éclairs.'

'Well Lil, if I can't get my hands on your buns, then your doughnuts will just have to do!' he winked.

'My Goodness, Alex O'Callaghan,' Lilly said blushing, 'Siobhan will have to watch you!'

CHAPTER NINE

'Alex is on his way, I just got a text from him. Lily practically gave him all the cream cakes out of the fridge and wouldn't take a cent. They're her gift to Amy for her party, isn't she so sweet…pardon the pun,' Siobhan giggled, eager to get away from the whole subject of babies. Emma had been her best friend forever almost and she found it so hard to lie to her about how she really felt about becoming a mother but she was sure Emma wouldn't understand! She was such a fantastic mother and was completely besotted with Amy. Siobhan could feel her face flush any time Emma mentioned babies or pregnancy. She had always managed to change the subject or insist that she didn't want to get too stressed out about it, that she was sure it'd happen when the time was right. Alex was really starting to pile the pressure on even more and it was getting harder to brush the subject under the carpet. He had started mentioning tests and she was sure that Emma was thinking along the same lines. The pressure was definitely mounting. When Alex had first talked about his desire to start a family, she knew she wasn't ready to become a mother. She had worked hard to achieve her career and she wanted to keep it. Plus, she had spent years sculpting her body to the way it is now so a pregnant body terrified her. Although she and Alex had talked about having children someday, neither of them really cared when that day was. Now that *someday* was upon her, she wanted to run away screaming 'Nooooooooo I'm not ready!!'

At the time, Siobhan didn't want to upset Alex's new-found dreams of a family when he was recovering. Plus she was hoping that she would warm to the idea herself. But time hadn't thawed her feelings towards it at all. They were more frozen than the ice berg that hit the Titanic! She just didn't want children. She didn't want to give up the life she had, the figure she worked hard to attain, the job she had and the life in general she enjoyed. She felt sorry for Emma being stuck at home with a child when she was free to go wherever she wanted whenever she wanted. She loved being able to go out to dinner at the weekend without worrying about babysitters. She loved throwing a few clothes into a bag and heading off for a weekend away at the last minute. She really didn't want to give up her life or swap it for one where she had extra responsibilities.

Sometimes she felt so incredibly angry with Alex. How dare he expect her turn into a baby making machine just because he had a sudden urge to play daddy? When he was running the show in the firm, there was no mention of babies and children but now that he was ready to play daddy, he just expected her to drop everything including her fancy lingerie and play mammy.

She was in a constant battle with herself, toying with the anger and guilt. She wasn't sure how much longer she could live like this. She wasn't sure how much longer she could get away with it anyway; she was going to have to decide what she was going to do. The whole situation was becoming far too exhausting. It had all gone on for so long now, she just couldn't see her way out of it. She couldn't come clean.

If only she had been honest to him about her feelings in the first place. He may have understood and they could have worked through it but now it was an impossible situation. She had been cheating him out of a child and lying to his face every single day for a year. How could they possibly move on from that?

'Ah great, Lily and Sean are wonderful, aren't they? What time is it now anyway?' Emma asked while opening a bottle of wine, snapping Siobhan out of the turmoil going on in her mind.

'It's only twenty past one.' She replied glad to be taken out of her thoughts.

'Oh, I'd say Aidan's parents will be here soon. They were coming down that bit earlier to go visit his grave. Anyway, we're all set now thanks to you, I'd never have blown all those balloons up on my own. Food is ready, all we have to do now is sit back and relax.' she handed Siobhan a nice glass of chilled white.

'We're starting early, aren't we? I don't want to be pissed when everybody gets here,' Siobhan was glad of a glass of wine all the same.

'Oh, we deserve it, a moment of peace before chaos begins.'

They went into the living room and collapsed onto the sofa. Amy was busy making a jigsaw puzzle on the coffee table. 'She loves those puzzles, she'd spend all day making them, takes after me that way, I'd say. There's no way Aidan would sit there doing that.' Emma looked at Amy patiently putting the pieces of the puzzle together. She was lost in her own little world singing to herself.

'Aidan used to get so frustrated putting flat-pack furniture together. I remember the day we spent putting together the book shelf in our room. Gosh, did he get mad! At one stage, I thought he was going to throw the whole bloody yoke out the window.'

Emma's eyes creased slightly as she laughed at the memory fondly. Siobhan looked at her with a smile on the outside and worry on the inside. She was waiting for Emma to have a little cry, but nothing. This whole situation was just too strange. Emma was chatting about memories of Aidan, his parents were on their way, they were probably at the graveside now, everybody was going to arriving shortly to celebrate little Amy's birthday. This was usually a time when Emma had a few moments of lament. But nothing, nothing at all.

'Emma, are you sure you're alright? I mean, I know this must be a little hard for you.' Siobhan asked gingerly.

Emma looked at Siobhan with positivity radiating out of every pore.

'Yes, I'm okay; I told you I feel like, well, I feel like Aidan is here with me today!'

'Of course he is, he's around you all the time, and I'm sure.'

'Yeah but, Siobhan, like I said earlier, I can feel him, not just a presence, more than that. There are times when the hair stands up on my neck and I can feel a sensation around me like he's putting his arms around me. At first I put it down to just freaky happenings but then I started thinking, what if it was Aidan. So now when I feel it, I stop and close my eyes and it lasts for ages, I love it, it's so comforting.'

Emma had a genuine contented smile on her face that had been missing for a long time. She'd been saying weird things lately but this was getting a bit too weird. Was she actually suggesting that Aidan was in the house? Like as a ghost or something? She knew it probably wasn't the right time to quiz her but she felt that she had to get to the bottom of what Emma was saying. 'Emma, how do you mean Aidan is here? Do you mean that he's actually here in the house?'

'Yes,' she smiled.

Despite the serious look on Siobhan's face and the frown lines between her eyebrows, Emma's mood could not be dampened. For a long time, she didn't know how she was going to be able to go through life without her husband and lately it seemed she wasn't going to have to. He was back where he belonged, with her and their little girl. That's why she was in such good form. She didn't have the same dread she normally felt on such occasions. She normally felt cheated out of a proper family day. She hated the feeling that she was celebrating something that they had created together and yet he never knew they had made such a wonderful child. It had always felt wrong. But, today, she could feel him around her from the minute she woke up. It was an incredible feeling. It was like she had met him for the first time all over again. She couldn't stop smiling. She felt safe all over again, like she had felt when he was alive. She felt loved and secure. She couldn't get him out of her mind and it didn't seem to bother her that he was out of reach.

It had started a few weeks before as a simple feeling. She had been vacuuming the stairs when, all of a sudden, everything seemed to get brighter as if a dark cloud had just revealed the sun's powerful rays and they was able to shine down ever so intensely. It felt warmer and she could feel the brightness on her skin.

She had stopped cleaning and stood up straight. There was no explanation. There were no windows directly influencing the brightness or level of light on the stairs. She put it down to tiredness and thought nothing more of it until the next week when it happened again. The next time it happened, she stopped vacuuming immediately and closed her eyes. This time she could feel something behind her. Like a heaviness. It was almost as if she could lean back and yet be supported by whatever it was.

She rang Siobhan straight away to tell her what had happened and that she was sure it was Aidan. Siobhan was very supportive and Emma was so glad that she didn't tell her to cop on or not to be silly. She had no intention of broadcasting the strange fact that she felt her husband had come back to her in spirit form but she felt safe telling Siobhan.

'Okay, so is it like the same heaviness you felt that time? Because that could be tiredness Emma.'

'No, it's more than the heaviness. It sounds crazy but it's like he's here with me in the house, following me around or just maybe looking after Amy. And when I pass him, he, I don't know, it's like he blows on my neck to let me know he's there or something'. Emma was beaming with happiness.

'He blows on your neck, what, do you feel his breath or something then?'

'Yeah, that's exactly it, I can feel his breath and I just get shivers all down my body. It's amazing, Siobhan.'

Siobhan was the one getting the shivers down her body now. She was already fretting over her friend just sensing the heaviness on the stairs but this was going a step too far. She knew this was why Emma was feeling so happy.

Siobhan's stomach fell. Was Emma heading for a breakdown? She'd been supportive during previous conversations but it was going a bit too far now. Emma was acting like Aidan was back and back for good. Never mind the state of Emma's mental health, this certainly wasn't healthy for Amy! Growing up with a mother who believed her husband was haunting the house.

'Oh, here's Alex now. Listen, just keep this to yourself. I know I can tell you but I couldn't imagine many people understanding.' Emma got up to let Alex in; Amy went running out to the door with her, screaming Alex's name at the top of her voice.

'I couldn't imagine too many people understanding either,' Siobhan muttered to herself as she watched Emma leave the room. She sat quietly looking around and suddenly felt very aware of the emptiness of it. She scanned the room for shadows or signs that Aidan was about. 'This is crazy, you silly idiot. Of course, he's not here. The man is dead and gone and Emma has to come to terms with that one of these days.'

She took out her phone and rang Jack. 'Hey, how are you? Yeah, I got here a while ago. Listen, I think we need to talk about Emma... I'm just very worried about her, Jack ... she's talking about Aidan being here ... no, it's more than that ... I gotta go, Alex is here but, look, don't be late okay ... yeah, see you in a little while ... bye.'

She threw the phone back into her bag and drank another sip of wine. She was going to have to tell Jack what was going on. Maybe, together, they could get Emma through this phase of hers.

CHAPTER TEN

'Everything okay?' asked Michael as he took a swig of his tea, sensing that Jack's phone conversation was quite worrying.

'Oh, it's my friend's daughter's birthday today and her husband isn't around to celebrate it unfortunately. He died before Amy was born, in fact he didn't even know Emma was pregnant!'

'Oh really, wow that's hard. What happened, if you don't mind me asking?'

'It's mad, actually, he was working in Dublin and he used to commute up and down. He worked all hours and all sorts of shifts so Emma was always worrying he'd fall asleep at the wheel or something. It's a great motorway but it's long and tedious, so easy to drift off if you're any way tired at all. But sure as it happens, he was driving home from a soccer match in the local pitch one evening and out of nowhere a tractor came out of a field onto the road, he swerved to avoid it but it was too late. He caught the corner of the tractor and was thrown off the road. After doing a three-sixty, his car smacked into a telephone pole.'

'Was he killed straight away?' Michael looked saddened at the story even though he didn't know any of the people involved.

'No, he was rushed to hospital and was in an induced coma for days, he had a serious trauma to his head and the swelling on his brain was severe.'

'Oh no, his poor wife.'

'Yeah, Emma, she was so strong throughout the whole thing, she never left his bedside for days, she stayed so positive and insisted he'd be fine. God love them, they weren't married all that long either. I've never seen how strong the human spirit can be until then, she was incredible. After the fourth day, the doctors brought him out of the coma and Aidan as we knew him was gone. There was nothing they could do, the damage to his brain was irreversible and he needed life support to stay breathing. It was so hard to accept. Emma refused to switch off the machine for a full two weeks before his parents convinced her that his spirit was gone and that he should be allowed to rest. She was numb during the funeral and then she just fell apart,' Jack paused, remembering, 'it was horrific. I had only moved to the place about ten months before the accident but I felt like they were my family from day one. I bought the semi-detached beside them and we hit it off great. I couldn't believe how lucky I was with such amazing neighbours. It was a terrible time! Emma went downhill so fast it was frightening. She didn't want to take part in life anymore, she didn't want to get up, to get dressed, to eat even, all she did was cry. We were so worried about her.'

'Ah that's awful, what happened to her?'

'Well, Joan, her mother called the doctor to the house several times and she was put on anti-depressants but then she started to puke everywhere all the time and her mother dragged her into the doctor's worried sick about her. I'd say that poor woman aged ten years during the whole thing with worry alone. Turned out Emma was pregnant. She was about three weeks gone when the accident happened but because they weren't even trying, she didn't notice.'

'Oh wow, that's unreal!'

'Yeah, so after she found out she was pregnant, she felt she'd been given a bit of Aidan back and gradually, day by day, she managed to climb out of the dark hole she was in. It wasn't easy though and, even when Amy was born, she was torn every time she looked at her. She suffered a little then with anxiety and all, but things were much better and again, day by day, she got better. Four years later now and, thankfully she's doing well. But days like this are hard though.'

'Feck, and we think we have problems!'

Both men sat in silence for a moment, both deep in thought. Jack allowed his mind to enter that dark place in his head. That same place that he spent the last twenty years trying to run away from. But after an agonising minute, he had to slam it out yet again. He started feeling physically sick, his stomach churned. He had to escape the sinister terrifying place quickly and shut the door firmly behind him. He simply couldn't afford to let any of the ominous thoughts follow him into the new life he had worked so hard to create for himself. They'd destroy him for sure.

'Jack, are you okay? You've gone a bit pale.' Michael looked at Jack with concern. 'Yeah, sorry, I was just thinking about it all. Listen, let's get another coffee and then you can tell me what you're doing back in Kilfarrig.'

Within minutes, Steve was carrying over coffees to the two men. 'Is there anything else I can get for you?'

'No, unless you fancy some lunch, Michael? I hear the food here is pretty amazing.' Jack flashed a cheeky grin.

'I'm good today, but definitely next time.' Michael felt a slight twinge of guilt as he spoke to Steve. The poor guy was looking at him like a child in a toy store with pleading puppy dog eyes. He was hoping Michael would order something. Michael wasn't sure whether it was because he wanted something to do or because he was so worried about his job that he was glad of any paying customers. Steve picked up the empty cups and walked back across the almost empty room.

'So Kilfarrig has got under your skin then has it? Can't keep away from the place.'

Michael smiled but Jack could see a sadness suddenly creep into his eyes.

'Well as you know, I'm thinking of moving down here. I'm viewing a place later on.'

'Oh yes, that's right! A city boy moving down to a little coastal village, do you think you could cope?'

'Ah it's great little place isn't it! That new shopping centre and cinema is state of the art sure!'

'Okay, you're being sarcastic now!' Jack laughed.

'No, it's gorgeous here, not to mind the cheaper house prices and rents. Sure, it's a perfect spot really. It started off as a little fishing village, didn't it?'

'Yeah, it did. There's still a lot of fishing done off the coast. The harbour is more full of sailing boats nowadays and tourist charters.'

'Do you know that the Priory Hotel group are looking for planning permission for a new hotel and leisure centre just outside the town? In fact, I think they're looking to create an 18-hole golf course too.'

'No I didn't know that! I have to say you really know your stuff on the place anyway, are you making Kilfarrig your specialty on Mastermind or something?' laughed Jack.

'Ah, I like to do my research on a place before I move there, don't know why really. It's a bit silly but I've never really been the spontaneous type. I really think about things before I act. Although I'm fairly desperate to move now and with this place being beside the motorway I'd be able to hop up and down to the city for interviews.'

'Ah sure, yeah, you couldn't find a better spot. It's a thriving little place really. I just wish this bloody place would thrive with it, money getting too tight to mention.'

'Don't talk to me, I hope I get another job fairly soon. I was never spontaneous but I was never any good at saving for a rainy day either, I was damn lucky to get a redundancy package but it's not going to last all that long. I reckon I'm gonna have to rent a shoe box and eat very little to make it last just in case another job doesn't come along as soon as I'd like.'

'Were you in a house in Dublin or an apartment or...?'

'I had a gorgeous apartment, fantastic view, right smack bang in the centre of all the action. Wasn't cheap though, rent was big money.'

'Did you share it with anyone, another lodger?' Jack wasn't sure but he thought that maybe he had just asked him a question that he seemed slightly uncomfortable with!

'Eh, well yeah, actually I did. That's the real reason why I'm in a hurry to move. I shared it with my ex. We lived there for almost a year and a half but things didn't work out and we decided it was time to call it a day. Cameron, my ex, moved out straight away and I stayed on but now that I don't have an income I just can't afford the place on my own and I couldn't imagine getting anyone else in. Too many memories. Ah I just want a clean break you know.' Michael looked at Jack with obvious hurt in his eyes. Whoever this Cameron girl was, he must have been madly in love with her. There was no mistaking the heartbreak he portrayed as he spoke.

'I'm so sorry to hear that, a year and a half is a long time to devote your life to someone.' Jack wasn't quite sure what to say to Michael. He had no idea how it felt to be in love. He could never bring himself to get close to anybody. He had accepted long ago that he'd live his life without love, he had to, he had no choice.

'We were together for a couple of years actually, we met in the States and then Cameron moved over here. But, yeah, it's a long time and well, I suppose, it's just something I'm going to have to get over. There's no going back.'

'What happened? Oh sorry, I shouldn't have asked that. It's absolutely none of my business.' Jack regretted prying into the other man's life. He couldn't bear people asking him his life story when he first arrived. He had hated how friendly the locals were in the beginning. Asking questions and waiting for answers. He thought they were all so bloody nosy.

'No you're grand. I guess we just grew apart. Cameron always wanted to move back to the States and I was happy here. Things weren't good between us and, soon enough, we were arguing every day. It was a hard decision but it had to be made. Cameron moved back to the States and, well, that was that. Gone!'

'Do you still talk to her or have you just cut all ties?'

Michael looked at Jack with a strange facial expression and didn't say anything for a few seconds. Jack could see he had made Michael uncomfortable.

'We just cut all ties that seemed the easier solution.'

'How are you finding it, the ties being cut, that is?'

'Hard, but I have to just get on with it, I have to accept it's over. We couldn't live with each other so what else could we do?'

'The question is, can you live without her?'

'I have to, I have no option, it's over. Anyway, look, enough about me, I certainly didn't mean to go on about all that! Why don't I sit down with you at some stage and we can thrash out a few more ideas to get this place buzzing again?'

'Yeah, that'd be great, I'd appreciate any ideas at all, you really seemed to know what you were talking about the last time you were here. And sure, look, why don't you give me a look at some of the places you fancy renting around here and I'll let you know what's a good spot.'

'Okay, I'll see what this place is like today but I'm going to go through the letting agents' listings again and I'll shortlist a few others also.'

'Tell you what, I'll be back in later after the party so why don't you pop in then?'

'Sorted.'

Jack sensed that Michael was back to his old chirpy self, but the hurt from his break-up was definitely lingering under his skin.

CHAPTER ELEVEN

'Well, that was a great day, little Amy was delighted with herself.' Seamus took off his coat and hung it on the coat hanger just inside the hall door. The drive home had been a quiet one. Himself and Joan were communicating less and less these days, but even he could tell there was something on her mind.

Joan never even heard her husband say a word as she filled the kettle. She stared out into the sea of green trees facing the back of her adorable little house. She loved the vastness of the woods – they were like a protective boundary right at the back of her garden. For many years, she'd resented living in Kilfarrig yet she never could fall out of love with the amazing scenery which surrounded her house. For her entire life living there, those woods were her solace, her place to disappear into when things got on top of her. Even now, she could hear the laughter coming from a young Emma and Siobhan as they played in them.

She made her way into the spotless sitting room and went about lighting the stove. The views from the window were just as astonishing. Sitting high up on Kilfarrig Hill, the house had spectacular views of the coastline and miles of sea reaching out to the horizon.

'Did you want tea, Joan, the kettle's just boiled?' Seamus popped his head around the door.

'Yes please, but I'm too full for any more food so the tea on its own will be fine for me, thank you.'

'I'm full to the gills with food too. Emma put on a fair spread alright, although what the hell was that birthday cake supposed to be? I gave my bit to Digger when she wasn't looking!'

'Ah sure, she tried her best, I suppose. She was never really a baker, was she?' Joan laughed to herself.

A few minutes later with a cup of tea in hand, they were both sitting down in front of the stove staring at the television. Seamus was flicking about the stations looking for something to watch. As he did so, Joan could see lots of programmes that she could have happily got lost in but she knew he was looking for something a bit more current affair-ish. He liked to keep on top of the news and what was going on in the country. Joan, on the other hand, was sick to death of listening to what was going on and all the bitching and moaning and giving out that was constantly on those stupid programmes. 'Nothing on the television, as per usual. How many bloody channels do we have these days and there's never anything good to watch,' he grumbled in her direction as he continued channel hopping.

Joan threw her eyes up to heaven. There were plenty of good and interesting programmes on but he just had to moan about something. You couldn't watch the soaps because they were all stupid and depressing in his eyes. You couldn't watch anything at all resembling a reality show because, in his eyes, they were all the most ridiculous silly things you could ever watch and unless there was an educational value to the programme you were watching, they weren't worth watching it. Needless to say, he was always on the Discovery channels and the news channels.

'She looked good today, I thought,' he said, looking over at his wife sitting back drinking her tea. She looked like a woman with a lot on her mind. She just stared into her cup without answering. He couldn't help but feel a little annoyed.

'Who?' she asked eventually, when the sound of his voice intruded on her thoughts.

'Emma, she looked good, didn't she? Haven't seen her that happy in a long time!'

'Yeah, I suppose,' mumbled Joan.

'What is wrong with you, Joan? Anyone would think you've have just come from a funeral not your grandchild's birthday,' he scolded.

'I'm fine, Seamus, just relaxing after the day that's all. I'm tired now.' Sounding a little less than convincing.

'Well, you look bloody miserable. I thought if anything you'd be best pleased to have seen our Emma and little Amy in such good form.'

Now it was Joan's turn to feel annoyed. She shifted in her seat and looked her husband in the eye. 'That is just it, Seamus. Emma was in great form, too much so. I was expecting her to be a little, well I don't know what I was expecting but…'

She didn't even get to finish her sentence when he butted in. 'Honestly woman, you weren't happy when she was upset and now you're not happy when she isn't upset. You're never happy, are you? What do you want from the girl, to spend the day in mourning? She has to get on with things. Sure, you were saying that yourself and the minute she actually seems to be doing just that, you're not happy with it. I don't know, I really don't.'

She was more annoyed now at how Seamus was talking to her and what she was hearing. 'I am happy that she's getting on with things, I think it's great that she's managing her grief better. But I know Emma inside out and I know that, normally, she'd have been feeling sad at some stage on a day like today. I think she was in great form, yeah, but it was a strange great form.'

Seamus looked at her puzzled. 'A strange great form! Absolute utter nonsense, Joan, you're just not happy unless you have something to worry and moan about.'

Joan sat up on the edge of the chair, visibly angry! 'I don't go around moaning about anything, Seamus. And even if I did, how would you know? You're hardly ever here anymore. Besides, I think I'm allowed to be concerned about my one and only daughter, don't you?'

The question was more of a statement than anything but he answered it anyway. 'Oh, here we go with the only child issue. Well, who have you to blame for that, Joan?'

His question was exactly that, a question. And a question that pushed Joan over the edge. She stood up almost shaking with anger. 'Don't you dare throw that back in my face again! I was doing what I thought was right for me and for us at the time. You didn't seem too bothered with more children either, you know, you can't put all the blame on me. You definitely didn't offer to give up your job and stay at home with Emma or any other child we would've had.'

'Joan, I was the principal of the school and you were only a class teacher. My salary was a hell of a lot more valuable to us and, besides, it was more of a woman's role to stay at home with children.'

'Huh, you sound just like your mother, Seamus. If she were alive, she'd be very proud of you and your backward views. I'm going to bed.' She walked out of the door, not waiting for any retort or smart comment from her husband. There was no talking to him sometimes and he'd often infuriate her to the point of boiling. She marched into her room and got dressed for bed, still reeling. She washed her face and brushed her teeth with such ferociousness her gums were nearly bleeding.

It was only after a few deep breaths that she calmed down and it was then the tears sprang into her eyes. Climbing into bed, she felt completely alone and upset. He had often pulled the "it's your fault we only had one child" card and it was hurtful to hear. She was glad his mother was dead and gone. Partly because she was an absolute cow to Joan and never approved of her modern ways of wanting to go out to work instead of being a conventional little housewife. But mostly because she'd have felt smug about how unhappy Joan was right.

Joan really regretted not having a larger family around her. She wasn't sure whether it was because she'd have just liked to have more children and grandchildren around her now in her older years or because she was so desperately lonely and unhappy in her marriage.

Herself and Seamus were supposed to be enjoying their retirement years together at this stage of their life. She had visualised them going on walks along the beach together hand-in-hand as an old couple. Going on cruises to see the world. Sipping wine in great companionship watching the sun set in the horizon. But the reality was a lot different. They were growing old and growing apart. Each day seemed to be a day further apart. Seamus kept himself busy after retirement. He stayed on the Tidy Towns committee and he never missed his card night every week with a group of other retired men that he liked to meet up with.

On the outside, anyway, he came across as a happy man, content enough with life but Joan could never really see a content happy man. He was always a grump at home and he had the cheek and the audacity to say she wasn't happy unless she was moaning. She knew she was anything but a moaner. But she had to admit that when they were together, that was all either of them could do. It was like just being in each other's company brought out the worst in them.

She was still awake when she heard him come down the hall to come to bed. She quickly rolled over onto her side so that her back was facing him when he got into the bed.

A few minutes later, he got in beside her and settled himself in, facing away from her also. He was asleep in minutes and began snoring. Each snore louder than the one before. She lay rigid beside him, enraged at just how easy sleep came to him and the snoring didn't help her anger. Each snore seemed to come very loudly from his throat right the way up to his nose and then he'd blow it out of his mouth making his lips quiver with a trout pout and flap so annoyingly loud! She could feel a great humongous red ball of intoxicating rage cultivate with great intensity in her chest as she lay beside him. She turned around on her back and thumped him on his arm. He moved and the snoring stopped for a second but it soon started again and this time even louder. Joan pulled the covers back with more than enough force than was needed and stomped off into Emma's old room. She sighed as she snuggled up into the clean crisp duvet. Sleeping in Emma's old room was becoming a familiar nightly event.

CHAPTER TWELVE

'You know something, Alex, your arssshhh looks sho sexy from this angle!' Siobhan slurred as she patted his ass.

Alex was thankful his wife weighed about as much as a feather as he carried her up the stairs over his shoulders. 'You know, you have to be the only woman who manages to get pissed at child's birthday party. You're a disgrace, you know that?' he laughed as he gently laid her down on the bed and sat down beside her.

'Ah now, I'm not to blame. Emma is the real culprit here, I'm the innocent one. She was the shuplier, I mean supplier. Besides, I didn't have much to drink all day. Shur it was only when Emma put Amy to bed did we really shart, I mean start drinking,' she slurred as she lay back and closed her eyes, allowing her body and mind to completely relax.

'I know, I left a perfectly sober wife when I went off to The Cellar with Jack for a pint and when I got back I found a drunken intoxicated mess sprawled out on the sofa or should I say two intoxicated messes!' he called back to her as he walked into the en-suite.

'You, my dear husband, are zagghherating, zagghherating, yeah, I mean exaggerating. We just had a few little glasses of wine to finish off the day, we deserved it shur.' The words seemed to be coming from Siobhan but she wasn't moving a muscle.

Alex emerged from the en-suite with a toothbrush in his mouth and a smile on his face. 'Ah, wasn't little Amy so cute with the bike, she loved it didn't she?'

'We, what do you mean we? I made sure to tell Emma that you insisted on getting her a bike, I mean, it's coming into the winter, you gobshite. Shur, what use is she going to get out of it now.'

'What are you talking about? You know, you can wrap children up and bring them out on bikes in the winter too? Imagine how nice it will be for them heading out in the winter, all wrapped up warm in jackets and big woolly hats and heading up to Lily's for a nice warm apple crumble. Amy on the bike and Emma walking alongside. I think it sounds nice, I can't wait to do that kind of thing with our own kids.'

Siobhan covered her face with her hands and groaned. Oh no, she thought to herself, not this bloody issue again and now he's moved onto kids, never mind one child. The instant anxious feeling in her tummy made her sober up pretty quickly!

Alex looked at Siobhan confused. 'What's wrong, honey?'

Siobhan got up off the bed and began to get undressed. 'Can we jusshh go a few hours without having to menshon bloody babieshhh?'

'What? What's wrong with you? What's so wrong with talking about our future?' Alex replied, astounded at her outburst.

'For feck's shhhake, Alex, all you ever want to do ishh talk about babieshhh. I've done nothing but talk about bloody babieshhh all bloody day. Emma was going on about it before the damn party, her mam was ashhhhking me all about how it'shh going, everyone was going on about how good a bloody father you're going to be and how lucky I am and hopefully it will happen schoooon. I'm sick to my back teeth talking about it.' Her voice rose steadily with each word and her face reddened with anger.

Alex was stunned at her reaction. He just stood still and looked at her with an open mouth. They'd never argued like this before. 'Siobhan, I don't understand, what's going on with you?' his face was scrunched up with total confusion at her outburst.

Siobhan was feeling like a volcano ready to erupt. All the pressure of getting pregnant that had been forced on her for the past twelve months was mounting to an all-time high and she wasn't going to be able to contain it much longer. 'I jushhh wish we could go twenty-four flippin' hours without mentioning damn babies. There's more to life than stupid babies, Alex. I'm more than a flippin' baby making things, you know, one of those things, yes machhhhine, that's it a machhhhine!'

'Damn babies? Siobhan, I can't actually believe you're talking like this. Anyone'd think you don't even want a baby! What the hell has got into you, what's your problem?' Alex shouted.

'You, Alex, you're the problem!' she yelled.

'What exactly is your problem with me?' he yelled back in confusion.

'Alex, you've never had to work for anything and now you decide you want a family. And hey preshhhhto! I'm supposed to click my fingershh or my pelvis or whatever and give Lord Alex whatever he wants.'

'You know something, Siobhan, I don't think we need a baby in this house because you're the biggest baby I've ever come across. I'm fed up listening to you carry on about how tough you've had it, how you had to work so hard, how I was handed it all in life. I worked bloody hard to get to where I am too, you know. I had to prove myself to my father and work hard to be the son I wanted to be for him. When he died, I didn't know how I was going to cope, I was scared, Siobhan. I've worked so hard to achieve everything in my life and I am so sick of you throwing all that back in my face,' he turned and marched out the bedroom door.

'Where are you going?' she called after him, as shocked as him at the tone they were using to each other.

'The spare room, and don't bother coming near me either!' he yelled back at her.

Siobhan jumped slightly as the spare room door banged shut. She was left standing in their massive master bedroom all alone. Feelings of dread rose inside her, had she said too much? They'd been married for the best part of ten years and this was the first time he had ever walked out of their bedroom to sleep in the spare room. She'd never seen him so angry before. Sure, they'd had fights before but she was always the one to storm out and head for the spare room. He always came in though and coaxed her back into their bed and they'd end up cuddling or enjoying passionate make-up sex.

This was frightening. She sat on the bed and searched her mind aimlessly to figure out what had just happened. He was the cool one, the one to never get heated. This was unfamiliar territory and it didn't feel good at all. She felt sick. Her chest felt tight and she couldn't breathe properly. Her stomach felt worse with apprehension. She lay on the bed in her underwear and began to cry. She could feel each and every single tear sting her face as they slid down.

Alex was fuming. He was totally and utterly sick to death with Siobhan acting like she was the only one who ever had to work for something. He climbed into the bed. It was funny, he thought to himself, it was a pretty nice room. It looked different when you were actually lying in the bed looking at it.

He switched off the bedside locker lamp and thrashed around for a moment trying to find a comfortable position. He closed his eyes but it took him ages to calm down, he was seething with anger. He could feel his chest rise and fall as the rage filled circled his body.

Siobhan had really pissed him off. She had such a hang up about other people and how easy life was to them and how hard she had to work at everything. Anyone would think she had a terrible life. He just couldn't understand her thinking sometimes. She had everything she could ever want. A fabulous house designed by one of the best architects in the city, a brand new car every bloody year nearly, a holiday at least once a year, weekends away to fancy hotels at the drop of a hat, enough money in the bank that she'd never need to worry.

And yet all she could do was moan about how easy everybody else had it. She couldn't see past her own nose sometimes. And there was poor Emma, widowed and a little girl to bring up on her own. She just got on with it. She had thrown her daughter a wonderful birthday party and sailed around as if she was the happiest woman in the world with everything she could ever want. And going to bed alone tonight without her husband. Well, thought Alex, Siobhan can have a taste of what it's like going to bed alone tonight too.

CHAPTER THIRTEEN

Emma did a final check on the doors before she went upstairs to bed. She couldn't believe the house was back to its normal tidy self after the day's mayhem. It was hard to imagine that only a few hours earlier there were plates of food everywhere, drinks, wrapping paper and presents. Although she begged them to leave the tidying and cleaning up at the time, she was thankful now that her mother and Siobhan had got stuck in when everybody left.

She filled Digger's bowl of water and patted him gently on the head. He was such a good dog. The poor thing was cast out to the back yard all day but he didn't seem to mind. All he wanted to do these days was lie around anyway. He was getting on in dog years but Emma was convinced he was pining for Aidan still. He was Aidan's dog really. As soon as Aidan moved down to Kilfarrig, he insisted on getting a little puppy. They visited the pound within weeks and he instantly fell in love with Digger, a two-year-old golden retriever.

'I better get a glass of water for myself too Digger, I think I had a little too much wine tonight.' She turned off all the downstairs lights and left on the one on the landing. She liked to have a bit of light shining into Amy's room in case she woke up.

As she did every night, she found it impossible to pass her daughter's door without peeping in. The peeping always led to actually going in and planting a gentle kiss on her head.

Tonight was no different. She quietly nudged the door open further. Emma's heart lifted when she looked in on Amy sleeping. She looked so peaceful lying there with such an angelic face. She crept over and carefully sat on the side of the bed. Amy didn't move a muscle. She took a deep breath, inhaling all of Amy's beauty as she did. It was incredible the amount of pure love she felt for the little girl fast asleep in her bed. Her heart felt like bursting. She smiled and stared through blurry eyes at her little sweetheart fast asleep. She reached out and gently pulled back a strand of hair off Amy's face. Amy stirred a little and Emma cautiously jumped back, repeating a motherly mantra over and over... 'oh shit...don't wake up, don't wake up, don't wake up, don't wake up....'

Moments later, she climbed into her own bed and snuggled up into her fresh clean sheets. She had changed all the bed clothes that morning, knowing how nice it was going to feel to snuggle up into the gorgeous smell of fresh clean pillow case and duvet after a long day. She loved burying her nose into them and smelling the fabric conditioner.

She lay still and content with a slight smile on her face. The light from the landing was creeping in ever so slightly into her room just enough as to provide a smidgen of brightness. Even though she had the big double bed all to herself, she always slept on the side she had claimed when she and Aidan first started sharing the bed.

Today had been a wonderful day and she was delighted with how it had all went. Everybody was in great form and Amy was absolutely spoilt rotten with all the presents. The food went down a treat, so much so that nobody seemed to have room left for the birthday cake. Most of it was still in the fridge. Strange she thought but she had to actually convince Amy that it was an actual cake and it was ok to eat.

But by far the most amazing part to Emma's day had been the miraculous connection she had felt to Aidan. She had no doubt that he was with her in spirit form. She could feel him in the house all day. Her smile grew as she closed her eyes and remembered the tingly feeling that would suddenly wash over her many times during the day. Being able to share the experience with Siobhan made it even more incredible. It made it seem more real, to be able to say it out loud to somebody. She was sure that it sounded crazy and she would never tell anybody other than Siobhan and Jack about it.

She turned so she was lying on her back looking at the ceiling and put her hands out on top of the duvet. She couldn't feel anything in the room or around her but she wasn't disheartened. 'Aidan honey, thank you so much for being there for me today. I could feel your essence around me, your presence, or should I say your spirit. It was such a comforting feeling to have you near me. Isn't Amy wonderful?' She waited eagerly for a sign of some sort, a reply, but nothing. 'I really hope you're happy with the way I'm bringing her up. We didn't get a chance to chat about raising children and our hopes and dreams for them. I just want Amy to be like you, kind, loving, smart, incredible.' She waited, looking at the ceiling waiting for a flash of light of something but nothing. 'I miss you so much, Aidan, so much that it still hurts every single day. I love you.'

She had often talked to Aidan at night before she fell asleep but, lately, she was half expecting something to happen to let her know he was listening. The highs she'd been feeling during the days that she had felt a connection to him were followed by lows at night when not a single sign was transmitted. She wanted to be able to communicate with him so badly. She was one hundred percent positive he was with her during the day and yet, at night, a shadow of doubt crept into her mind asking unwanted questions like, 'Was I just imagining it?'

'Aidan, I know you were here today, I know you were with me, I could feel you, I know I could. I know you wouldn't mess me around. Please, please give me a sign that you're here now. Anything, anything at all.' Seconds went by where she was almost afraid to breathe in case he made a sound and she wouldn't be able to hear it. But nothing. 'Please Aidan, show me a sign. I need you, I need you so much.' Again, she waited. Nothing. Tears began to flow. She turned over, curled up in a ball and cried herself to sleep.

CHAPTER FOURTEEN

Jack woke up feeling refreshed and completely recharged, even though the night before had turned into a lads' drinking session rather than a business chat. Alex had ended up going back to The Cellar with Jack after the birthday party where he was introduced to Michael.

Soon, the three men were joking over a few beers like old friends. Alex was sensible and only had the two beers, but Jack and Michael made up for it by gradually becoming stupidly drunk. Steve, being sensible, thought they were too intoxicated to be trusted to stay in the bar so he called them a taxi before kicking them out.

It was only when the taxi pulled up outside Jack's house did they remember that Michael was actually staying in a B&B on the other side of town. Jack insisted that Michael kip in the spare room for the night and Michael was too drunk to care where he slept.

Jack could hear Michael snore as he passed the spare room on his way down the stairs. Even with the sore head, he felt good. He felt different. For the first time in a long time, he felt positive. He realised while talking to Michael last night, or what he could remember of it anyway, that he was actually being extremely negative over everything lately. He never really believed in people's attitudes being a big part of their financial success or life success. But Michael was a great believer in what he called 'the universe' and how if you asked for it, you received it. It was all a bit way over Jack's head but Michael was trying to explain to him over their eight beer that negativity would breed negativity and that Jack had to change his attitude.

By the eleventh beer, Jack had come to realise that he was actually dreadfully negative about the business. By his twelfth beer, he was convinced that his negativity was driving the business into the ground and it had nothing to do with the aftermath of any recession. By his thirteenth, he came to the conclusion that it was all bullshit and the recession was the real perpetrator but that maybe his negativity wasn't helping.

So today was a new start, a positive one. He was damned if he was going to let anything close down his bar for good. He wasn't going to let this rough patch beat him and he was going to do his damnedest to turn the bar around.

Alex woke up feeling like all the muscles in his back were knotted up and twisted. He couldn't believe how upset and angry he had got with Siobhan. He rarely let fly at her like that! He felt terrible. Everything was definitely getting on top of him these past few months. Trying to conceive for a full year now was starting to bother him. Siobhan had told him to be patient, that it could take a very long time, but he honestly thought it would have happened by now. It was fun in the beginning having all that enjoyable sex. And, he had to admit, he always liked to cuddle up with Siobhan afterwards and wonder if they had just made their son or daughter.

But now it was just getting frustrating. These days, he felt like giving his sperm a pep talk before he jumped into bed with her! To tell them to get their swimming caps on and go like an Olympian up that pathway to reach that egg waiting there patiently for the winner of the sperm race!

He was only in his early forties and he had often heard of men in their sixties fathering children so he was sure it wasn't his age. He always had a loaded gun and he never had any trouble pulling the trigger and shooting out the good stuff. He wondered if maybe he was shooting blanks.

What if it turned out he couldn't have children, he couldn't give Siobhan what she wanted? How could he look her in the face and know that he was the cause of all the frustration and disappointment they felt each month? He knew she was putting on a brave face for him but, deep down, she was bitterly disheartened when she got her period. She was like clockwork, every twenty-eight day without fail she would get it and the hope that maybe, just maybe, this month was crushed.

That was obviously why she lashed out at him mentioning children again last night.

'Oh, I'm such a gobshite,' he muttered to himself as he threw back the duvet. Sitting there in his boxers, he thought about the fight they had and what she had said. He had been really hammering home the babies issue a hell of a lot in the past year. If he was feeling anxious that nothing was happening, then she must be sick with anxiousness. Alex knew Siobhan always got what she set out to do, so not being able to get pregnant must be killing her. All his anger disappeared and his attitude softened. He stood up, stretched his arms up over his head, and headed for the master bedroom.

Siobhan felt terrible. She lay awake exhausted from a night of practically no sleep. She tossed and turned all night. It was all getting too much! She was dreading the morning coming so much that she just couldn't drift off. Alex had never left their bed before so she couldn't help but feel that this was the beginning of the end. This was serious now. She'd had so much to drink last night, she couldn't exactly remember what she had actually said. Alex, however, was going to remember every detail. She fretted over how much she had let slip in the heat of the moment. Was he going to put two and two together and come up with 'my wife has been lying to me for a year, the devious witch?' After the way he stormed out of the room last night, she knew he was capable of leaving.

She closed her eyes as she thought of life without him. How would she cope? She loved him so much and the thought of him leaving was way too painful. Then again, she thought, why would he be the one to leave? She was the one cheating him, she was the baddy. Babies, she thought, bloody babies, why couldn't I just be a normal woman and want one, I wouldn't be in the stupid mess then. She tried to picture herself wheeling a pram down the street and meeting up with other mothers for play dates. No, it wasn't for her. She was happiest when she was pounding away on her treadmill and in the office sorting out all sorts of legal issues. But the reality of the situation was that if she was to peel away what made her happy, she would be left with one vital core, her husband. Nothing would make sense without him. Was she going to lose him now? She was terrified of the answer.

Emma was awoken up to a bright and cheery four year-old pulling her eyelids open. No, she screamed inside, it can't be morning already.

Surprisingly Amy had actually slept in past her usual wake-up time but the previous night's wine was tugging on Emma to turn over and fall back into a nice long slumber.

'I want breakfast, Mammy, I want breakfast. Mammy, Mammy, I want breakfast, I want break...'

'Yeah, in a minute, Amy, I'm just waking up.'

'I want breakfast, Mammy, I want breakfast, I want breakfast Mammy, I want...'

Emma crawled out of the bed reluctantly and threw on her nightgown. 'Aidan, if you're around, the least you could do is make the bloody breakfast,' she said out loud as she walked out the bedroom door.

Jack heard Michael moaning as he came down the stairs.

'You know something Jack, I think we drank The Cellar dry last night!' He looked a little worse for wear in his wrinkly clothes which he obviously slept in and ruffled hair. Jack poured him a coffee and went about cooking a fry-up.

'A few ol' sausages and rashers will put you right.'

'Oh, food, no I couldn't!'

'Wait till you smell it, you'll be right as rain when you get it into your belly, soakage, man, soakage.'

'What has you so chirpy this morning, then?'

'Michael, I'm taking your advice, no more wallowing in self-pity. From now on, I'm going to be nothing put positive and I'm going to pull The Cellar back up from its knees. You were dead right last night, I've been way too bloody negative and, as you say, negative thoughts bring negative situations.'

'Eh, did I say that? What a load of crap, I must've been really drunk!' he laughed.

Alex gently opened the door to the bedroom and walked in softly just in case Siobhan was sleeping. She was wide awake though and looked like she hadn't slept at all.

She sat up in the bed as soon as she saw Alex with a look of dread all over her face.

'Morning, honey.' Alex walked over to the bed sat down and took her hand in his.

The knots in her stomach eased a little, she wasn't expecting him to do that.

'Morning, how did you sleep?' her voice was a little wobbly.

'Not great. It was silly of me really to storm out, I can never sleep without you,' his face was so loving that it made her feel sick with guilt.

'I'm so sorry for fighting with you, Alex. I guess I had too much to drink and it had been a long day.'

'No, I'm the one that should be sorry, honey. I had a really good think about the whole situation and it hasn't been easy on you, I can see that now. I've been putting you under so much pressure with the pregnancy issue and that just wasn't fair.'

Siobhan couldn't believe what she was hearing, he was sorry for piling the pressure on. He had actually realised that it was all too much for her and that he needed to back off. This was incredible, just moments earlier she was expecting him to come into the room, still angry and demanding to know what was going on.

She had seriously thought about coming clean about being on the pill and throwing it all out there. Now, he was the one sorry for the row and for the pressure she was under. Maybe they could get through this after all. The knots in her tummy were almost gone.

'Siobhan, it's been hard the past few months and it's getting too much for us. I think we should deal with this head on now. We can get through this.'

Siobhan felt the knots beginning to tighten again.

'I think it's time we saw a fertility expert.' Alex searched her face for a reaction. His words were like a wrench, which seemed to reach into her tummy and tightened the knots to the very last.

CHAPTER FIFTEEN

'What's Santy bringing you for Crispmas, Illy?' Amy asked with her eyebrows burrowed into a questioning form.

'Oh, I think he's going to bring me a lovely cuddly teddy bear, Amy. Won't that be nice?' smiled Lily as she placed Amy's cookie in front of her.

'A teddy?' said Amy, frowning, 'but aren't you too old for teddies?'

Emma jumped into the conversation very quickly to save any further embarrassment. 'Why don't you tell Lily what you're getting, honey?'

'I'm getting a real rocking horse that makes real horsey sounds when you press his real ears,' she shouted out with pride, 'oh and a big big big surprise!'

'Oh lovely' Lily said, cocking her head to one side for added effect.

'Yeah and Tracy said she was going to get Mammy a big fat viberatorer. What's a viberatorer, Illy? Mammy keeps telling me to ssshhhh when I ask.'

Tracy chocked on her latte and Emma took on the colour of Santa's red coat.

'Okay, well maybe your mam will explain that to you when she gets home love,' Lily chuckled. 'you enjoy that viberatorer now, Emma, won't you.' She was still laughing to herself as she walked away.

'I keep telling you to watch what you say around her, I told you she is a real little parrot at the moment, picks up on and repeats everything!' Emma scolded Tracy harshly.

'Sorry but it *was* funny. Anyway, look, can I borrow Amy over the weekend for a few hours? That new children's film is out and I need a child to go see it with me, I'd look fairly odd going in on my own.'

'Sure, it'll give me time to clean the house for Christmas, Aidan's parents are coming down and I want the place gleaming. Plus, I might attempt to make a Christmas cake, I'll make you one too if you like?'

'Ah no, I'm okay for cake, thanks anyway. I, eh, I don't really like it too much!' Tracy said rather quickly.

'Yes, you do, you love Christmas cake, what are you talking about? You're always scoffing it in the staff room so the rest of us grab a slice and hide it in our lockers! Remember last year, Mrs. Doyle made the staff a fabulous cake for Christmas and you had it half eaten before lunch time!'

'Oh yeah, I suppose it's alright, it's just that my mam has baked a couple already so really there's no need to make me one, but thanks anyway.'

'But you said you're mother wasn't making any this year, her knees are acting up again aren't they? She's going to your sister-in-law and she has done the lot.'

'Oh yeah but, look, don't go making any for me please, it's too much hassle.'

'No it's not.'

'Yes it is.'

'No it's not, especially seeing as you're bringing Amy off to the cinema for a few hours.'

'Okay, then, what I really mean is it's too much hassle on me!'

'What?'

'Well, I'll have to pretend to be delighted, take the cake home and I use the term "cake" very lightly here, try and dispose of it safely, and believe me that means not digesting it in any way, then lie to you for weeks afterwards, then try and deal with the guilt of lying and, frankly, that's all too much hassle!'

Emma looked stunned.

'Emma, honey, I love you but I gotta tell you, your Christmas cakes are, well, shall we just say, complete disasters!' Tracy bravely admitted, patting her friend's hand.

Emma was so offended that she hadn't even noticed her mam and dad sitting at the table right next to them.

'What's wrong, love? You look terribly upset.' Joan asked.

'Nothing, but can you do me a favour, mam? Can you make me a Christmas cake when you're doing yours?' Emma asked with a pout.

'Already done, dear, you know… just in case your cake didn't work out,' smiled Joan, not minding the devastated look on Emma's face. 'Oh actually, speaking of Christmas,' she continued, 'you haven't forgotten to ask Jack to dinner have you?'

'Of course not, he's delighted. I think he has a thing for you, mam, you want to watch out, dad!' joked Emma, getting past the cake thing quite quickly.

Seamus barely looked up from his paper. Joan wiped some imaginary fluff from her cardigan. 'Oh Emma, he's such a lovely boy, I can't see why you wouldn't…'

She didn't even get to finish her sentence before Emma butted in, annoyed, 'Don't even say it, it's not now or ever gonna happen.'

'Leave her alone, woman, will you?' Seamus reprimanded, finally taking his head out of the paper to say something.

Joan didn't even flinch at his grumpy tone, she was just glad she had said something worthy of his attention!

'Come on Amy, help Granddad pick out a lovely sickly bun.'

'Oh dad, she's just had a massive cookie, don't fill her with more rubbish before she goes to bed,' groaned Emma. 'then again,' she thought to herself and then shared aloud, 'you're the one putting her to bed so it won't make a difference to me.'

'Guess what, Granddad,' piped up Amy all excited, 'mammy is getting a big fat viberatorer for Christmas!'

'Oh right, very good,' coughed a mortified Seamus.

'What is a viberatorer? Illy doesn't know what one is, I already axed her!' Amy declared with her big inquisitive eyes looking up at her Grandad.

'Amy, will you stop telling people that? Tracy I'm going to kill you!' Emma spat out.

Seamus and Amy quickly left the table before Emma blew up altogether!

'So, Tracy, what are you doing for Christmas?' Joan asked, eager to move on from the viberatoter. 'Would you like to join us for dinner?'

Emma noticed that her mother was asking everything and anything that moved to dinner this year!

'Oh, thanks a million, Joan, but I'm going to my brother-in-law's this year, his wife cooks enough food to last a year!'

'Oh that will be nice for you. What about Siobhan and Alex, Emma, what are their plans?' Joan continued, hoping to add a few more to the dinner table. The company might make up for the loneliness she was feeling these days.

'They're going to Alex's mam's and Siobhan's mam is going to join them for a few hours. There's a Christmas dinner in the Everglades but Siobhan wanted her mam to share the day with her. Although by the sounds of it, Catherine wants to get back to the nursing home early because they're having Christmas drinks in the afternoon and watching old movies.

'Sounds like a lovely place, doesn't it, though then again it would have to be for the cost of it every month, wouldn't it!' Joan blurted out. 'But just imagine all the company you'd have in a place like that, always having someone to talk to!' she continued.

She'd always warned Emma to never ever put her into a nursing home but now she wondered if it was such a bad thing after all.

Emma and Tracy carried on with the conversation, not noticing that Joan's gaze had wandered. 'Right, Joan, come on,' butted in Seamus, 'we've bought some lovely little cream cakes for after dinner, didn't we, Amy?' he said, ruffling the child's hair.

'Right, come on so, Amy, let's get you back to the house so we can make a start on it, do you want to peel the carrots?' Joan asked as she stood up.

'Oh yes please, Nana,' Amy jumped up and down excitedly, 'and then you can tell me all about mammy's viberatorer!'

CHAPTER SIXTEEN

Siobhan spent most of the week in the office trying to avoid Alex. He was desperately trying to pin her down to a date for a doctor's appointment. Ever since their row, he was being an absolute dote and she couldn't stand it. She felt like she had her foot constantly glued to the accelerator and the guilt had gone up a gear while she was doing one hundred and fifty kilometres an hour the wrong way down a motorway with no brakes.

'Siobhan, earth to Siobhan.' Julie was standing in Siobhan's office waiting for her to sign some letters but Siobhan was miles away. Julie wondered what was going on. Alex had only come into the office one day that week and Julie had to send home some urgent paperwork with Siobhan last night that he needed to sign. They couldn't have had a row because anytime he rang to speak to her he sounded in terrific form. It was weird, though, that he rang the office to get in touch with her; usually he just rang her mobile. Siobhan was definitely acting strange and it was getting frustrating.

'Oh, sorry, Julie, here they are, all signed and ready to go. Why don't you head on home, you deserve an early finish.' Siobhan didn't even look up at Julie as she spoke.

'Oh, that'd be lovely, if you're sure.' Julie was gobsmacked. It was a very rare occasion when she got to leave the office early. It was weird, but she wasn't complaining.

'Absolutely, have a good weekend.' Siobhan finally looked up and smiled but she was still miles away.

Julie quickly placed the letters in their assigned envelopes, franked them, grabbed her coat and ran for the door.

It was only when her tummy began to rumble did Siobhan realise it was well past knock off time. She sat at her desk wondering what to do. She wasn't too keen on the thoughts of going home to face Alex and all his enthusiasm regarding doctor's appointments and fertility treatments. She rang Emma and arranged to go back to her house for a takeaway and a bottle of wine.

Alex was disappointed when Siobhan rang to tell him she was going over to Emma's for a takeaway, he really wanted to sit down with her and figure out the best time for them to arrange a visit to the doctor's. She'd been working so hard all week he didn't want to pester her but a week was nearly gone now since he mentioned fertility experts and he was eager to take the first step.

He still felt a pang of guilt for sleeping in the spare room the previous weekend after their fight. He hadn't really thought about the pressure she must have been feeling to conceive and since then he was trying to make it up to her. He had suggested they go away to their usual spot for a spa treatment and some well-deserved relaxation but, bizarrely, Siobhan declined. He wondered if she was still mad at him since the row; she was a little distant but she insisted it was simply because she was so busy at work and tired at night. He decided to head down to Jack's for dinner and a few beers, he could certainly do with a few.

Two empty plates and an empty bottle of wine later, the two girls sat back on the sofa gazing at the telly. 'Amy is so good for going to bed, isn't she? She just lay down after her story and cuddled into her teddy.' Siobhan was surprised at how easy it was to settle Amy down to sleep. She had visions of a toddler running around the house screaming at bedtime. She certainly couldn't believe Amy was so good.

'Just think, in another while, you could be doing that every night.' Emma grinned over at Siobhan.

'Doing what every night?' Siobhan asked, acting clueless.

'Putting a little one to sleep, silly! What are you like, eh? Where's your head at all?' Emma giggled.

'Oh, yeah right, well, I just hope they'll be half as good as Amy if that is the case.'

'How are things going anyway?' Emma wasn't too sure about asking the same old question again, she felt like she was beginning to sound like a broken record. And if the record wasn't broken, she was sure that Siobhan must be getting to the point where she'd be happy to break it!

'Emm, well, Alex is keen to go see someone; I think he wants to go see Dr Kennedy just to get the ball rolling,' Siobhan replied, not too enthusiastically.

Emma was surprised that there was any progress. Usually, Siobhan didn't have a whole lot to say on the matter, even if she didn't sound all too convinced about the doctor visitation. 'You don't seem too sure about going to Dr Kennedy.'

'I just think it's all way too early to be involving doctors and specialists. I mean it can take so long to get pregnant and the more pressure, the harder it is.'

'Yeah but, with Alex being in his early forties, he probably wants to move things along, that's all.'

'We're still young. A lot of couple are opting to have children in their later years these days and, sure, I'll probably only have the one so it's not as if we're rushing to raise a large family or anything.'

'Well, look, I think it's a good thing to make an appointment. You never know, even by starting the ball rolling there, you may feel more at ease and fall pregnant in no time,' Emma said, trying to sound upbeat.

'Yeah, anyway, enough about that. I'm not here to talk about pregnancies and babies. How are you?'

Siobhan was instinctively aware that Emma wasn't in great form, even though she was trying her best to act as if she was. 'Are you okay, Emma, you don't really seem yourself tonight?'

'Yeah, I'm fine.' Emma seemed surprised at the question. She had worked hard to look composed.

'Come on, it's me you're talking to. You don't seem happy at all, I can tell.' Siobhan wasn't going to let it go, half afraid to let the baby conversation creep back in.

Emma threw her head back on the sofa and looked up to the heavens as if looking for an answer. Eventually, she decided to let her guard down and drop the obviously not-so-good acting. 'Nothing has happened all week,' she sighed.

'What do you mean, nothing has happened?' Siobhan looked at her intently.

'Nothing has happened, nothing at all. I haven't felt Aidan around me, I haven't felt his presence at all.' She took her head up off the sofa and looked over at Siobhan with tears in her eyes. 'It went from being amazing, absolutely amazing to nothing at all. I could feel him, Siobhan. He was here, I know he was, he was here and now, now he's not, he's just disappeared.' She had a look of despair about her which tugged at Siobhan's heart big time.

'Emma, honey, I'm sure Aidan is here in spirit but physically he's gone and I really think you need to accept that and try to move on with your life. I know that sounds harsh, but for your own sake and for Amy's, you need to start living each day for you and for Amy. Not for the chance that you might feel Aidan's presence around you. Even if he was here, or if he is here, it will never be in body, it will never be the same. You have to let go, honey, you have to move on.' Siobhan's whole body was leaning towards Emma as if she was waiting to catch her tears in case she became overwhelmed with emotions. But it was a dangerous place to be, Emma became overwhelmed with emotions alright, anger and fury to be exact.

'What do you mean if he was here, do you not believe me now? Why would I make that up? And I'm sick to death of you telling me to move on. Ever since he died, you've been on my case to move on. I can't move on. He was my life, Siobhan, Aidan was my life, so I can't move on with it when it's dead, can I?'

Siobhan was shocked. 'Emma, how can you say that? You've a wonderful daughter upstairs, she's your life now, she's your future. You have everything to live for and I'm sure Aidan would turn in his grave to hear you talk like that.'

'Don't you dare talk about my husband turning in his grave! You have absolutely no idea what you're talking about. You're so bloody lucky, Siobhan, and you don't even know it! You have your husband, you climb into your cosy bed every night beside him, you wake up every single day beside him, you work with him, you can see him, hold him, touch him.' Emma's rage simmered to a whimper.

Siobhan quickly moved over till she was practically sitting on top of Emma. She threw her arms around her friend who was now a blubbering mess. 'I know, I know, I'm sorry for upsetting you, honey. I'm just worried about you and I desperately want to see you happy again.'

'I don't think I'll ever be happy again, not without Aidan. I love Amy with all my heart, of course I do, and this is not about her. If I didn't have her, I couldn't cope but life without him is hard. I loved him so much, I love him so much still.'

'I know you do pet, I know you do.' There wasn't much more Siobhan could say, or more to the point, was willing to say. 'Why don't I open another bottle of wine? We could do with another glass and then I'll ring Alex, tell him I'm gonna stay here for the night?'

'Don't be silly, I'm fine. You don't have to stay here. I'm hardly going to do anything stupid now, am I? As you say, I have an amazing little girl upstairs and, God knows, I love her so much.'

'I wasn't even thinking that, Emma, I know you wouldn't leave Amy. I just think it would be nice, we can throw on one of your DVDs and just chill out.'

Alex was on his second pint when his phone beeped.

'STAYIN IN EMMAS SHE NEEDS COMPANY, HOME IN THE MORNING, LOVE U X'

'Well that's just great' he muttered, a bit too loudly.

'What's up?' Michael asked as he drained the last of his bottle.

'Oh, the missus isn't coming home tonight. She's staying in a friend's and I wanted to talk to her about something, but sure there's always tomorrow, isn't there?'

Michael wasn't sure whether Alex wanted him to answer him or not.

'Well then, if that's the case, you can stay for another surely. Jack, two more here please when you're ready.'

Alex wasn't arguing, he didn't feel like going home to an empty house. He was never any good at being on his own and hated the idea of not sleeping beside his wife.

Jack brought over the three beers and joined the two lads. 'Well, what's the craic here, any news?'

'Alex here is a single man for the night, his missus is staying with her pal tonight, isn't that right?'

'Oh, is Siobhan staying at Emma's tonight? God, their cackling better not keep me awake.' Jack rolled his eyes up to heaven but was smiling away.

'Well, I suppose it'd make a difference wouldn't it, it's usually you keeping poor Emma awake with all your cackling, and not the same type of cackling the girls would be getting up to, if you know what I mean.' Alex nodded the head at Jack and looked over at Michael with a big grin.

'Oh, tell me more, a ladies' man are you Jack?' Michael slagged him.

'Any word on somewhere to rent yet?' Jack asked, brushing off any Spanish inquisitions into his love life.

'Oh yeah actually, I think I finally found an apartment to rent, it's on Peter's Lane. I viewed it today and it's fairly decent,' said Michael, good-humouredly changing the subject without Alex even noticing it.

Alex thought out loud, 'Peter's Lane, Peter's Lane? Oh yeah, that's the one down from the Italian. Are the apartments nice? I'd imagine they're fairly small, no?'

'Yeah, it was small but, sure, I'm only renting and the rent is reasonable. I'm not too keen on the parking, though. I'd feel more secure if my car was in a drive or locked in, you know.'

'Ah, you're in a fairly safe place, believe me,' Alex tried to reassure him.

'Hey, I just thought of a brilliant idea. Why didn't I think of it before?' Jack's face lit up and he suddenly came alive as he spoke. 'Why don't you move into my place?'

Michael looked at him astonished. 'Oh, I didn't realise you were looking for a tenant.'

'I'm not, but when you think about it, it works out great. I could do with a few extra bob seeing as this place is not pulling in as much cash as usual. Sure I have two spare rooms, you could rent one and I'll even do you a good deal on the rent seeing as you've been offering me good advice to get this place up and running again.'

'It's a deal!' Michael put out his hand and shook Jack's.

'This calls for a celebration. Steve, another round over here please,' called out Alex.

CHAPTER SEVENTEEN

Michael stood out on the path and took a minute to simply admire the house, his new home for God only knew how long. He couldn't believe his luck. Out of all the new housing estates and apartment complexes built in the past couple of years in the town, none had really taken his fancy. But Jack's house had a unique character to it. The little cul-de-sac was quiet and private, in the shape of a circle, with five sets of well-maintained semi-detached houses all gathered around, nice and cosy. Two red brick piers stood tall but unassuming at the entrance with a dark green tidy hedge either side. The line of maturing elm and spruce on the drive in were subtly welcoming.

Jack lived in the fourth house from the entrance which was attached to Emma's on his left. Leaning on his car, Michael studied both houses and started to feel a glimmer of hope that the future was starting to look up again. It had been hard splitting up with Cameron but life in Kilfarrig seemed to be on the up.

His thoughts drifted into the air and were carried away by the cool south easterly winds as two women and an adorable little girl emerged from number three, the house next to Jack's. A big friendly golden retriever ran past them and straight over to Michael with his tail wagging. Michael immediately got down on one knee to pet the dog and commented on how friendly he was.

Emma looked over to see a young handsome man down on one knee, talking to Digger. Of course, Digger was absolutely loving the attention and the good old rub behind the ears that the man seemed all too happy to give.

'I'm so sorry. Digger, come here boy. You must be some sort of dog whisperer, he's usually very wary of strangers, usually a great guard dog,' Emma lied through her teeth. Digger was no more a guard dog than Amy was. He was a clumsy lovable creature that would lick a burglar rather than bite one.

'Oh, You must be Emma, I'm Michael. I'm actually your new neighbour, I'm moving in with Jack, he's renting me one of the spare rooms.' Michael held out his hand and smiled at Emma, thinking how pretty she was. Jack had talked a lot about her but had never mentioned how attractive she was in a sweet way. She came across confident but in a funny kind of shy way.

'Oh yeah, Michael, pleased to meet you. Jack has mentioned you before; you're in marketing right?' she said, shaking his outstretched hand.

'I didn't know Jack was looking for a lodger, he never said!' Emma looked confused, she knew things were not going well for Jack but he'd never said anything to her about needing to take in a lodger.

'It was a spur of the moment decision really. I've been down here on and off for a while and, well, it seems like the perfect place to relocate to. I was paying a fortune for rent in Dublin and I can't afford it anymore since I was let go.'

Michael looked past Emma's shoulder at the sight of the other woman helping the little girl stuffed into a winter jacket, hat and scarf onto a little pink bike. 'That must be the adorable little Amy that Jack was telling me about,' he smiled at the bundle of jacket and hat trying to peddle the bike with its stabilisers down the short driveway towards Emma. Amy somewhere inside, peeping out.

'Yeah, that's Amy, my daughter; hiding among all those layers. Say hi to Michael, Amy, he's going to be our new neighbour.' Emma beamed with pride as the coat peddled towards her.

When she reached Emma's side, Michael bent down and held out his hand. 'Hello there, little lady, how old are you then?'

A little face poked out from under the hat and mumbled something about being a really big grown up.

'Wow,' laughed Michael, 'you are a really big grown up, able to ride your own bike and everything. You're a smart little girl, aren't you?'

'Uncle Alex showed me how to peggle it,' Amy said, self-pride radiating from every pore.

'Well, I think Uncle Alex did a very good job.' Michael felt a sudden pang of sadness as he remembered Jack telling him how Amy's father had died before she was born.

Siobhan, who had been busy trying to put the lead on a very excited and squirmy Digger, looked up at the mention of Alex's name. Michael was quick to catch her eye, 'You must be Siobhan, I was out with your good husband last night,' he said as he walked over and stretched out his hand towards her.

'Oh yeah, Alex has mentioned you before alright.' She hid her surprise that Alex had gone out. When she text him that she wouldn't be home last night, he had texted back, telling her to have a good night but no mention of going out himself.

'Oh don't believe a word! I've only ever seen him when we're drunk so whatever he has said doesn't count, right?' he laughed as he looked back at Emma and Amy.

'Oh well you'll have to pop in now for a glass of wine seen as we're neighbours.' Emma said quite casually with a smile on her face.

'Oh absolutely that sounds good, you can fill me in on all of Jack's antics so I'm fully prepared now that I'm moving in.'

'Well, as long as you don't mind extra company in the house the odd Saturday night and an extra person for coffee Sunday mornings, you'll be fine,' laughed Emma.

'Oh yeah, I've heard he's a bit of a Jack the lad alright. Sure maybe I'll pop over to you on a Saturday night when he has company, for the glass of wine so.'

Siobhan watched as the two carried on with the banter. It was nice it was to actually see Emma smile and joke in another man's company. Maybe this new guy moving in was going to be a great thing. Alex had mentioned that he seemed to be a nice fella the last time he had a drink with him.

'Anyway, we better get going before the weather changes and we're caught in a shower. We're heading up to Lily's for a coffee. Sure, I'll be seeing you around then, neighbour.'

'He's seems lovely doesn't he?' Siobhan said in a hushed voice as they walked away.

'Yeah, he does, very nice,' Emma agreed.

Mmmm, watch this space, thought Siobhan, watch this space.

'Would you like another toasted rasher sandwich, Alex? You practically inhaled that one,' laughed Deirdre as she refilled his cup with hot tea.

'No thanks Mam, but that was delicious, just what the doctor ordered.' Alex sat back and rubbed his full belly. The ferocious hangover was almost gone now.

'Aw sure, it's lovely to sit down and have lunch with you on a Saturday. It was a lovely surprise. Shame Siobhan couldn't make it, don't tell me she's working or killing herself on that bloody walker? The girl doesn't see how skinny she is.'

Deirdre was very fond of Siobhan but worried that she was so fanatical about her weight. 'No, she stayed in Emma's last night actually but I'm sure she'll have been for a jog before I get home,' Alex said offhandedly as he stirred his tea.

'Oh, is everything alright?' Deirdre had never spent a night away from her husband in all the years they were together, apart from her stay in hospital having each of the children.

'Yeah, I think she just wanted to spend some time with Emma, that's all. Poor Emma is still finding her feet a bit I think, it's still hard on her.'

'Oh, I thought she was doing much better these past few months. Siobhan had said she was in good form, no?'

'Ah yeah but, sure look Ma, these things take time, don't they?'

'I know love, sure I still miss your father so much, tis a great loss.' Deirdre hung her head and stared into her tea.

Alex's heart went out to his mother. She was still beautiful and elegant and too young really to be rattling around in the big old house on her own. He reached out and gently rubbed her hand.

'Anyway, let's not get all morbid. How are things going with yourself and Siobhan, any news on the baby front?' she asked carefully.

'No,' Alex said with a big sigh that came all the way from his big toes.

'It's just not happening for us.' Alex looked at his mother and she could see the sorrow and disappointment in his eyes. It hurt her to see him in such anguish.

'Maybe you should talk to Dr Long for some advice, pet. Sure your father knew him well and he was very kind to me when your father passed. He's supposed to be brilliant, do you know him at all?'

'Yes I do. Siobhan handled his divorce a couple of years back. He's one of the leading fertility specialists in that pirate clinic isn't he? I was actually just going to make an appointment with our own doctor, Dr Kennedy, but now I think I might see about Dr Long. Only thing is, I just can't bring myself to pick up the phone. What do I say, "Hey John how are you? By the way I can't seem to get my wife pregnant!" A bit of a delicate subject, isn't it, so I was just going to go see Doctor Kennedy to get the ball rolling on it all, make it less…I don't know, less of a big deal, I guess.'

'Look love, it's nothing to be ashamed of or embarrassed about. I think you should give him a ring. Maybe he can do you a favour and see you sooner rather than later.'

'Yeah, maybe. Poor Siobhan, it's all getting on top of her too, you know. Can you imagine what's going through her head? She has succeeded at everything else and this is one thing we seem to be failing at. If I feel this bad, I can imagine how she feels.'

Deirdre looked at him, surprised. Surely, Alex knew exactly how Siobhan was feeling. 'Have you spoken to her about it, love?'

'Yes and no. We kind of had a bit of a tiff and it was fairly obvious that the pressure of not conceiving was getting to her. I know it's a difficult subject for her, Ma, she can barely look at me and I know it's because she feels a failure. But the thing is, who is to say the problem lies with her? It could easily be me. I could be the one with the problem and it's killing me to think I could be the cause of all this frustration.'

CHAPTER EIGHTEEN

Emma was pleasantly surprised to find that she had managed to actually enjoy the day. It was a long time since herself and Siobhan had spent so much time together and she really appreciated her friend's company. She had been feeling rather down lately. She had lost the feeling that Aidan was around and it hurt so much. She felt as though she was beginning to grieve again. She had been so sure of his presence but she felt nothing lately except pure loneliness. If it hadn't been for Amy, she'd have lost her mind completely. When she had felt his presence, she had felt alive again and happy with life. Now, she just felt rotten.

She yawned as she slouched back on the couch and cuddled into Amy. They were both wrecked after the day with Siobhan. They had walked the full length of the beach, spent ages pushing Amy on the swings in the park and stopped off in The Cellar for a coffee. If she didn't know better, she'd have thought that Siobhan didn't want to go home! Amy laughed as the animated fluffy lion pounced playfully on a butterfly only to open his paws and let it go again. Digger caught Emma's eye as he wagged his tail for a moment, making her smile at him flat out asleep on his side.

'Digger must be having a nice dream Amy.'

'Why mammy? 'Amy looked up at her mother full of wonder.

'Because he just wagged his tail.'

'Why?'

'Because he wagged his tail honey.'

'Why mammy?'

'Because dogs wag their tail when they're happy.'

'Why mammy?'

'Well, because I suppose that's how they show they're happy because they can't smile.'

'Why?'

'Because, I don't know, they just can't smile. So they wag their tail, then we know they're happy.'

'Why?'

'Because that's the why, Amy! Oh look, the films over, time for bed now!' Perfect timing! 'Right madam, up you get, let's go get you into your lovely comfy jimjams.' Just as she had thought, there were no arguments at all. Amy jumped down off the sofa and went over to give Digger a goodnight hug. Digger looked up at her with big brown eyes, wagged his tail and laid his head back down again. Funny, thought Emma, he normally jumps up as soon as they get up off the sofa, he must be wrecked too.'

'Look mammy, he wagged his tail again, he must be trying to smile.'

'Yeah, he's happy.'

'Why mammy?'

'Alright now bed time, come on face and teeth please.' Emma marched her up the stairs before another bout of the whys completely took over.

Amy was already drifting off to the land of sleep when Emma returned to the living room. Digger looked like he hadn't moved a muscle. 'Come on, Digger, get your dinner,' she patted her leg as she called to him. 'Come on Digger,' she called him again, but he just looked up at her for a second and put his head back down again. 'Weird dog, I've never known you to knock back your dinner before. Ah well, I'll put it in your bowl and you can get it later. Hope you're not feeling sick though.'

She filled up his dog bowl with meaty chunks of dry dog food and filled up his water bowel with fresh cold water. 'Gosh, no wonder you're not running for your dinner, don't think I'd be running for that either.'

Aidan was the one who had insisted on feeding him dry food, he had always said it was much better for his teeth. Not to mention the fact that picking up his poo was a lot easier after dry food. Emma giggled at the memory of Aidan coming into the kitchen giving out one day after she had fed him a more appetizing looking tin of juicy dog food. 'That bloody dog food ran out of him, Emma, I had to scrape up his bloody shite, don't give it to him again.'

'Now, what do I want, what do I want,' she asked herself, standing in the kitchen. 'Mmmm, think I had enough wine last night .... oh yeah, hot chocolate.'

Moments later, she was curling up on the sofa again with a hot mug of hot chocolate. Sipping it, she flicked through the channels looking for something to get stuck into but she came across nothing that took her fancy. She finally settled on a movie that she had seen before with Aidan. It was a romantic comedy and when it first came out, she went to see it with Aidan in the cinema. Well, she actually dragged him to see it with her. She remembered laughing like a hyena at it in the cinema but, this time round, she wasn't finding the hilarious bits one bit funny.

The familiar old feelings of unbearable loneliness and sadness were creeping in again. Digger never moved an inch as she hopped up off the sofa and climbed the stairs. Two minutes later, she came back down, snuggled up in a dark blue hoody, and plonked herself back down on the sofa. Aidan's hoody was a permanent item of clothing for months after his death and it was only in the past few months that she had left it in the wardrobe. But tonight, she needed the comfort and she immediately felt better wrapped up in the safety of his favourite clothing. She always felt closer to him when wearing it. She drained the last of her hot chocolate, lay down on the sofa, and curled up into a comfy position. She tried to focus on the film but her eyes wouldn't stay open so she settled for just hearing the telly instead before drifting off into a peaceful sleep.

'No Aidan, I like wearing it...no, I like it……... stop.' Emma reached out her hand in front of her as if pushing somebody away. 'Stop, it smells of you... no…. it's mine now….it smells like you….' She smiled as she stopped giving out long enough in her sleep to take in the scent in the air around her. 'It smells of you... your lovely smell.'

She opened her eyes gently but remained in the same position, inhaling the air around her deeply. All of a sudden, she sat up like a dart on the sofa and grabbed at the blue hoody as if protecting it. Confused and dazed, she looked around as if expecting to see someone beside her. But the scent she had been dreaming about was still lingering, calling out to her senses. She inhaled deeply again and then began taking short sniffs of the air like a sniffer dog looking for drugs.

'Oh my God ... Aidan ... I can still smell you, I can still smell you ... you *are* here ... you *are* here with me.'

She closed her eyes and began to cry tears of joy. Digger got up from where he had been lying all night and came over to her. He nudged his head off her leg and wagged his tail. Through her tears, she could see him look up at her and she flung her two legs off the couch and hugged him tightly.

'He was trying to take the hoody, Digger. He told me to take it off and put it away. Can you believe that, boy, can you believe that?'

She lifted her head and inhaled the air again, but this time there was no scent, it had faded away just as her tears had. Digger got up and went back over to the corner of the room and sat down beside the black leather bucket chair. Emma was elated. There had been no mistaking the scent of Aidan in her dream and she could still smell it when she woke up. So, there was no mistaking the fact he had just visited her. She was over the moon. But why she was dreaming about him trying to take the hoody off her? If he was around her in spirit, surely he knew how comforting it was to her and he'd hardly try to take that away from her. But she's been able to actually smell the scent of Aidan's favourite aftershave not only in her dream but even when she woke up. Even when she was sitting up and fully alert. It couldn't have been from his hoody, her mother had thrown it in the wash many times. 'If you insist on wearing this, then it has to be washed now and again, Emma,' she had said one day as she gently prized it out of Emma's hands.

Delighted, Emma switched off the TV and stood up. 'Come on Digger, out to the toilet, good boy.' Digger jumped up and waited for her to open the back door before he ran outside to relieve himself. 'Lazy dog tonight, you could have told me you were dying for a pee boy,' she said as she rubbed his head on his way back in. Instead of curling up in his bed in the kitchen, he made his way back into the sitting room and parked his golden behind back down beside the same chair again. Emma followed him in with a bewildered look on her face. 'What is going on with you tonight Digger?' she asked as she went over and bent down beside him. He licked her face, looked up at the empty chair, and then flopped down into a comfy lying position. Emma's face turned white as she looked up at the chair. 'Oh my God, Digger, do you see Aidan? Is Aidan in the chair?' Digger managed to look at her with his eyes only, too tired and comfortable to lift his head off the ground. Emma gazed at the chair in disbelief. That is why he hadn't budged from there all evening. Aidan is here, in this chair. She went into the kitchen, grabbed Digger's bed and brought it back into the living room to where he was lying. 'Here boy, get up and let me put this down, you can sleep here from now on.'

After five minutes of simply staring at the chair, she eventually switched off the light and went upstairs. Amy was sound asleep as she looked in on her. Quietly bending down, she planted a soft kiss on her forehead. 'Don't worry, sweetheart,' she whispered, 'Daddy's looking after us.'

Siobhan heard her phone beep as she was just getting out of the bath. Who is texting me at this hour, she wondered. She dried off and smothered her body with her favourite shea butter cream.

Alex had arrived back from his mother's around eight but she hadn't really chatted to him. Instead of settling down to watch telly with him, she opted to run a few miles run on the treadmill followed by a long and luxurious bath ... alone. Baths were normally something she enjoyed sharing with Alex and their deep Jacuzzi bath was more than a comfortable fit for two bodies, especially when they were wrapped up together.

Gently towel-drying her hair with one hand, she reached for her phone with the other as she sat down on the bed.

YOU WON'T BELIEVE IT, HE CAME TO ME AGAIN TONITE & DIGGER CAN SEE HIM TOO, IM SO HAPPY, TALK 2MORO XXX

'No way! You're right, Emma, I don't believe it. I thought you were over all this stuff!' she muttered, annoyed. She had spent a lovely day with

Emma and was happy that her friend hadn't really mentioned Aidan that much during the day. It wasn't that Siobhan wanted Emma to forget about him, but she really wanted her friend to start living again. Earlier today, Michael, Jack's new lodger and Emma had hit it off and Siobhan had fingers crossed that maybe this guy would be the beginning of something new for Emma, even if it was only a distraction. The de-stressing effects of the long soak in the bath had well and truly worn off Siobhan now. She quickly dried her hair and popped into the bed, knowing that she would not be able to sleep. She grabbed the phone and started playing solitaire.

Alex was surprised to see Siobhan still awake when he came into the room almost an hour later. 'Can't sleep, love?'

'No,' she sighed heavily.

'How many games have you played now?' he grinned. Once she got going on the solitaire, she could never put it down.

'I've lost count, but I did beat my time,' she said flatly.

Alex undressed quickly and went into the en-suite to brush his teeth. Siobhan put the phone away and switched off the light on her side of the room. When he came back out, he was surprised that Siobhan had turned her light off and was lying on her back facing the ceiling. Lately, as soon as he came into the room, she turned her back to him. This was progress at least. She hadn't really spoken to him since he came in and he was sure she would be asleep by the time he was ready for bed.

Maybe he would give Professor Long a ring in the morning, he thought. If Alex himself was the reason they couldn't conceive, maybe he could sort it out or at least come to terms with it himself before helping Siobhan come to terms with it. She wasn't handling all this pressure of not conceiving too well; maybe he could just do this one thing himself without having to drag her through the whole process too.

He climbed into bed beside her. 'Are you alright?'

'Yeah, I got a text from Emma tonight. I really thought she was turning another corner but it looks like she is right back in the middle of madness again.' She turned her head towards him and he couldn't help but notice that her eyes were the greenest he'd ever seen, but there was no sparkle in them, not tonight.

'Is it Aidan again?' he asked gently, stroking her head with his hand.

'Yeah, she said he came to her tonight and that Digger can see him now too, Alex, what are we going to do? She's losing her marbles, as far as I can see. I really thought she'd come to her senses but now she seems to be back in cloud cuckoo-land again. What can I do to help her, Alex?' she said softly, tears running down the side of her face and on to her pillow. His touch was comforting and this made her cry even more.

'I don't know honey, I don't know,' he said, throwing his arms around her, holding her close as the tears came harder and louder.

Siobhan cried her heart out solidly for what seemed like an eternity. When the crying died down to quiet little sobs, she searched her mind for the reason she was crying in the first place. She was sure it had started due to her concern over Emma but, somewhere along the line, she was pretty sure she was crying because she had missed her husband. She had missed his touch over the past few weeks and she had missed him. He had been her rock for so long in her life, a constant friend and supporter of everything she did and wanted to do. But he would never stand by her if he knew how she had tricked him for so long.

She stopped crying and looked up at Alex. Even with his eyes closed, she could see the compassion on his face for her. She knew he was fully aware she was avoiding him but he never pressured her into telling him why exactly. He had gotten into his head that she was as upset about their failure to conceive as he was. He had talked about seeing doctors and wanted to pin down a date. She had avoided the dreaded conversation all week. I can't do this anymore, she thought, I can't go on deceiving this man. I have to do something.

Alex opened his eyes and looked deep into hers. 'I love you Alex,' she said from the very bottom of her heart. 'I love you and I never want to be without you, I never want to lose you.'

'You're not going to lose me honey. I love you too and, believe me, nothing bad is going to happen.' He kissed the top of her head, closed his eyes and held her even more tightly.

CHAPTER NINETEEN

'Thank God it's Friday, eh? It's been a long week, that's all I can say.' Jack refilled Emma's glass and sat down.

'Too true!' Emma and Michael agreed in unison.

'Where is the little princess tonight?' Jack asked.

'Oh she's with my mam for the night, she picked her up from school today, she takes her the odd night to give me some time to myself although usually I count down the hours till I see her again.' She laughed at the irony of it all. She longed for a night alone to have some peace and quiet and to be truly lazy, but as soon as she got it she couldn't wait to get Amy back again.

'So you decided to come over here and drink all my wine then did you?' laughed Jack.

'Well, I actually wasn't expecting you to be here tonight, you are always at the bar on Friday nights so I had planned a nice relaxing bubble bath for myself but I suppose this will have to do.' she said as she held up her glass and grinned.

'Cheeky. I have given myself a well-deserved night off. It's been a busy week and a busy day. Steve can manage without me tonight. It's great, I feel like there's light at the end of the tunnel. Thanks to you, Michael, that meeting on Wednesday went brilliantly and Joe O'Reilly was dead keen at today's meeting to get together and come up with something for both businesses,' Jack said.

Emma was thrilled to see Jack looking so optimistic again. Ever since Michael came on the scene and began advising Jack here and there about what he could do to liven things up at the bar, Jack had become confident that the bar would be able to ride out this troubling time. He'd even asked Emma for ideas on how to make the bar more attractive for mothers to pop in for lunch or a coffee before or after shopping over at the shopping centre.

'Oh, so what will yourself and Joe be doing? You treat him to a free dinner and you get a free ticket to the cinema?' asked Emma, giggling.

'Well, smarty pants, you're actually not far off it. We're trying to work out a deal so that if you have a two-course meal in The Cellar, you'll get two free tickets to the cinema that night. Or, if you go to the cinema, you get a voucher for two drinks for each ticket. We've to work out the details but I really think it'll be good for both of us, won't it, Michael?'

'Yeah, I think it'll pull in a lot of business. Like I said initially, people are willing to go out but they do want to spend wiser.'

'Yeah, and I've teamed up with Rebecca from Halo too.'

'Oh, the new salon a couple of doors down?'

'Yeah, she's going to give them a half price voucher for a speciality coffee and choice of scone for here to all her clients. Then we are going to do something similar for her. What do you think?' Jack's face was glowing.

'That's a great idea. I always feel like a new woman after a haircut and I do actually feel like I want to go somewhere to show it off and not just home again. Bravo, Jack, great idea. Only thing is, I didn't think you served coffee and scones. Isn't The Cellar more of a complete lunch menu?' Emma looked confused.

'It was, but now I'm going to do a simple tea, coffee and confectionary menu just for people who fancy a bite to eat but not an actual lunch. And I'm having the painters in next week to lighten and brighten up the place, like you suggested,' said Jack proudly.

'Crikey, you're busy, aren't you?' giggled Emma again.

'Well, as long as you don't start raking in shitloads of money in the next few months and decide you no longer need a lodger, that's okay,' Michael said in jest. He had spent most of the week sitting down with Jack going over marketing ideas for the joint. He was thrilled to see Jack all excited about moving forward too. When he met him only a few months previously, he seemed like he was just about ready to give up on the place.

Emma drained the last of her wine and stood up. 'Right gentlemen, I'm off. I think I'll have that long soak in the bath after all. Ever since we mentioned it, it's been calling out to me. I'll pull the door after me, so don't move a muscle. See ye tomorrow no doubt,' she called after her as she went into the kitchen and rinsed her glass in the sink.

'Will you bring in the bag of roasted peanuts in the press over the microwave there before you go?' Jack called into her.

Emma came back in a few seconds later and threw his peanuts at him, 'What did your last slave die of?' She laughed, walking towards the front door.

'She didn't do what she was told,' called out Jack, stuffing a handful of roasted peanuts into his mouth and offering Michael the bag.

'So have you any family Jack, brothers, sisters, parents?' Michael asked while taking a fistful of peanuts.

Jack took a sip of his drink before answering, 'No, my folks are passed away.'

'Oh, sorry to hear that, Jack. Have you any siblings?'

'Yeah a brother, but we're not close. Are you hungry at all? I might throw on a pizza,' Jack said, legging it out of the room at the same time. Shit, thought Michael, touched on a raw nerve there big time.

CHAPTER TWENTY

Emma woke up with a smile on her face. She'd been dreaming about Aidan again and it had felt so real. They'd been walking along the beach with Digger and it made her want to jump out of bed and head over to the beach for a walk before Amy got home. She felt as though it was something she had to do yet she didn't know why. It was a fairly chilly December morning! She jumped out of bed despite the cold and pulled on a pair of jeans, tied her hair back and brushed her teeth.

She searched around the room for Aidan's really warm and cosy blue hoody. 'Where the hell is it? I definitely put it on the end of the bed last night. Aidan, if you've hidden it, I won't be impressed, you know how much I love that hoody.' She searched the house for another few minutes with no luck and then decided to give up. Disappointed, she got a warm red fleece out of her wardrobe and put it on. 'Come on Digger, let's go for a walk.'

The cool sea breeze was refreshing on her face as she walked along the beach next to the growling waves roaring onto the sand as if to catch her feet. She closed her eyes for a moment as she walked and took in the sound of the waves as they crashed ferociously before retreating back out to sea, leaving a white bubbly residue behind.

The hypnotic effect of the crashing sound was rudely interrupted by Digger who had promptly found a stick hidden between the rock armour up on the backshore. He threw his new exciting play item at her feet and barked direct orders at her to throw it into the waves only for him to dive straight in and retrieve it. She shook her head and laughed at him.

She picked up the stick and fired it into the sea with all her might and shivered as she watched Digger dive full force into the freezing cold waves, which seemed to swallow his golden body as he eagerly pounded his way through the water to retrieve it. Never one to let down his breed, he quickly reached the stick which was bobbing in and out of sight, grabbed it between his teeth and headed back to Emma with his head tilted above the water, prized possession safely tucked in mouth.

As always, as soon as he reached the sand, Emma ran away from him a little, knowing that he'd immediately drop the stick and shake his entire body, sending cold smelly drops of water all over her if she was close enough.

'Ah, Digger, do you have to do that?' she yelled at him as he shook drops of salted water in her direction, drenching her legs especially. He responded only by picking up the stick and throwing it at her feet and barking orders yet again to throw it into the water, challenging her to throw it as far as she could.

She stood for about twenty minutes throwing the stick enjoying the obvious fun he was having. Even though it was early, blustery and there was nobody else around, she felt full of life watching him enjoying himself.

'My Goodness, Digger, you dogs really do have a layer of blubber under your skin, don't you? Or else, you're just a mad thing who really doesn't mind freezing your balls off,' she shouted after him as she fired the stick back into the oncoming waves.

'Oh, I'd say he's a mad thing alright. I wouldn't fancy freezing them off myself anyway.'

Startled, Emma spun around to see a man all huddled up into his jacket grinning at her. Mortified that anyone had heard her shouting out the word balls, she couldn't help but feel the heat rise up into her cheeks. He probably wouldn't notice anyway, seeing as her cheeks felt red and raw from the salty wind.

'Oh, sorry, I didn't realise there was anyone around.' He came over to where she stood and looked out at Digger fervently making his way back to shore with the stick firmly in his grip. 'He's an energetic little fella isn't he?' he said, nodding towards Digger.

Emma looked at the man standing beside her. He was slightly taller than her and seemed to have a good size build, his dark curly hair waving about wildly in the wind. She couldn't really get a good look at his face as the bottom half of it was lost in his jacket which was zipped all the way up to keep the harsh breeze away from his face. She didn't really know what to say to him. Here she was on the beach, swearing like a sailor while her face was scalding from wind burn and her hair was dripping with grease.

Digger landed in between the two of them and shook the sea off himself, giving both bodies either side of him a good drenching before wandering off up to the rocks to take a long undignified but satisfying wee against an unknowing boulder.

'Oh, I'm so sorry, he's drowned you.'

'Oh, don't worry, it's fine, it'll dry out. Really, it's not a problem,' he replied, looking at her with kind reassuring brown eyes.

'I haven't seen you around here before. Are you on holidays for a while?' she asked, mortification melting away slowly.

'Kind of something like that, I suppose. Right now though, I'm looking for the nearest pot of hot tea and maybe a nice rasher sambo. Any suggestions at all?' He lifted his head to expose his strong jaw covered in dark bristly stubble. It suited him, it almost drew a line up to his cheek bones. She shook her head, disgusted at herself for allowing her mind to wander and admire his face. He looked familiar!

'Oh sorry, I just thought you were a local maybe. Sorry to have bothered you, you looked to be enjoying yourself there, or well your dog did anyway.'

Digger was now happily sniffing the rest of the other boulders protecting the coast from the erosional effects of the hungry sea.

Emma shook her head again, shaking herself out of the spell she was in while examining the guy's face. 'I am local, sorry. Yeah, there's a great place not too far from here, you more than likely passed it on the way down, I'd say. Lily's, they do amazing breakfasts. Digger, come on, boy.'

The two of them began to walk in unison back along the beach towards humanity. She left him at the door to Lily's, refusing his offer to join him for a cuppa. Walking away, she couldn't help but wonder what his reasons for visiting the town were. It sounded like he was here for more than a little break away.

It was lunch time when she pulled up outside her mother's house. The wind had not let up and the trees behind the house were swaying and singing as the wind whistled through them. Emma smiled at the sight of smoke coming from the chimney.

She ran in the back door and was greeted by the heat in the house and the smell of fresh fruit scones. 'Oh yummy, they smell nice.'

'Hiya love, we're in the sitting room.' Amy and Joan were huddled over the coffee table, busily studying jigsaw pieces. Amy leapt up and ran into Emma's arms. 'Mammy mammy, Granny and me made scones, they're in the kitchen.' Emma hugged her daughter as if she hadn't seen her for a week or two.

'You're here early, love. I wasn't expecting you till after lunch at least.'

'I know, but sure didn't I miss this little scallywag and besides I could smell the scones from town, so I had to follow my nose.'

'You have a big nose, mammy,' Amy giggled as she pinched Emma's nose.

'Oi you, little rascal.' Emma sat down on the couch and began to tickle Amy till the little girl was red in the face and dribble started to spill out of her mouth.

Joan watched them, delighted to see her daughter in good form, pleased that whatever was bothering Emma had seemed to pass.

Emma drove home, happy to have her little darling with her again. At home, the guy she had met earlier on the beach popped into her mind and she wondered again what he was doing in the town. He reminded her of someone, but she couldn't tell who for the life of her. She put him to the back of her mind and settled onto the couch, nice and comfy with a gigantic bar of delicious chocolate. All set for a good Saturday nights viewing of some sort of reality TV.

Later that night, she fell into bed, already in a sleepy mood. Snuggling up into the duvet, she felt all warm and cosy within minutes. 'Goodnight Aidan, love,' she said as she reached out to flick off her bedside lamp. But before she even reached it, the bulb flickered a few times, making the room bright and dark for a few seconds, finishing off with light again.

She couldn't help but smile. The flickering was a sure sign of goodnight from Aidan. 'You know, you could go away and learn how to communicate a little better. I'm sure if you tried hard enough, you could manage a few words.'

The light flickered again and this time the bulb blew, leaving her in complete darkness. 'Okay, okay, I was a bit cheeky, I know, asking for too much. Night, love,' she giggled, turning over on her side before drifting off into a long and peaceful sleep.

'How was Emma today?' Seamus asked casually as he got into bed beside Joan.

'She seems grand,' Joan answered, without taking her eyes off the book she was reading.

Seamus had been away all day and wasn't home long. She was used to this now and it didn't particularly bother her, but she sure as hell wasn't going to drop her book and make conversation with him just because he was home and wanted to chat. He wasn't too worried about Emma and thought Joan was making a mountain out of a molehill, so she had stopped trying to talk to him about it. In fact she had stopped trying to talk to him about anything really!

CHAPTER TWENTY ONE

Siobhan worked up a real sweat during her jog. She had run solidly for six kilometres without even noticing and without making a dent in her worries. Her head still overflowing with crap. Even though Alex seemed to have calmed down completely about visiting the doctor, her own guilt was starting to consume her. And what about Emma? Each call from her was getting weirder and weirder. On the phone, Emma would chatter away about how Aidan would play their favourite song on the radio, as if he was saying he was there. Another time, she had asked for a sign from Aidan that he was in the room with her and the next thing the bulb went. And, now, Digger was sleeping in the sitting room because he liked to be close to Aidan who was sitting in the chair in the corner of the room. It all completely freaked out Siobhan. Emma must be having a break down.

The water from the power shower fell onto her body like a heavenly soothing waterfall. The steam clouded up the glass blocks separating the open shower from the rest of the room. She lathered her silky skin with shower gel, closed her eyes and took a deep breath. She was calling around to Emma's later and not looking forward to it. What was she going to say if Emma started going on again? She was afraid she'd fly off the handle and tell her to cop the feck on to herself, but she knew that was not the way to approach it. Maybe it was time to involve Joan. Emma wouldn't be happy but she felt had to do something.

'What do you want Amy? Sausages, mash and peas with loads of scrumptious gravy or chicken nuggets, veggie mash and beans or you can have pasta either?' Emma was reading out The Cellar's new children's menu, feeling rather impressed with the choices available.

'Fish, mammy, peas,' Amy replied, vigorously colouring in the page of funny looking characters with her special cup of crayons.

'Oh, the fish comes with beans but I can give her peas instead if she'd prefer them.' Steve was eager to please with the new menu and worried about getting everything right.

'No I like beans, I don't want peas.'

Steve took the order into the kitchen, looking a bit confused. He guessed he was going to have to learn all about kids seen as he was a new daddy himself.

'The menu is brilliant, Jack. The new adult menu is brilliant too. Mmmm, everything sounds absolutely delicious.' Emma was still reading the menu as she spoke.

Jack was eager to hear what Emma thought of it all. He'd never catered for children before on the menu. The old days of just appealing to the upmarket posh wealthy ladies who lunch were gone, along with the expensive glassware and cutlery. He kept all that upstairs where the ambience and posh glassware suited the more refined customer. Downstairs was more chilled out now, and gave her somewhere else to drop in for a coffee. Emma loved popping into Lilly's for a cappuccino and a quiet read of her book, so now she had two choices.

Michael walked into the bar with a great big smile on his face. 'Hey guys, guess what? I got a job. Finally, I got a job.'

Jack and Emma were delighted and both stood up to give Michael a hug.

'Well done, that's great news. Is it the one you really wanted?' asked Jack.

'Yep. Can't tell you how relieved I am.' Michael sat down opposite Amy and loosened his tie. 'And that's not all, Cameron called and wants to meet up.'

Jack sat down beside him, the smile still there but a little more forced now. 'Oh.'

Emma had heard all about the break up from Jack but Michael had never spoken to her about Cameron, so she felt a little awkward. She also noticed that Jack's demeanour had changed slightly.

'Mammy, I farted and I think it might be a smelly one like the one you did in the car this morning.' Thanks Amy, for saving the awkwardness, she thought as her face turned a dark shade of red.

'Right, well, missy, we better go now. Siobhan's popping over for coffee. Thanks a million, Jack, that was absolutely delicious.'

She made sure Amy had her belt on right before popping into the car herself. As soon as she turned the key, one of Aidan's favourites came blasting from the radio. It was a common occurrence these days that the radio would be playing some song of significance to Emma. Either a song she had first danced to with Aidan, a song that he used to sing any time he was vacuuming or washing up, or a song that they both loved. Siobhan told her she could find significance in practically any song that she heard. And that Emma was subconsciously attaching a time, a place or certain significance to every song that came on in the car and that it was nothing freaky at all. But Emma knew better. She knew that Aidan was coming to her in the songs and, somehow, he was managing to play certain songs at certain times to tell her he was there and thinking of her. Now, in the car outside The Cellar, she smiled as she listened to one of Aidan's all-time favourite's belt out of the speaker and envelope her in memories of him. She closed her eyes for a second and said a little silent 'Thank you, I'm thinking of you too', before driving off.

'That's really great news about the job, Michael, you must be thrilled.'

'I won't lie to you, I'm absolutely over the bloody moon. I was beginning to think I'd never get another job. You've been more than reasonable with the rent, Jack, but things were starting to look a bit worrying on the money front.'

Jack felt his stomach start to churn with anxiety and he had no idea why. 'So, what's the plan now then? Are you gonna look for a new bachelor pad back up in Dublin?'

Michael searched Jack's face to see if there was any sign of what he wanted the answer to be. Was he still welcome as a lodger or did Jack want him out? They'd become such goods mates in the past couple of months, he'd be sorry to leave. Then again, although he was getting over the pain of his split with Cameron, he couldn't help but feel a major pull of the heart when they had talked on the phone. Now, he could sense an uncomfortable awkwardness between himself and Jack as they sat there. 'Well, I hadn't thought about moving back up to Dublin actually. I don't think I could afford to pay rent on my own really but, look, if you want to have the house back to yourself, I certainly don't mind.'

'Hey, no, not at all. I didn't mean it that way! I'm happy enough to have you stay in the house, so you're welcome to stay.'

Michael relaxed slightly but could tell that Jack hadn't.

'Spit it out, Jack, what is it?'

'Nothing, it's great, the new job and all. And, look, if you want to move back to the city that's great and all, but I really am more than happy to share the house, honestly.' Michael was feeling ill at ease again. He knew there was something still on Jack's mind.

Before Michael had a chance to say anything else, Jack stood up and started clearing away the table.

CHAPTER TWENTY TWO

Siobhan pulled up outside Emma's house a little later than arranged. She wasn't sure what Emma was going to come out with today and she wasn't sure if she even had the energy for it. She switched off the ignition and held her face into her hands for a second as if trying to escape the world and all the worries it brought. She heard a car horn beep behind her and looking in the rear view mirror, she could see Michael pull up.

'Hey Siobhan how's things, haven't seen you in a while, working hard eh?' He walked over to her noticing the dark circles under her eyes.

'Yeah I'm actually mental busy at the moment but it's not a bad complaint in this day and age I suppose, any luck on the job front yourself?'

'Actually yes I got a job offer that I'm very happy with and yeah I think it's a perfect position for me so I'm very happy needless to say.'

'Ah Michael that's great news, I'm delighted for you, Alex will be thrilled to hear that.'

'Speaking of Alex I was trying to ring him there to see if he fancied a pint tonight, call it a celebratory drink, but eh I couldn't get through.'

'Oh I actually haven't seen Alex all day, he was up and gone early this morning, come to think of it he never really said where he was going, I assume he's off on the golf course or something, or maybe he's off with a fancy woman.' Michael joined in with Siobhan as she laughed the notion away. He genuinely found the idea of Alex off with another woman as a bit of a joke, anybody could see that Siobhan was the only woman for Alex and he could tell that even though Siobhan had joked about it she certainly had no doubts about his faithfulness either. They spent another few moments talking about the weather and how Alex was mad in the head to be off golfing on such a bitter cold day, before parting ways. As Siobhan walked up towards Emma's front door her thoughts turned to Alex. He never said a thing to her about where he was going and she hadn't heard from him all day. It was strange but she wasn't worried. She wasn't going to win any prizes for communication lately but things were definitely on the up and up for them. She had felt so much closer to him again lately. Emma opened the door with a big smile on her face and a four year old frog hanging onto her leg.

'Where's Uncle Alex, Sivvy?' she asked with a disappointed look on her face.

'Do you know something Mr Green froggy, I have no idea.' Siobhan said as she picked Amy up into her arms.

'I'm not a man frog silly, I'm a girl frog.' Amy said, giggling.

'Oh, silly me!' laughed Siobhan.

Emma looked at her in concern, despite her laughter, she didn't quite look herself. 'Is everything alright? With you and Alex?'

'Oh yeah of course it is, I just haven't seen him all day, I bet he's somewhere trying to play golf.'

'In that weather?' asked Emma with a tone of surprise in her voice.

'You have no idea the amount of passion that man has for golf my dear.'

The three of them went into the kitchen and Emma put the kettle on. Amy ran back to the table to complete the jig-saw she was doing.

'Help me Sivvy.' Siobhan took off her coat, sat down beside Amy and began searching for pieces to fit into the puzzle.

'So any news Emma.' She was hoping Emma would fill her ear about idle gossip she had heard during the week or funny stories about work, anything except the same old shite she was hearing about Aidan lately. She was relieved when Emma started telling her all about Jack's new menu at the bar and how well he was doing. She was thrilled to hear of course how Jack's bar had seemed to turn a corner for the better but she was even more elated to hear Emma discuss something other than her dead husband sending her signs. An hour went by and there was absolutely no mention of ghosts, spirits, songs or light bulbs. Siobhan had allowed herself to relax completely and was enjoying Emma's company. They were rabbiting on about everything and anything so much so that Siobhan had almost forgotten all of the worries she had been carrying around for the past few weeks. They went into the sitting room and switched on the telly for Amy, she was feeling tired and Emma put on one of her favourite DVD's to sit back and watch. Siobhan remarked on Digger's new sleeping place and how comfortable he looked flat out in his bed. Within minutes however she could feel her stomach tighten back to that familiar dread she had around Emma lately. Emma went into a detailed account on how Digger was able to see Aidan and how he even appeared to play with him. Emma's skin glowed as she told Siobhan about the dog's new relationship with the spirit of Aidan. Siobhan felt sick at the thoughts of her best friend being so happy about something that sounded so weird. Looking out she had noticed that Michael's car was gone and replaced with Jacks. Perfect she thought, she could have a chat to Jack and see what he thought. They had to do something at this stage.

'Anyway look Emma, I better go, I actually want to pop into Jack before he heads back down to the Cellar for the night shift, to congratulate him on his new menu and all.'

Siobhan stood up and went towards the kitchen for her coat. Emma followed her not noticing the change in atmosphere, 'Oh okay, we must have lunch there soon, I'm heading up to Aidan's parents for lunch tomorrow but maybe keep next Saturday in mind.'

'Yeah sounds good.' Siobhan gave Emma and Amy quick kisses goodbye and ran for the door.

Jack was looking back through some old photos of himself and Conor when they were younger. With a stabbing pain in his heart, he remembered how close they were. Even though Jack was two years older they were more like twins. They went everywhere together and whenever Jack was about you would know Conor wasn't too far behind. They had their own circle of school friends but outside school they were inseparable. Conor looked up to Jack so much and was so proud of his older brother and Jack was mad about Conor. Being sons of the only publicans in the village they were well known in the community and their parents proud as peacocks of them. That was before it all went horribly wrong of course. Conor was doing his Junior Cert and Jack was studying for his Leaving Cert when things changed dramatically. After the big fight Jack vowed he would only stay long enough to do his exams. As soon as he was finished he packed a rucksack and left his family home and never looked back. He went to Spain and spent years working in bars. Although his parents could have well afforded to send him to college he didn't want to take a cent off them. Too many words had been said. He had done really well in his leaving cert. A result of spending the last few months of it as a hermit in his bedroom studying. Not really out of choice but because he felt he could no longer be part of the community. His father had stopped him from working in the bar and Conor didn't want to have anything to do with him. He thought back to how well he did in his exams and how he could have easily walked into any course in any college or university at the time. But it wasn't to be and instead he fled the country in shame. The painful thoughts of his past were abruptly pushed to one side of his head when he heard someone rapping on his door rather forcefully.

'Jack, we have got to do something, this is starting to get all too crazy, she's bloody lost it you know,' Siobhan didn't wait for an invite and hurriedly marched past a puzzled Jack into his kitchen. She was shaking her head as she helped herself to large cup of coffee out of the machine, 'she's really bloody lost it Jack, I'm telling you'.

'First of all hello, secondly would you like a cup of something and thirdly what the hell are you on about, who's lost it?' Jack asked as he began to refill his own cup. By the look of Siobhan he felt he was going to need it.

'Emma has bloody lost the whole entire damn plot, I just had lunch

with her, I'm telling you she is in coo coo land Jack, what are we gonna do?'
She slumped down on one of the bar stools at the kitchen island and stared
at Jack with a seriousness on her face that looked almost scary.

Jack sat opposite her. 'Look Siobhan, whatever it is it can't be that bad,
so just calm down a minute and tell me what happened.'

'Well according to Emma, now Digger is communicating with Aidan,
apparently he only sits in the one corner of the living room now and stares
at the wall. Oh and yesterday he was playing ball....with Aidan.' Both
Siobhan's voice and eyebrows rose as she spoke.

'Eh, what exactly do you mean, playing ball with Aidan, I don't
understand,' Jack was looking even more puzzled.

'You don't understand??? Join the fecking club, she walked into the
living room last night after putting Amy to bed and there was Digger
playing ball, throwing the ball around, crouching down and growling and
wagging his tail. Emma said he only does that when your interacting with
him, he gets all excited and crouches down on the ball if you go to take it
away. So she automatically assumes now that Aidan was there actually
playing with him. This has gone far enough now, Jack. She smells him in
the morning, feels his arms around her at night, he plays songs for her on
the radio and now he's bloody playing ball with the bloody dog.'

'Look, I agree that it does seem a bit strange but if it makes her happy
to think he's around well then isn't that a good thing?'

'Jack, she is going insane, she needs to get on with her life, she needs
to let go, we all loved him so much and God knows he is missed every
single day but this is not right, she is not living her life, for feck's sake Jack,
she thinks she's living with a ghost, we have to do something, I can't stand
seeing her like this, it's not good for Amy either, what are we gonna do'.
Siobhan's face was overflowing with worry and concern.

'I don't know, I really don't, it's such a delicate issue, if she is having
some sort of breakdown then forcing the issue might do more damage!'

'Well, we have to do something Jack, the way things are going she'll
soon be setting a place for him at the table. We won't know where to sit
when we go in case we're sitting on him!'

'Okay your exaggerating slightly now, it's not that bad, she misses him
and yeah maybe we should try and help her move on, I don't know, maybe
if we approach the subject of his clothes again, maybe it's time to empty his
wardrobe, get her to pack that blue hoody away, what you think?'

'Yeah, that's not a bad idea, having all his stuff around can't be
helping, She still keeps his aftershave on top of the cabinet in the en-suite
and even though she did donate some of his clothes to charity she still held
onto so much. It's as if she's holding onto it in case he comes back, has she
even really accepted he's gone at all?'

Why don't we ring her Mam, tell her our concerns, I'm sure she's noticed too and is just as worried, of course you know that when I say we ring I actually meant you'. Jack eyed Siobhan with a slight smile on his face.

'Actually, I was thinking of doing that, I'm glad you said it too, I'll definitely do it now, in fact I might just go see her, it's not really something I would feel comfortable talking about over the phone, "Oh hey Joan, how are things, by the way I think your daughter is gone mental", definitely think it's better to talk to her face to face.'

'When will you go see her?' Jack asked.

'As soon as I possibly can!' sighed Siobhan loudly.

'Maybe you should wait until after Christmas now though?'

'Yeah maybe, but as soon as possible after Christmas then I'm definitely telling her!'

Emma cleared away the coffee cups. She felt so good to be able to share her experiences with her oldest friend in the world. She was sure that Siobhan wasn't totally convinced about Digger playing with Aidan. The look of disbelief was a dead giveaway but she felt lucky to have someone to confide in. As mad as she sounded she knew her friend would only ever support her. She was certainly a wonderful listener. There was no way her mother would be so understanding, Emma chuckled to herself. Her mam would have her sectioned into the mental home for sure. There was no way she could or ever would share what was going on with her, she just wouldn't understand, not the way Siobhan understands. Emma knew herself it all sounded freaky but she was in no doubt at all that Aidan was around her and in their home. She was feeling a closeness to him. She had no idea why he was here but she was happy he was. She didn't want to let the feeling go. She didn't want to let him go, again.

CHAPTER TWENTY THREE

Alex walked up the steps to the clinic with trepidation and damp palms. The clinic itself was very clean and fresh looking, bright colours stood out on the walls and a spotlessly shiny wooden floor led the way from the front door to the receptionist in the foyer.

He felt a little more at ease when he saw how private the reception area was. As it was, he felt like he was carrying a huge sandwich sign telling everyone he was a failure in the family making department. He was glad he'd decided to come on his own though. God only knew how poor Siobhan would feel. He checked in with the receptionist who told him to take a seat in the waiting room; she assured him Professor Long would be with him shortly. He was surprised to see that the room was almost full with couples young and old. He nodded at a young couple as he sat down beside them. They were staring into space and holding hands. At least he knew nobody there and nobody would recognise him. Sky News was playing away on the forty-two inch flat screen television on the wall and Alex was glad to have something to focus his attention on while he waited. Everybody was very quiet almost as if it was an unspoken rule that you couldn't speak while you were waiting.

Within a few minutes, an attractive nurse came in and called his name. He stood up quickly, apprehension flooding in. Now that he was in an actual clinic, he was so nervous he wanted to run out the door again. The pretty nurse walked him down to Professor Long's office, opened the door, smiled at him and told him she would be back for him when he was ready.

'Ah Alex, how are you? It's been a long time since I've seen you. How is your mother keeping?' Professor Long stood up from his massive mahogany table and walked around to shake Alex's hand. He was only about eight years older than Alex but Alex immediately felt inferior to the tall strong looking man in front of him. He was cursing his sweaty palms, feeling embarrassed that Professor Long had touched them. Now, he'd know how weak Alex could be.

'Mam's great, thank you and thank you so much for fitting me in. I really do appreciate it. I couldn't believe it when your secretary told me you have a five-month waiting list!'

'Oh yes, I'm snowed under at the moment. Is Siobhan not with you today? I was expecting to see her with you.'

'Well look, to be honest, she doesn't even know I'm here today. I didn't want to put her under any pressure if I could help it. I know things are getting to her and she's feeling the strain of the situation a hell of a lot. So at least this way, I can find out if it's my fault we're not conceiving and, if so, what I can do about it.'

'Okay Alex, usually we see the couple first and talk things through but seeing as it's yourself, I'll make an exception. But, really, you should think about sitting down with Siobhan tonight and discussing your visit with her. If it turns out that there's no issue with you and you have to tell her that, it can actually do more damage. It'd be like saying, "I passed the test so you must be the one who's failing."'

'Well, I think she feels like that anyway. These past few months have been tense at home. Sometimes I feel she's avoiding me like she's feeling guilty or something. I thought that maybe if I researched things properly or got myself checked out first, I could save her some hassle.' Alex was beginning to feel uneasy again. He'd been sure he was doing the right thing by visiting the clinic on his own first, but now he wasn't so sure. How would she feel if everything was okay with him? Would it be a kick in the guts for her if he was perfectly able to father a child and it was her fault they were having problems. As it was, she seemed to flinch if he came near her and she was never in the mood to have sex anymore.

After a full health check, a discussion about diets and exercise and a detailed and embarrassing discussion about the ins and outs of his sex life, pardon the pun, Alex was directed down the hall again by the pretty nurse. They came to a door and she handed him a small cup and told him to take his time. Red as a beetroot, he took the cup and walked into the room, glad there was nobody in the corridor. There was a stack of pornographic magazines on a table and, even though he was alone, he could feel the heat of his face extend down his neck. He wouldn't even pick up a magazine for fear of what was possibly on them. Instead, he opted to press play on the DVD player instead. He just couldn't relax and the sight of the woman's tits flying everywhere on the telly was doing nothing for him. He switched it off and thought of Siobhan.

After the deed, he sat back and wished he had told Siobhan about the bloody visit after all. He could have done with her support. Or given the situation, he thought humourously to himself, he could have definitely done with her lending a hand! He certainly didn't enjoy having to come on his own, in more ways than one. He took a deep breath before he opened the door and tried to calm himself. It wasn't too far to Professors Long's office; if he took long strides, he'd be there in three seconds flat. Nobody would see him.

Sure enough, on his second stride, the door he was passing opened and a man walked out. 'Hey Alex, how are you? What a place to bump into someone, eh?' The man looked weirdly at ease considering he was standing in a fertility clinic corridor with his sperm in his hand. Alex was just grateful the other man didn't hold out his hand for a handshake. 'Err, Harry Belfield, yes how are you? I hope everything is going well for you now that all that mix-up is sorted out with the deeds.'

'Yes, yes, it all worked out great, thanks to you,' said Harry, looking as if he was all set for a good old chat.

Alex quickly jumped in and excused himself before Harry could say another word. 'Great, well, must rush, good to have seen you again.' He began to walk away when, horrifyingly, the other man juggled his little container into his left hand and held out his right towards Alex. 'Yes, good seeing you again.'

Alex shook hands quickly and made his way back to the Professor Long's office, wiping his hand relentlessly. Feck's sake, of all the times to bump into someone, it would have to be with sperm in your bloody hand.

A little while later he sat into his car, glad the ordeal was over, for now at least. It would be a week before he was going to hear any result back. All he had to do now was figure out how he was going to approach the subject with Siobhan.

CHAPTER TWENTY FOUR

Emma was lost in thought as she strolled down the cereal aisle in the supermarket. Chocolate hoops for Amy and granola for me. Actually, I really should try harder to get Amy to eat more healthy in the mornings, she thought as she threw the boxes into the trolley. It was already overflowing with Christmas goodies, so chocolate cereal wasn't really going to make much of a difference. She started humming to one of her favourite Christmas songs. She'd been dreading Christmas again, but this year she didn't feel as empty and lonely, knowing that Christmas spirit wasn't the only spirit in her house this year.

Eyeing the cinnamon candle in her trolley, she smiled, remembering how it was one of Aidan's favourite things about Christmas, the lovely Christmassy scent. That, and a huge Christmas wreath on the door.

In the toiletries aisle, she was reaching for a box of tampons singing the Christmas song louder and with more emotion when the sound of a 'hello' startled her so much she jumped. Down went the neatly packed display of incredible comfort tampons. Her two arms sprang out immediately to stop the falling boxes but it was too late. With five boxes of tampons around her ankles and a red face, she turned to find the stranger from the beach smiling back at her.

'Ooops, my fault, sorry. I didn't mean to frighten you, let me get them for you,' he said as he bent down to retrieve the boxes.

'Nooo, it's alright, honestly, let me.' Emma grew scarlet as he stood up and handed her all five boxes. She noticed his face had also turned a bright shade of red as he'd just realised what he was handing over. They both stood looking at each other for a few moments without saying a single word.

'Okay, well, nice seeing you again,' he spluttered as he turned and walked off in a hurry.

Emma let out a breath that she didn't even realise she was holding.

'How bloody mortifying,' she muttered to herself as she threw the tampons back onto the shelf. Just then, she could see the stranger walk back towards her causing her tummy to flip spectacularly.

'Sorry, look eh, I know it's Christmas Eve tomorrow and you're probably very busy and all, but do you fancy meeting for a drink later maybe?' the silence dragged on, 'Or….a coffee even?'

'Actually, you know, I'm really busy at the moment, but thanks anyway.' Emma blushed again.

He turned to leave. 'Okay, well look, have a good Christmas and, sure, I'll probably bump into you in Lily's at some stage again.' He walked away for a second time, moving faster than an Olympic power walker this time!

Joan and Amy settled down in the coffee shop with their Christmas shopping all around them, packed up in brightly coloured shopping bags. Even though it was freezing outside, Amy insisted on a bowl of ice cream while Joan ordered a mug of steaming hot coffee and a fruit scone.

'Hey Amy, out Christmas shopping, were you?' called out Michael as he came over. He ruffled her head and gave Joan a wink.

'Oh hello, Michael. We've been shopping all morning and now we're going to treat ourselves, aren't we Amy?' Joan was delighted to be finally sitting down. 'Won't you join us?' she asked, pointing to the spare chair.

'Don't mind if I do,' he said as he plonked down on the chair. 'Sure, how could any man refuse to join two beautiful ladies such as yourselves?' he chuckled.

Well, Seamus does, she thought to herself, remembering this morning's conversation with him.

'I'm bringing Amy Christmas shopping this morning. Would you like to come too?'

'Ah sure, what would I be doing traipsing around the shops? You know I hate that sort of thing, Joan!'

'So, tell me, Michael, what are your plans for Christmas Day, will you be going home?'

Jack had just reached the table, carrying a coffee for Joan and a massive bowl of ice-cream for Amy.

'God yeah actually, I've been so busy here the past few weeks, I haven't even had time to think about Christmas myself, thank God,' he said while placing Joan's order on the table, 'so what are you doing for Christmas Michael, I never asked. Going home?'

'Nah, the folks flew over to Sinead, my youngest sister yesterday. They wanted to spend it with the grandkids, seeing as they don't see much of them. Leslie is having the in-laws for dinner for the first time, so I didn't want to land on top of her. Besides I'm looking forward to a few quiet days. It's been such a mental time getting used to the new job and that. Not that I'm complaining, mind you!'

'Well, if you don't mind a few hours of madness, we'd love to have you over for Christmas dinner, Michael.' Joan said politely.

'Oh no Joan, I couldn't intrude. You've enough to be doing already. Seriously, I'm fine, it's no big deal at all.' Michael felt slightly awkward.

'Oh believe me love, you wouldn't be intruding. Sure, the more the merrier, that's what I always say, isn't it, Jack?'

'Yep you sure do. Besides, you haven't lived until you've had one of Joan's Christmas dinners, they're amazing,' Jack said patting his belly.

'Well, I suppose it'd be a shame to miss out on that, wouldn't it?' Michael laughed. 'That's settled then,' cheered Joan. 'Christmas dinner at mine it is!'

Christmas tunes were blaring from the radio as Joan worked away happily in the kitchen. Everything was on time and smelling pretty good. The turkey was cooked to absolute perfection and the apricot stuffing smelled mouth-wateringly delicious. Joan was just taking the honey glazed ham from the oven when Lily arrived into the kitchen with a casserole dish full of her bacon and onion sprouts. Sean followed closely behind with a tray of salmon and cream cheese pastry squares. 'I have the pudding in the car, Joan,' he said handing her the tray. 'Not great for the hips but heaven for the lips!' he winked.

'Goodness, guys, you've done too much!' Joan said as her eyes danced appreciatively over the lightly covered tray.

'Ho ho ho, merry Christmas everybody.' Michael and Jack piled into the kitchen carrying what looked like the contents of Jack's bar stock.

Before Joan got to even say hello, a tiny person came crashing excitedly into the kitchen also.

'Look, look, look, Santy brought me this, look, look!' Amy was almost screaming with delight, still holding the latest and greatest baby doll that appeared to be weeing all over the tile.

'Oh!' Michael said, squatting down to inspect the freakishly real-looking doll.

'Hi everyone, happy Christmas,' Emma bellowed out as she entered the overcrowded kitchen carrying chocolates and wine.

The Christmas music could only just be heard over all the chatter in the kitchen but Joan was thrilled to have a house full. Let the fun begin, she thought, popping open a bottle of fizz.

A couple of hours later, everybody was sitting back in their chairs rubbing their bloated tummies. They were all a bit quieter now and groaning from food overload. But Joan was still full of happiness, the chatting and banter over dinner brought a new lease of life to her lonely soul. She had lost faith in love and had begun to think that it was only for the young. That it inevitably faded as the years passed. But witnessing the love between Lily and Sean restored her faith a little that love and tenderness could exist between old married couples. It just didn't apply to her marriage.

Over in the corner Jack couldn't help but notice that Michael's face went pale as he checked his phone.

'Everything alright?' he asked all concerned.

'Eh yeah, yeah, it's grand, it's just a message from Cameron! I wasn't expecting that.' he said, looking dumbfounded.

'Oh, what does she want? Just to wish you a happy Christmas?'

'Eh yeah.' he managed to splutter out as he took a gulp from his wine.

Jack could see Michael was shaken from the text. There was obviously more to it than just a happy Christmas wish! He didn't really know what to say, Michael didn't seem to want to talk about it so he cleared up some more of the table and went into the kitchen.

At the sink, Emma was standing there, holding the gold cross that hung so elegantly from its gold chain that Aidan had bought her for their first Christmas as a married couple.

'You alright, Emma? You were far away there!' he laughed, putting his arm around her.

'Oh Jack, I never heard you come in.' she jumped, slightly startled.

'You look happy today, Emma. I know it's still just hard for you but I'm so proud of you.' He squashed her closer to him and kissed the top of her head.

'I am happy, Jack. Yeah, I want Aidan here with me in body but he's here with me in spirit!' She turned towards him, beaming from ear to ear.

'Yes, of course he is pet. He's up there looking down on us, jealous that we're all getting pissed and he's not,' he laughed.

'Yeah,' Emma smiled, 'but it's more than that. Promise you won't think I'm gone all weird but, well, a photo of Aidan and myself fell off the shelf this morning! Obviously it was Aidan saying "Happy Christmas." I bought him a candle and put it beside the photo frame so I think it was also his way of saying thanks.' She paused for a second wondering whether to continue or not. Feck it, she thought, she had to tell someone.

Jack smiled out of awkwardness more than anything else. Was Emma suggesting her dead husband had knocked over the frame?

She took his silence and smile as a good sign, giving him a big hug and sighing at how wonderful her day was turning out so far.

That night, Joan got into bed absolutely exhausted. She had enjoyed every second of the day. Seamus was already in bed and snoring his head off. She tossed and turned for a while trying to get comfortable. It had been a while since she had slept in this bed and she had become more used to Emma's old bed. She finally settled, lying on her side with her back to her husband, sighing deeply as it was the first time all day she had felt lonesome.

CHAPTER TWENTY FIVE

Wonderful childhood memories came flashing back as Siobhan entered the gate to Joan's house. She loved spending time here when she was younger. The house itself was quite modest and dwarfed by the amazing woods behind it and the full sea views in front of it. Sitting beautifully on the side of Kilfarrig Hill, it was the most picturesque place where anybody could ever wish to live.

Joan was like a second mother to Siobhan while she was growing up. Although she didn't visit her as much these days, Siobhan always felt mothered as soon as she was in Joan's company. She was nervous about her visit today though. When she had arranged a time to call over the phone, she knew Joan could sense something was up. She had only shut the car door when front door opened.

'Siobhan darling, how lovely to see you. Come in, come in, I've the kettle on and fresh scones bought in this morning. I was just whipping some cream.'

Siobhan smiled. No matter how much she had grown and changed over the years, Joan still saw her as the sweet-toothed child she once had been.

Half a scone and a bucket of tea later, a stuffed Siobhan felt she had talked enough about life's trivial matters. It was time to broach the subject of Emma's diminishing state of mind.

'You know, dear, it's wonderful that you've come to visit and I'm thrilled to see you but something tells me there's more to the visit than popping in for a little chat.'

'Eh, actually yeah, there is something I would like to talk to you about. I, well, eh, well it's like this, I, eh.' How was she supposed to tell Joan that Emma, her one and only precious daughter, was having a mental breakdown.

'Siobhan love, I've never known you to be backwards about coming forwards. What is it, have you news for me on the baby front?' Joan treaded carefully, she knew there was something going on with Siobhan and she knew things were not what they seemed .

'Good Lord no, nothing like that.' Siobhan waved her hand away in a manner that was a bit too blasé.

Joan's eyebrows rose slightly and Siobhan knew she had answered that question too quickly and with slightly too much relief in her tone for someone supposedly trying for a baby for ages. Joan reached over the kitchen table and placed her warm hand on top of Siobhan's.

'You know, sweetheart, there's absolutely no shame in not being ready for children. They're a big commitment and motherhood can be scary, but you have to be open and honest about it, especially to Alex. He has a right to know how you really feel. I can imagine how much pressure you must be feeling and that pressure is only going to mount, you have to be honest here.'

Siobhan's eyes welled up and big fat blobs fell down her face. She immediately felt relief but shame all at the same time.

It took her a few moments to compose herself and she was glad that Joan had got up to get her a tissue. She wasn't sure she'd be able to look her in the eyes. Plus she could feel her nose about to run and she didn't fancy Joan seeing snot all over her face, no matter how motherly she was.

'How did you know?'

'Emma tells me you've been trying for quite a while now. And I guess it would be reasonable to assume you'd have gone to see a doctor by now but Emma says you're not keen. And, well, to be honest love, I can see a little bit of myself in you.'

Siobhan looked up intrigued. 'How do you mean?'

'Don't get me wrong. I don't mean to sound like I grew up in the dark ages or anything but, back in my day, it was more than an assumption that when you got married, you'd have children. It was also more than an assumption that when you had a child, you'd be the one to stay at home and rear it. It was the norm.'

Siobhan listened intently.

'When I moved here all those years ago as a young primary school teacher, it wasn't long before I met and fell in love with Seamus. We courted as you did back then and there was no question he was the one for me. I guess marriage was the next step. We were only married a short time when he became principal. The fact his father was the previous headmaster was a great help I suppose. Anyway, I soon fell pregnant with Emma after that and it was only then did I realise that it was assumed I'd leave my job when she arrived. I was naïve, I suppose, I never really thought about what would happen after I had Emma. I thought I'd get a childminder and go back to the job I loved. Seamus's mother was disgusted with that idea. In her eyes, a child should be at home with its mother and that was it. Seamus was great but childrearing and home-making were a woman's responsibility in his mother's eyes and she had no problem letting me know.'

'So what happened, what did you do when Emma came along?'

'I felt I had no option but to leave my job. The job I worked hard for and studied hard for. I felt I had no other choice. Kilfarrig became so backward to me then, I became really homesick for the city, for where I felt women had a better chance in life to be themselves.

'Anyway, when Emma was born, I loved the bones off her, needless to say, but I got very down. I guess I had postpartum depression but back then nobody really knew much about that or had even heard of it. I struggled and myself and Seamus hit a bad patch for a while. I resented his mother for putting so much pressure on me. But Emma was a wonderful baby, thank God, and things eventually got much easier. I spent a lot of time in Dublin with my mother and she was a great support. I think that was what got me through the depression. Once Emma reached school-going age, I looked to get my job back and it was as if God was looking down on me because I was able to walk back into it without any hassle.'

'Sounds like you had a tough few years. Did things get easier once you went back to work?'

'Actually, yes and no. I stayed working, as you know, and was very happy but I was so scared of being put in the same position again and, well, going through that terrible time of depression, I refused to have any more children. Seamus was disappointed but the depression nearly tore us apart. Neither of us knew what was going on and he couldn't cope with my constant moodiness and crying. I was hard to live with and there were times I was sure he'd leave. In fact, there were times I even wanted him to leave. Emma became the only thing in my life that gave me any joy and, even at that, I don't think I was ever really happy. It was a difficult time and, to be honest, even though I know now that none of it was my fault, I still feel guilty.'

'But you shouldn't feel guilty, you were unwell and, what's more, you didn't even know.'

'That's the thing about it though love, guilt gets under your skin and becomes part of you. Even after all these years, I feel bad for being so anxious when Emma was a baby. I feel like I lost out completely on her first year. I was always so down that I couldn't bring myself to enjoy life with her. So yeah, I still feel guilt and I've one huge regret too.'

'What's that?' This time Siobhan reached over and put her hand on Joan's. She wasn't sure if she was imagining it but the earlier warmth in the older woman's hand had seemed to be gone.

'I regret my decision never to have any more children. When I look back on my life now, Emma is the most important part of it. I worked up until my retirement and then that was it, nothing. Years of working and suddenly it's time to quit and, believe me, then you sit down and really take stock of your life. I regret not having a bigger family, fatter family albums or having a brother or sister for Emma.' Her eyes teared up and Siobhan could see the regret in them.

'So you see darling, I was a little like you in a way, scared, but please think about what you want and be open with Alex, he's a good man and you're a good girl, sort out how you feel and what you want and don't end up with big regrets like me.'

Siobhan couldn't help but feel compassion for Joan. She was a wonderful person to have in her life and Emma was lucky to have such a lovely mother. Then the thought struck her, Emma, she had come to talk about Emma and had completely forgotten about it altogether. Looking at Joan now, whose eyes were wet with dormant emotions now escaping, it was probably the worst time to bring up such a sensitive issue. But she knew the Joan would want to know.

'Joan, thank you so much for telling me all that. I'll think about your advice, I promise.' She hesitated and the older woman instinctively knew that Siobhan had something important to say and, all of a sudden, she knew it was something that was going to affect her.

'The thing is, I'm actually very worried about Emma.' Siobhan treated every word with care. As if saying it gently was going to soften any immediate fears rushing to Joan's head. For the next hour, she spilled out all her worries and concerns about Emma and all the weird things she was experiencing.

Later that evening, Siobhan drove home in silence, although her head was buzzing. She thought of Joan's face aging before her with worry for her one and only daughter. Joan's words of advice ran through her mind. And she wondered how Alex would react if she came clean about the real reason she was not getting pregnant. She could feel her stomach turn at the very thought of telling him. This was one big mess she had created, and if she didn't fix it soon, it would cost her dearly.

CHAPTER TWENTY SIX

'Sorry, Siobhan, you forgot to sign these papers and this letter needs to go out today. Also, Mr. Adams phoned again, he's heading into a meeting but asked if you could email over the report you were working on, he said he really needs to read it today.' Julie stood looking at an unusually disorganised Siobhan. It was becoming a bit of a frequent event. Usually she was the pinnacle of professionalism but these days professionalism seemed to be given a back seat. It was hard to work with her like this. Julie had absolutely no idea what was going on with her. Alex had come in the normal three days and was on top of his game so to speak. He met all his clients, dealt with all his paperwork, made his calls and did it all with a smile on his face.

'Sorry Julie, here I'll get straight onto that now. Can you pull out the Lawson file for me, please?' Siobhan smiled up at Julie as if she didn't have a worry in the world. But she couldn't hide it. She was seriously on edge and had been all week. She was expecting Emma to ring all week to rant and rave at her down the phone for telling Joan all about her 'experiences' of Aidan in the house. But no call came. She wasn't too sure how Joan was going to deal with it. They had both agreed to keep in touch but she had heard nothing yet. It was nerve wracking. She wanted to ring her and ask what was going on or how they were going to deal with it but at the same time she wanted to give Joan time to take it all in. It must have been a shock to hear your only daughter was going insane. Joan had seemed very down as it was and Siobhan got the feeling all was not well in her world at the moment.

Alex was feeling very nervous; he didn't even notice he was tapping his foot on the floor at a hundred miles an hour annoying the couple beside him. His palms were sweaty again and he hated every moment he had to sit in the waiting room. He was intimidated, waiting to hear whether he was a real man or not. He had done a good job over the past few weeks putting the test results out of his head. His relationship with Siobhan had improved, it was like old times before the pressure had got to them. But now he was here, waiting impatiently. He wasn't impatient to hear the results but just to get out of the place. Just as the involuntary tapping of his foot was reaching boiling point for the couple beside him, a cheery good looking nurse called his name.

His heart thumped in his chest as he made his way to Professor Long's office. He was sorry now he had got in touch with him at all. Maybe it hadn't been such a good idea to have an acquaintance examine your manliness. Maybe he should have just gone to Dr Kennedy and waited for a referral to a fertility expert he wasn't acquainted with.

'Good morning, Alex, good to see you again, take a seat.' Professor Long indicated to a chair and proceeded to tell Alex the results.
It was good news! His tests had come back fine, in fact his sperm count was quite high and there was absolutely no reason for him to be unable to father a child. He was swamped with relief. Then Professor Long burst his bubble.

'Would you like me to make an appointment for Siobhan now, Alex, or would you like to talk to her first and give me a ring later? I'll fit you in within a few days so when you get through to Mary in reception just ask to be put straight through to me.'

Professor Long could almost feel Alex's dread. How was he going to tell her that their inability to conceive lay at her door? She'd be heartbroken.

'I'll talk to Siobhan tonight and I'll ring you on Monday to make an appointment.' Alex stood up as he spoke and thanked the Professor again for the news and all his help so far. So far, thought Alex to himself, this was just the beginning of a long road and God only knew what lay ahead of them.

Driving home, he decided he would whisk her away for the weekend. If he was going to open up such a delicate discussion with her, surely it would be better done in a five-star hotel room after a couple of spa treatments and an exquisite meal. He'd pack her bag and be all ready to go the minute she came home from work. Better still, he'd ring Julie and see if she could cancel any of Siobhan's meetings in the late afternoon and clear her schedule for an early departure from the office.

Lily carried a full Irish breakfast over to the rugged-looking handsome man sitting by the window immersed in the daily paper. He was unshaven and unkempt looking but it only added to his attractiveness. His full head of dark brown hair had slight bits of grey going through it although he didn't look old enough to have any grey hairs. Lily was glad he didn't attempt to hide the grey with dye; the speckles of grey suited him. They gave him a mature appearance and added to his charming looks.

'Here we go love, a full Irish with no black pudding, I put on an extra bit of bacon there, you look hungry.' Lily smiled down at the young man as she placed his plate in front of him. He looked up at her and his eyes smiled as much as his mouth, as the lines around them creased. 'Thank you, I am hungry actually. Must be that lovely fresh sea air, I'm not used to it.'

'Are you here on a holiday?' Lily asked, feeling very drawn to him. He looked familiar.

'Yeah, kind of. It depends. I don't know really,' he said, starting to butter a slice of toast. Lily instinctively knew that that was all he wanted to say. 'Well enjoy your breakfast, love,' she said as she turned away. She had just reached the counter when she heard the door open.

'Morning, Lil, it's my turn this week,' Emma said cheerily, walking up to the counter.

'Oh yes, fruit scone Friday. I have them here for you, love. See anything else you like?' smiled Lily mischievously.

'Eh....actually you know what, Lil, that chocolate roulade looks delicious. I think I might splash out and get some slices of that, I have that Friday feeling.' Emma giggled like a little kid.

'Oh Emma love,' laughed Lily, 'I wasn't talking about the roulade!' she raised her eyebrows very suggestively as she nodded her head in the direction of the gentleman mopping up his runny egg with his toast.

Emma looked around puzzled and then caught sight of who Lily was referring to. She looked back at Lily with a smile on her face and threw her eyes up to heaven.

'Honestly Lily, you are one red blooded woman. How does that poor hubby of yours cope, eh?' she laughed as she handed over the money for the scones and the roulade. She was about to leave the coffee shop when the subject of Lily's interest called out to her.

'Hey, how you doing, how's that lovely golden retriever of yours?' he said, standing up to speak to her. He had finished his breakfast and looked more than satisfied.

'Hi again, you're becoming a bit of a regular her in Kilfarrig, aren't you?' Emma blushed a little; she knew that Lily was looking at them curiously as they chatted.

'Yeah, I am, I guess. It looks like a few people are in for a treat with their tea this morning anyway,' he said casually, pointing to the delicious items in her hands.

'Yeah, it's a good way to start the weekend. Anyway, I better get going, nice to bump into you again.'

'Yeah, you too, see you around sometime maybe.'
Emma smiled but didn't say anything back. She had the feeling he *wanted* to see her around. She felt a little flustered as she left. The last thing on her mind was dating anybody and she was sure she'd never feel like dating anybody again. After all, she had her husband, the fact he was dead didn't seem to bother her at all.

Joan and Amy were busy making banana muffins when Emma came in the door after school.

'Hey, Mam. Hiya sweetheart, did you have a good morning in crèche?' Emma made a beeline for her daughter and gave her a big hug and a

108

squeeze.

'Yeah, Mammy, were you a good girl at school today?' Amy asked innocently.

'Oh yes, I was a very good girl. Were you a good girl today, too?'

'I was a good girl, Mammy.' Amy looked as proud as punch of herself.

Joan felt uneasy. She so desperately wanted to grab Emma and ask her what was going on in her head. But she knew she had to tread very carefully. Seamus was of no help whatsoever. He dismissed the whole thing as just some silly nonsense that Emma would soon snap out of. According to Siobhan, however, it had been going on for a good while now and even the fact that Siobhan had come to Joan was saying how serious the situation was. She put the muffins into the oven and put the kettle on.

'Would you like me to hold onto Amy for the night, you can go out and have a few drinks with Siobhan or something?'

'Ah thanks Mam, but no I'm shattered so I think it'll be a date with Friday night TV for me.'

'Ah alright, but she's always more than welcome, you know that sure don't you?' smiled Joan.

'Thanks, Mam. Where's Dad?' Emma was playing with Amy's hair, she felt like she hadn't seen much of her father in a while. Any time she called to the house, he was always out and about doing something or other.

'Oh God only knows, probably at some Tidy Town meeting or something.' Joan laughed as she said it but there was a definite sharpness in her voice.

'Jack told me Dad is doing that new wine tasting course he's running upstairs in The Cellar on Thursday nights now.'

'Yeah that's right, he seems to be enjoying it.'

'Why didn't you do it Mam, you'd have loved it too. I was surprised you didn't, it's a big hit, there are a good few doing it. Jack is delighted; a good few of them stay on after it for a few drinks.'

'Ah sure it's just not my thing. Tea or coffee?' Joan knew too well how successful it was. Seamus hadn't come home till all hours last Thursday night and, although he wasn't drunk or anything, it was obvious he had a good night out. She was really hurt over the wine tasting course. She'd have loved to have got out of the house and done something like that but he hadn't even bothered to ask her if she wanted to go with him. She tried to keep the hurt out of her voice though so Emma wouldn't notice. The last thing she wanted was to reveal her marriage of countless years was a complete misery to be in.

'I'll have a quick cuppa coffee, Mam. Just popping to the loo.'

On her way back from the bathroom, Emma peeped into her old bedroom. Even now, there was always something lovely about taking a little peep into her old room. She couldn't believe her eyes; it was full of her mother's things. Her dressing gown and night clothes were sprawled across the freshly made bed. Her book and reading glasses were on the bedside locker, her slippers were on the floor beside the bed and a few of her clothes were folded neatly on the chair near the window. Emma was puzzled; why was her mother sleeping in her old room? A feeling a dread came over her. Her parents' marriage was as solid as a rock or at least that's what she had believed all her life. Shutting her old bedroom door, she walked back to the kitchen, her heart beating slightly faster.

Joan was carefully taking the muffins out of the oven and the smell of fresh baking wafted throughout the house.

'Mam, why are your things in my old room?' Emma blurted out. Straight away, she could tell from her mother's face that all was far from well.

Joan placed the tray down and walked slowly over to the kitchen table.

'Amy darling, why don't you go into the living room and make that puzzle again, you're so good at it.'

Emma watched her mother as she sat down on the chair almost in slow motion. She could see a hint of a broken woman in her which was unfamiliar territory. 'Emma love, things are just not great between your father and myself at the moment, that's all, and I've moved into your old room to give us a bit of space.' She tried to sound calm but she knew her daughter could read her like a book. Things were seriously wrong with herself and Seamus and after what seemed like a lifetime of getting on with things and making life and marriage work, it was all starting to fall apart now. It was like there was nothing keeping them together anymore, there was no common interest. There was no sexual interest. There was no reason to pull together and work like a team anymore. It was all going downhill and very fast.

'Mam, please don't try to spare my feelings here, I'm a big girl you know. I can tell that things are obviously not going well so don't try to cover anything up here.'

Joan looked at her daughter and felt a real sadness. Here she was struggling with her own issues, grieving her husband and her own marriage still and now she was finding out about that her parents' marriage was falling apart. It all seemed so unfair, but she had to be honest with her. 'I really don't know what's going to happen in the future, but to be honest with you, love, it really doesn't look too promising.'

'What happened? I thought you and Dad were rock solid, I thought you were so happy together, even at Amy's party you were so united. How long has this being going on?'

'We haven't been getting on for a while, love, but things are going from bad to worse at the moment, I think it could even be time for us to think about a separation.'

Emma was stunned. 'A separation, are you serious? After so many years, how can you be thinking of separating now? Mam, you've got through all the hard stuff, you've got through all the shitty life stuff together, you are supposed to enjoying yourselves now, enjoying your retirement, everything you have worked for, not thinking about separating. Have you tried counselling?' Emma was clutching at straws.

'No we haven't gone down that route and to be fair, love, we do have a lot of life experience and if we feel that it's not working then I think there is not a lot we can do about it. We've grown apart and we, including you, must accept that.' Joan began to feel strong again. It was as if she was saying it out for the first time that it wasn't working anymore and that her marriage was over. She'd been thinking it for such a long time but had never said it out loud to anybody. It was strange to be saying it with such definition but it felt good. Like she had just accepted it herself.

'Accept it? Mam, are you crazy? You've been married for over three-and-a-half decades. Decades, Mam, not years, decades! And now you decide that it's not working and it's all over? How does Dad feel about it all?'

'Your father's not happy either, Emma. We're making each other more miserable by the day.'

'Miserable!! I can't believe it. You have each other, you have this house, you have a lifetime of memories and you're miserable. Do you not even realise how lucky you are to even have all that? For the love of God, Mam, you have each other. What I wouldn't give to have what you have. I lost my husband, I had my marriage taken from me and, here you are, throwing your marriage away.' Emma began to shake with a combination of anger, fear and sadness. Tears filled her eyes as she looked at Joan who was now lost for words.

After a few seconds of silence, Emma left the kitchen to fetch Amy.

CHAPTER TWENTY SEVEN

'Congratulations, Michael, that's great news, well done. Oh, I'd love to but I'm taking Siobhan away on a surprise spa break. She's been under a bit of pressure lately so I'm going to surprise her, it's only for the night though so maybe we'll catch up tomorrow night for a few. Okay then, listen congrats again, cheers Michael, bye bye bye bye.'

As soon as Alex hung up, he ran upstairs to throw a few of Siobhan's things into an overnight bag. He'd booked a deluxe room, one of her favourite spa treatments and a table in the exquisite restaurant. She'd be surprised and delighted.

Siobhan closed her front door and leaned down to slip her high heels off her tired and sore feet. She was surprised to see the lights off in the kitchen and, come to think of it, she wasn't greeted with any aromas escaping from the wok that would usually tantalise her taste buds as soon as she walked through the door on a Friday night.

'Honey, are you home?' She ran up the stairs and headed straight for the master bedroom. 'Honey?' She was beginning to wonder where Alex was when she walked into the room and saw him sitting on the bed.

He was facing away from her.

Siobhan stood at the door slightly bewildered. 'There you are, didn't you hear me calling you?'

He didn't reply, he didn't even turn to look at her. She scanned the room quickly and saw an overnight case standing beside the wardrobes and another one on the bed open. It was packed with her clothes and she could see some toiletries and a hairbrush also. 'What's going on, are we going somewhere?' she asked, walking over to see what was going on. Why was he just sitting there? Something was wrong, she could feel it!

He sat facing the window and didn't even look at her as she approached him.

'Alex, what the hell is going on? Are you feeling sick, is it your heart?' She crouched down beside him in panic. His face was hard, his eyes were cold.

He turned his head towards her and his eyes pierced her with an intensity she had never experienced before, making her uncomfortable. She shifted slightly beside him, searching his face for clues. Then her eyes fell to his hands and a cold sweat enveloped her. Within that split second, her whole world fell apart.

'Alex, it's not what you think. I can explain. It's a really old packet and I just forgot to throw them out, that's all.'

She waited desperately for him to say something but he just looked at her in disgust. 'Alex, please, you're over-reacting here to something silly.' She laughed a little to make it sound more convincing.

He stood up and walked towards the door picking up his overnight case on the way. Panic coursed through Siobhan's entire body and her heart began to race. 'Alex, this is silly, please!'

'Silly, you think this is silly, Siobhan? You think this is funny, you think I'm so ridiculously stupid that I'm going to believe your pathetic lies?' He dropped the case, walked back towards her until he was within an inch of her body, moved his face right up to hers and spoke, low and serious. 'You've lied to me, deceived me, deprived me, treated me like an idiot for so long and now you have the nerve to stand there and call this situation silly. You're a lying bitch, Siobhan, and I will never forgive you for this.'

She could feel his breath on her skin and the hatred with every word. Tears blurred her vision for a second but she was still able to see him pick up his case again and walk out of the room.

'Alex, please, I'm sorry, let's talk about this. You can't just leave, we need to talk, please,' she begged as she ran down the stairs after him.

All she saw was his back as he slammed the front door behind him. She dropped, sobbing, on to the bottom step of the stairs.

It was a cold wintery Saturday morning. Emma knocked on Tracy's door. While she waited for her to open it, she gave Amy another kiss on her forehead and told her to be a good girl for Tracy.

'Where are you going, Mammy?'

'Oh, I just need to go and see Nana about something, that's all.'

Just then the door opened to reveal Tracy looking very tired. Emma was sorry to have to ask her to mind Amy for the morning after teaching primary school kids all week, but she really needed to talk to her mam again. She had to get to the bottom of all this nonsense before her parents decided to do something really stupid and actually split up.

Joan and Seamus sat at the kitchen table with two steaming mugs of strong coffee in front of them. 'So we're agreed then, a separation is the best possible solution here?' Joan looked at Seamus. Although she was sad their marriage was over, she also felt a huge weight lift off her shoulders. No more carrying around the burden of a loveless marriage. Of course, once it had been full of love but that love was long gone.

Seamus nodded his head in agreement. 'I'll move out and get an apartment in the town and, sure, there's no point in selling the house. We might as well do as we had always planned and leave it to Emma. You stay

here, you love this place anyway. I couldn't imagine you anywhere else.'
Joan looked at him graciously although, deep down, she was pissed off at
him for thinking that he was better capable of moving out and moving on.
She was just as capable of starting a fresh life without him and she wasn't
stuck in any rut, especially now that they were parting ways. The house was
part of her now though and it would have been awful if she did have to
leave.

'I'll speak to Alex on Monday and see about sorting out the separation
and all. Is that okay with you, Joan?' In the past few years, he called her
Joan all the time. It used to be 'honey' but, like the love, 'honey' was also
long gone.

'Yes, that sounds good. I don't want this to become a war, Seamus. If
we can do this as amicably as possible, that would be for the best especially
considering Emma and Amy.'

Seamus stood up and laid one hand on her shoulder for a few seconds
before picking up his suitcase and walking out the back door.

At the table, Joan's tears fell freely, tears of sadness, tears of loss, tears
of fear, and tears of relief. At the sound of the back door opening, she
looked up to see Emma standing in the doorway.

'Mam, what's wrong?' Emma was at her side within a flash rubbing her
back in comfort.

Composing herself quickly, Joan gently took Emma's hand in hers.

'I'm glad you're here love, although your father wanted to talk to you
too. We...'

'Well, where is he, will he be home soon? I dropped Amy into Tracy's
this morning so I don't need to be back for a while yet.'

'Your dad is gone love, we decided to separate.'

Emma fell onto the chair. 'Gone? What do you mean gone, where's he
gone? Sure this is his home!'

'He's going to rent an apartment in town and sure, that will only take a
few days to sort, so in the meantime he's going to stay in the hotel.'

'In the hotel? Really? Can you not work this out or at least let him stay
here till he sorts something out?'

'Emma, you have to understand. Once we decided to separate, it was
what we both wanted. It wasn't a case of throwing your father out, he
wanted to go too.

The last thing Joan wanted was for her daughter to think she was the
big bad wolf in all of this mess; it was hard enough without looking like the
baddy.

'Well, why on earth didn't Dad come stay with me? Surely that's much
better than staying in a lonely hotel room after you've been kicked out of
your own home!' Joan's buttons were well and truly pushed now. Seamus

wasn't an innocent party in all of this, he shared some part of the break up too.

'Emma! I did not kick your father out! This was what we both wanted and he was more than happy to go to the hotel. He hasn't spent much time here over the past few months anyway so it wasn't such a big deal to him. Besides, we didn't want to bother you with all this, it's our issue to deal with. You've enough on your plate as it is.'

Emma's head shot up. 'What do you mean, I have enough on my plate?!'

Joan's face softened; she'd wanted to have this conversation with her daughter for a while now but this was not how she wanted to broach the subject.

'Nothing, love, we just want to sort this out ourselves. We're big enough to deal with it, so we don't want you worrying.'

'That's a politician's answer, Mam. I asked you what you were implying when you said I had enough on plate. Now, can you actually answer that?' Emma was insistent now because she had seen a glimmer of pity on her mother's face as she had said it. Taking a deep breath, Joan looked at her daughter's beautiful face, so full of fresh frustration and anger.

'Darling, Siobhan came to speak to me about, well, about your visions or how should I put it? Well, with how you think you've been feeling Aidan's presence around you these past few months.'

Emma stared at Joan, her mouth hanging open. Joan saw her opportunity to continue. 'She's worried about you, pet. Frankly, we all are!'

'Hold on a minute, who do you mean by "all"?' Emma demanded.

'Well, Siobhan and myself … and, well, Jack too.'

'Right, I see! So all this time I've been confiding in Siobhan, she's actually been thinking I was imagining it all? All those times she sat and listened to me, bloody smiling and encouraging me to talk, she was actually thinking in her head that I was going mad? You mean she never believed me, at all? Jack either? They both pretended to understand and got together then to talk about how flipping crazy Emma is!! And now you, you think I'm mad too. How dare she tell you anyway, how dare she?'

'Listen to me, love. We're all just worried that maybe things are getting on top of you, that's all. I mean, it can't be easy bringing up a child on your own while you're grieving for Aidan. It's nothing to be ashamed of that you may have conjured up ways to hold onto him, but you know, honey, it's not healthy. You don't want Amy thinking her dad is a ghost in the house, do you? Maybe you should go back and see that psychiatrist again.

'Seriously, I cannot believe I'm hearing this, Mam! That's why I never said anything to you. I knew you definitely wouldn't believe me,' Emma cried out. 'How do you explain all the things that have been happening then? Anytime I feel down and I really miss him and need him, he sends me a sign, like I'd turn the radio on and one of our special songs would be playing, our wedding photo fell down on the day he proposed. Digger will only sleep beside his favourite chair and even barks at it and all the times I can actually sense him beside me!'

'Oh darling, lots of those things can be explained away. Any song on the radio can be significant if you want it to be. Digger likes his comfort and now you let him sleep in the sitting room so he sure as hell isn't moving back to the kitchen and maybe you......'

'Maybe this, maybe that….maybe I'm not imagining things, Mam. I can smell him, Mam, I can actually smell his favourite aftershave especially at night. I can physically feel a presence around me. At night, the bedroom light flickers when I talk to him!'

'Oh love, I had no idea things have been this bad for you. You need to face this for what it really is,' Joan said, placing her hand on Emma's arm.

'Which is?' Emma asked sadly, ignoring the urge to yell out that things hadn't been bad, they'd been amazing and that the past few months had been so happy when she had felt Aidan around.

'A case of you not letting go, darling. You need to let go, for Amy's sake too.'

Emma felt sick. Not only did her mother think she was going crazy but she thought that her craziness was going to affect Amy.

'Thanks for your thoughts on it all, good to know you think I'm gone mad too!' she abruptly brushed her mother's hand away, stood up and walked out.

Tears slid down her face as she drove angrily towards Siobhan's house, fuelled with feelings of total betrayal by her two supposedly closest friends in the world. All this time they had been gossiping about her and the state of her mental health! She tore up Siobhan's driveway and nearly took the car door off its hinges as she banged it shut. Then she almost put the posh brass knocker through the hall door as she slammed it to get Siobhan's attention.

'I'm coming, I'm coming. Jeez, hold your bloody horses!' Siobhan took her time walking through the spacious hallway, pinching the bridge of her nose. She was in no mood for visitors! If she was at all surprised to see Emma fuming at her door, she hid it well. She grunted some sort of hello and headed back to the kitchen.

Emma stared after her for a second. The usually pristine Siobhan was decked out in a woolly dressing gown, her hair unruly and she slowly dragged her bare feet along the cold tiles. Okaaay, this was unusual. Nevertheless, Emma marched after her into the kitchen, all set to rant and rave. But the state of Siobhan stopped her in her tracks! Siobhan was sitting at the table, staring into a cup of black coffee with big fat tears cascading down her cheeks and free-falling onto her dressing gown. An empty bottle of wine sat on the island with a red wine-stained glass at the sink. Siobhan's pale face sported two great black circles framing her sunken eye sockets.

'Siobhan, what's wrong?' all of Emma's rage took a back seat as she quickly crossed the modern kitchen to where her broken friend sat now whimpering.

'He's left!'

'Huh, left? Who, Alex? What do you mean? I don't understand!'

'He's left me!'

'What do you mean, left you? What are you talking about?'

'Oh for flip's sake. Alex has left me, he's gone, moved out, left, understand now?'

'Bloody hell! What is it with you married people today? What the hell happened, why is he gone? Don't tell me he's seeing someone else?'

'No of course not, he'd never do that. He's a good man, one in a million…and now I've lost him…' said Siobhan, breaking down again.

'Oh no, not you, you weren't…'

'No don't be silly, he was all I ever wanted! I would never be un…'

The crying got worse.

'What, what is it?' Emma was really concerned now.

'I was going to say that I'd never be unfaithful, but if I'm honest with myself that's exactly what I was being,' she sniffed. 'I hurt him, hurt him really badly and he'll never forgive me!' Siobhan looked at Emma with desperation in her eyes, almost begging for Emma to make it all better.

'You know how badly he wanted a child?'

Emma just nodded.

'Well, I feel so ashamed, I don't know how to put this but well, I…' She put her hand over her mouth wanting the words to stay in. 'I deliberately stayed on the pill to make sure I wouldn't get pregnant, he found the pack last night and flipped out. He packed his bag and left.'

Emma was stunned. 'You mean all this time you guys have been trying, you've actually been on the pill??'

'Yes!' Siobhan held her hands over her eyes, unable to look at her friend.

'But you were both so determined, so focused on it. I can't believe it, this whole time you were…'

Siobhan butted in anxiously, 'No, I wasn't determined. It was Alex who was determined, not me! I didn't want a baby, I never did but somehow I was roped into planning for one and it was never my plan, never! He's the one obsessing about it, it was driving me insane! I didn't know what to do!'

'Did you not talk about kids?' Emma asked carefully, afraid to get her head bitten off again.

'Yes, of course, and we both agreed that the firm was our baby, our life, that our careers were the priority. But then he had his stupid heart attack and the thoughts of dying obviously changed his priorities. Never mind the fact that I never changed mine. But I was so relieved he was okay that I just went along with it till he was stronger to talk about it properly. Then he got obsessive and it just seemed to spiral.'

'But do you not remember all the little chats we had about it, how it wasn't happening for you and you were both upset and disappointed?'

'Bloody hell, Emma, are you really so caught up in your own stupid daydreaming to notice that I was uncomfortable with it every time *YOU* brought up the subject? Did you never notice that I tried to squirm my way out of talking about it? *YOU* were the one insisting on bringing it up all the time, not *ME*!'

Daydreaming?! Emma suddenly remembered her reason for banging on Siobhan's door in the first place. Fury suddenly hit her cheeks, flashing them red.

'Daydreams! Oh yeah, now they're daydreams! Seems like Alex is not the only idiot sucked in by your lies … for months, you've pretended to be there for me and, all that time, you were talking about me behind my back.'

'What are you talking about?' Siobhan asked, shocked.

'You blabbing to my mam! I thought you were a friend, I thought you understood me, but the whole time you thought I was bananas.'

'Well, I'm sorry you see it that way. I really am, but I only told your mother because I was worried about you.'

'Well, why didn't you talk to me rather than opening your big mouth to my mam? You never once made me feel I was going crazy or making it up, you were always happy to listen to me; I actually thought you were happy for me.'

'I never thought you were making it up, I just thought…think that maybe you haven't fully let go and that you've allowed your grief to play tricks on you.'

'So, you think it's all been in my mind?'

'Emma, please, just stop this nonsense. My husband has just left me, I'm not in the mood for you and your dead husband. Move on!' She might as well have punched Emma in the chest. Emma stood towering over Siobhan, stunned at how low her friend could stoop.

'How dare you! How *DARE YOU*! I'm not surprised Alex is gone, he deserves better.' With that she left.

Emma was still reeling from Siobhan's cruel words as she dialled Jack's number. It was clear the other two thought she was mad and needed to get her act together but she wanted to see what Jack had to say for himself. Was he being two-faced and insincere all this time too?

'Hey, how's it going?' he answered, sounding rushed. It was the middle of lunch time at The Cellar but Emma didn't care.

'So it seems you think I've gone mad too, then!' she spat the words out viciously.

'Sorry, Emma, what are you talking about? He didn't have time to try and guess. And it sounded like Emma wasn't in the mood for games either.

'So you think I've gone mad too? Christmas Day, standing in the hall, I told you about the photo frame. You smiled and listened so attentively, you nodded your head when I told you and everything! So, tell me, did you believe me or did you think I had gone crazy?'

The penny dropped. Emma had obviously been to see her mam.

'Look, you're upset at the moment, so can we talk about this when I've a chance to talk to you properly. I'll come straight home after this lunch time rush.'

'Just tell me, did you believe me or not?'

'Please, let's talk about this later; I want to talk to you properly...'

'Did you or did you NOT?' she yelled.

Jack didn't know what to say so he said nothing.

'Right, I see. Thanks, Jack, thanks a million!' She ended the call, throwing her phone down on the passenger seat where it bounced off and flew onto the floor.

'Thank you very much indeed, Jack, and you too, Siobhan, and you too, Mam!' she muttered. Then she did the only thing left she could do and burst into big fat tears.

CHAPTER TWENTY EIGHT

Tears were still falling fast and steady as Emma pulled up outside her house. It was only when she got out of the car that she noticed the stranger from the beach walking up the path towards her.

'Seriously, what are you?' she shouted angrily, 'some kind of psycho stalker?'

He looked surprised to see her. 'Oh hello, I didn't expect to see you. I didn't know you live here!' he stammered slightly, taken back by her accusations.

'Yeah right, that's why you just happen to be walking up towards my house, is it?' she said smartly, one hand planted firmly on her hip.

'What?' he asked, totally confused by her obvious annoyance at him.

'Look, do I have to spell it out for you? *I am not interested in you, Okay?*!! And no amount of asking me out, handing me boxes of falling tampons or stalking is going to change that! So just turn around and piss off ... please!' A few uncomfortable seconds passed by.

'Eh, this is embarrassing but I was actually looking for this house here...' he said, pointing to Jack's.

'Right,' she snarled, 'how convenient!'

'I was, I'm looking for Jack and I believe he lives here.'

Emma stared at him for what seemed like forever with her mouth open.

'Oh, I'm so sorry ... I ... I thought ... I'm so embarrassed now...' she groaned and threw her hands up to cover her face and started bawling her eyes out again.

He rushed to her side and placed a hand on her shoulder. 'Oh please, don't cry, it's okay. In fact, you're right, I do look like a weirdo stalker really, with my ordinary brown hair and distinguished-looking green eyes, not to mention the big silly grin!' His attempt to make her smile worked as she took her hands down and smiled a little for the first time that day.

'That's better. I prefer to make people smile than cry! So, about Jack, do you know if he lives here?'

'Are you a friend?' Emma asked.

He paused, seeming to ponder the question himself for a moment.

'Yeah, well, we grew up together.'

'Oh right, he never talks about home. Look, he should be home in a little while if you want to wait. I can make you a pot of tea to make up for accusing you of stalking me. Oh, and I baked a delicious chocolate cake yesterday ...'

'Oooh, chocolate cake, how could I refuse?'

Within minutes, he was wishing he had refused! He sat at the kitchen table, battling with a slice of supposedly chocolate cake-slash-chocolate rock more like. He finally got the fork to slice through it, but he had to use such force that the fork hit the plate with a thud and a piece of cake went flying across the floor bouncing a few times before it came to a stop.

'Lovely cake!' he lied, 'Lily should watch out.'

'Oh thanks, yeah I thought it turned out better than expected alright.'

Gosh, what were you expecting, he asked himself, trying to crunch on another bit. 'If you don't mind me saying, you looked upset when you got out of the car. Are you alright?' he asked.

'Yeah, I'm fine. I'm just mad in the head apparently!'

Despite her laughter, he knew someone had really upset her.

'Well, as a crazy stalker, I feel I can safely say you don't come across as someone who is ready to join our CSA just yet.'

'CSA?'

'Crazy Stalker Anonymous!' The pair of them burst out laughing.

'Sod it,' she said, 'you may end up thinking *I AM* mad, but I'm gonna tell you something.'

He sat up straight and gave her his undivided attention.

She told him everything she had felt, experienced, and sensed in the past year. He listened carefully to everything and didn't butt in or look shocked at any of it.

'I suppose you think I'm mad then.' It was a statement, not a question.

'No, no, not at all, Emma. I truly believe everything you just told me is possible.'

'Really?' she sat up with a new sense of relief. Someone believed her. She couldn't be mad if someone believed her.

'Yes, of course! Who's to say our loved ones disappear from us after they die? Think about it! Who can actually say that for a fact? I believe he was communicating with you.'

'It's so good to hear that. The very people I thought would believe me, well, they let me down big time,' she said sighing heavily. 'My mother wants me to go see a psychologist.'

'It's not their fault. Some people just don't have an open mind to this type of this stuff, that's all. I don't think it's a question of whether your husband is still around, it's more of a question of why he's still around?'

'I never actually looked at it that way,' she said, mulling over his words, 'I'm pretty sure he just wants to be around me and Amy.'

'Well, although I believe people can revisit their loved ones after they pass on, I also believe that their time after death is supposed to be peaceful, hence the term "rest in peace". I think they come back because they have a reason to.'

'Like a mission or a purpose?' she quizzed.

'Yeah, kind of. Death is natural, it's part of life. It's a natural progression, so I believe it's easy and natural for the person to move on because that's what they are supposed to do. But it's not as natural for the……..'

'The person left behind!' she finished the sentence for him.

'Exactly.'

'So what are you saying?'

'That maybe Aidan is still here because you weren't ready for him to leave?'

'He can't move on until I let him go, you mean?'

'That could be it.'

They sat in silence for a while. Emma was trying to process what he had just said. Was it really her who was stopping Aidan from resting? Was he still around because *she* couldn't or wouldn't let him go?

The sound of a car pulling up next door broke her train of thought.

'There's Jack now,' she said, standing up. 'Thank you so much for listening to me and for not judging me as a mad person.'

'No problem, I hope it all works out for you.' He walked towards the door with his heart in his mouth and his palms were wet with anxiety produced sweat. He wanted to run back through Emma's house, bolt out the back door, and run as far away as he possibly could.

Outside, Michael was trying to calm Jack down. 'Jack, don't worry, you'll sort this out with her in no time.' He had never seen him in such a state.

'You didn't hear her on the phone, she was gutted that we didn't believe her!' He shut the car door and jumped the wall in one go. Michael promptly followed. He was just about to ring the bell when her door opened. Jack nearly died when he came face to face with his past!

'Conor!' he eventually spat out, 'what the hell are *you* doing here?'

Conor hadn't been sure what kind of reception he was going to get, but this was about right, he reckoned.

'Hi, Jack,' he murmured, 'long time, no see.'

'What are you doing here?' repeated Jack harshly.

Emma butted in. 'I was upset, Jack, as *you* well know and your friend here kindly listened to me and without judgement at that!'

Jack roared laughing, a freaky nasty laugh. 'He's no friend of mine ... and judging people is all he's good at ...' he said sternly, keeping his eyes on Conor.

Emma began to feel nervous. Sure, she was mad at Jack but she knew he was a top guy with a great sense of judgement of character. If he was being this rude and ignorant to this guy, there must be a fairly good reason! Who had she just left into her house? And into her mind?

Conor could sense Emma's unease. He looked at her, saw her concern, and told her exactly who he was.

'I'm Jack's brother,' he said solemnly.

'His brother?' Emma gasped, 'but why didn't you just tell me that?' Then she turned to Jack, surprise etched on her face. 'But I thought you had no brothers?'

'I don't,' he replied quickly, 'we may be related by blood but, as far as I'm concerned, he's no brother of mine!'

Conor sighed loudly before putting his hand out to Michael who stood beside Jack, looking as puzzled as Emma.

'You must be Jack's...'

'Friend.' Jack said quickly.

Michael shook his hand, wary of the situation unfolding.

'Look, why don't I go in and have a coffee with Emma while you two go and... catch up?' he offered politely.

'I'd really love a chance to talk, Jack, please,' Conor pleaded.

'Where's Claudia, does she know you're here?' Jack asked.

'Who's Claudia?' Emma asked.

'His wife,' Jack responded, 'and Flynn, where is he?'

'Son?' Emma guessed.

'Right.' said Jack.

Emma felt sick. Who was this guy? It was all so weird. How come he only came to see Jack now and yet she'd seen him around the place so many times. And how dare he ask her out when he was married and with a son at that!

'I'll put the kettle on, Michael,' she said, walked indoors. Obviously, Conor's opinions about her letting Aidan go were just so he could be in with a chance. Snake! Perhaps he didn't even believe her in the first place, seeing as he was turning out to be a bit of a liar.

'That was awkward.' Michael said as he sat down. He spotted the chocolate cake on the table and hoped to God Emma wouldn't offer him any.

'Yeah, it was. Jack never talks about his family, ever. It must have been a shock for him to suddenly see his brother standing at my door.'

'Why do you think he got so angry?'

'I honestly have no idea. He keeps that side of his life to himself. But if I know Jack at all, I know it must have been something big to make him turn his back on his family.'

Michael nodded in agreement as Emma came over with two steaming mugs of coffee.

'Now,' she said as she produced a knife, 'how much of my delicious cake do you want?'

'Well? You didn't answer me, where are Claudia and Flynn?' Jack fired his house keys on the island and leaned against the counter with folded arms.

'Flynn died, Jack!' Conor looked ashen as he said the dreaded words.

'What?' Jack asked, not sure he heard correctly. He stood up straight and unfolded his arms, momentary forgetting he didn't want to let his guard down.

'Claudia went to wake him one morning and he...... he was......' He couldn't finish the sentence. 'Claudia was inconsolable. She got depressed. I didn't know what to do. I was supposed to be strong for her but I couldn't keep it up. I started to drink at night when she went to bed. Then, eventually, I'd have a drink before she went to bed. Then it got earlier and earlier and eventually I was totally depending on alcohol to kill the pain. But, by then, things were really bad between us. She moved back to Sweden and I ran the pub into the ground. Lost everything.'

'Why didn't you tell me?' Jack was stunned and pissed off that, although he had never seen his nephew, he wasn't given the chance to say goodbye. When Conor emailed to say Claudia was expecting, Jack couldn't have given a shit. However, when he emailed again telling him of Flynn's birth and sending him a photo of a tiny little being wrapped up all snug in a blue cosy blanket, Jack had found it hard to maintain his stubbornness and not reply. Now he felt a twinge of regret.

'Well, when you didn't reply to the wedding invitation or any of my emails, I didn't bother. What did it matter, what did anything matter? My boy died and it was the end of the world, so nothing else mattered.'

'I'm so sorry to hear all that. I really am! I'd never have wished any such thing on you.'

'I know ... thanks.' Conor hung his head.

'When did it happen?' Jack asked solemnly.

'Two years, eight months and three weeks ago to be exact,' Conor replied with unmistakable tears in his eyes. Silence took over for a few seconds.

'Why are you here?' Jack asked, calmer now.

'To see you. I've lost everything. Flynn was here for a short time but he was my world and he changed it for the better. He made me realise how important people are, how important family are. Then I lost him and I lost Claudia and then I lost everything else. I've been sober now this past eight months, I've got myself out of the rut I was in and I'm trying to put my life back together. Although I'm not sure what kind of a life that can be, but I need to try. Look, I've been seeing a counsellor for the past few months and I realise just how important it is that we can ... well, you can ... Oh, God, I've tried before to say sorry but I'm here now to do it properly, to apologise in person ... to your face, for everything.'

'You made my life hell!' Jack blurted out, frowning.

'I know,' he admitted shamefully.

'You turned my own parents against me, you made sure I had no friends, you fuelled all the nasty gossip around the school and the entire village about me and then stood by and laughed while I was bullied rotten! And if there was nobody around to bully me for your amusement, you just went ahead and bullied me yourself!'

'I know, I know ... believe me, I know! I was horrible to you and I'm ashamed about it.'

'You were supposed to be my brother. My family.'

'I know, I know, I was anything but family. I wasn't a brother, I didn't look out for you ...'

'Look out for me?' Jack sniggered, 'did you not hear what I just said? You were my biggest and meanest bully.'

'I'm so sorry, Jack. I know now how much I hurt you, I was young and really stupid and thought I was only mucking around. I never thought that I was really hurting you as much as I did. I'll never forgive myself for causing you all that pain!'

'Mucking around?!' Jack mocked. 'You did a hell of a lot more than mucking around, you destroyed me. Do you know that before I left, I seriously contemplated killing myself? But I was terrified! I couldn't do it, so I decided to get out instead.'

Conor was gutted hearing just how much he had tormented his brother.

'Oh Jack! I'm so sorry, I really messed up, didn't I?'

'Yeah, you sure did.'

Conor got up and passed Jack with his head down. Jack could see the years of regret in his damp eyes. The pure guilt etched in the fine lines around his eyes and across his forehead. The years of torment didn't exactly leave Jack, but the sight of his broken brother did lessen the weight of it slightly. Conor was just about to open the door when Jack called to him. He stood looking at the handle and then turned to face Jack slowly.

'Why don't you stay in Kilfarrig tonight and maybe we can meet up tomorrow and, well ... talk some more?'

'Really?' Conor asked, surprised as hell.

'Look, I don't know how we can get past all of this stuff but let's just meet up tomorrow and take it from there.'

'Yeah, that sounds great. Thanks Jack, I won't let you ...'

Jack interrupted quickly before he could make empty promises that Jack wasn't so sure his brother could keep. 'Don't go getting your hopes up for a rosy family reunion, I'm far from wanting to get all friendly and cosy with you. This visit of yours could end up with you going back home without a brother at all, do you hear me? Don't get too cocky here!'

'I understand, I really do. Look, all I'm looking for is a chance, even a small one, to make it up to you,' Conor blurted out.

'Just one thing, nobody knows about my past and I want to keep it that way!'

'What ... you mean in all these years, you never ...' Conor exclaimed.

Jack cut him off abruptly again. 'No, and don't bring it up again, ever!'

CHAPTER TWENTY NINE

Michael could see Conor leaving next door and heading down the driveway. He didn't look happy. 'Right he's gone, I'm gonna go in and see if Jack's alright, you coming?'

'No I should have collected Amy ages ago. I'll just give the brother from hell or whoever he is a few minutes to make sure he's well and truly gone, I don't even want to drive past him!'

'Okay, I'm off, I'll catch you later,' Michael said, a bit surprised that Emma wasn't rushing into see if Jack was okay too.

Jack was at the kitchen table looking at a photo of two young boys when Michael appeared.

'Jack, are you alright? That was pretty tense out there.'

Jack's eyes remained on the photo as he handed it to Michael.

'We were seven and nine in this photo. We got on well those days despite the normal killings that go on between two young brothers.'

Without saying a word, Michael sat down.

'But then we just grew apart, had nothing in common and became enemies.'

'You became enemies? That's fairly drastic behaviour for two brothers, isn't it?' Michael knew there had to be more to the story.

'Brothers don't just turn dog on one another, especially at such a young age for something as simple as having nothing in common.'

'We just began to grow apart and we were so different. He loved soccer, he was popular and such a big hit with the girls in the village, he was really good looking but he knew it and was such a cocky bastard.'

'I couldn't imagine you were too much different then.' laughed Michael.

Jack looked at him for a second before continuing. 'Actually, I was. I was fairly heavy at the time, had no interest in sports whatsoever, I had bad skin and, to top it all off, I was really shy. I used to stumble over every word almost. It drove my father mad. I can still hear him shouting at me, "For feck's sake, lad, just spit it out will you!" It wasn't a great way to be when your dad was a pub landlord. He expected us to work in the bar cleaning the glasses and ashtrays, but he was embarrassed by my "social awkwardness" as he called it. Conor teased me non-stop. I became even more horribly self-conscious and began to hate myself even more.'

'That's rough, alright, strong feelings there for a young fella.'

'Yep, it was pretty shitty alright. I just didn't fit in, it was terrible. All my so-called school friends began to tease me then too. I was fat, shy, ugly and couldn't even get my words out. I wanted to end things so many times!'

'I can't believe Conor didn't protect you.' Michael asked, frowning.

Jacked laughed, 'Yeah, he was the biggest bully of them all! It never stopped. Even when school ended and the other bullies went home, I still got it. Twenty-four seven, he made my life hell.'

'What happened then?'

'I decided to study my arse off! I figured I might as well seeing as I had no social life and every time I opened my bedroom door, he would do or say something horrible. I befriended another loner in my year. He was bullied rotten too ad had no friends either, so we ended up being friends out of pity for each other more so than anything else.'

'That's good, though, that you got another friend and just got on with it, isn't it?' Michael said, hopefully.

'Nah, because we were both victims of the bullies, my brother included, we only studied or ever met up in his place or mine. When he came to the pub, we stayed out of everyone's way and studied in my room but, sure, within months Conor had told the entire village we were both gay and he'd walked in on us kissing!' Michael's face fell. Jack noticed, because he'd intentionally zoned in on it to see what reaction he'd get. Nevertheless, he continued. 'Things got worse then, I was bullied far worse. Beaten up a few times and even ridiculed by my own dad. He didn't want me seen in the pub, he was so ashamed of me.'

'So he believed Conor then, he thought you were gay?'

'Yep, he said I was a freak and he didn't know how he came to have a son like me. I tried to tell him I wasn't, but it made no difference.'

'God, that all sounds terrible. What a horrible thing to have to go through. No wonder you didn't want to see your brother all these years!'

'Yeah!' he sighed, downbeat.

'So what happened then?' asked Michael, his brow furrowing.

'Straight after the exams, I moved to Spain and got a job in a bar. I became really obsessed with the gym and weights, lost all the weight, rented a tiny apartment in a shitty area and had hardly any money to live on but I was happy for the first time in my life! I regret now not going on to college. I aced my exams and could have got any course I wanted, but I just wanted to get away from my so-called family. I'd have gone to Australia if I'd had the money, but Spain was as far as I could get.'

Well, you shouldn't have any regrets now anyway. You've a thriving business here and you've made a great life for yourself with brilliant friends around you. The tables seemed to have turned. Your brother seemed fairly desperate to sort things out with you.'

'Yeah,' Jack said taking a deep breath, 'he lost his little baby to cot death, his marriage broke down, he took to the drink big time, and he ended up running the pub into the ground. I'm sure Dad would be turning in his grave now that his precious pub had to be sold off.'

'Oh right, wow, tough!'

'Imagine all that pain? Imagine your child dying, that's unnatural, isn't it? I actually feel bad for him.'

'That's fairly tough, alright.'

'Anyway, he's here now and wants to make amends, have some sort of brotherly relationship, I guess.'

'That's good, isn't it?' asked Michael cautiously.

'Yeah, well, we'll see,' Jack sighed, less optimistic, 'we'll see.'

Emma had just arrived home from collecting Amy when Siobhan rang. She ignored the call, talking to Siobhan was the last thing she wanted. Her head was racing and she was beginning to feel anxious. The old familiar big black cloud was rumbling around in her tummy and her breathing was slightly quicker than normal.

When Conor had been here, she actually felt at peace and so normal. Not only did he seem to believe her, but he seemed to understand her. But he was obviously only acting, telling her what she wanted to hear. He'd been eyeing her up for weeks now and he was already married! What a total scumbag! She felt weak all over for trusting him. But then again, she felt weak for trusting Siobhan and Jack too. Who could she trust? Could she even trust herself? She decided that the best course of action was distraction and what better way to take your mind off things than to ask your father to move in with you!

Seamus was thrilled when Emma asked her to stay with him until his apartment was ready. He didn't fancy staying in a hotel and staying at home was way too awkward now. Besides, it would give him a few weeks to properly catch up with Emma and find out what was going on in her life.

Alex was still as mad as hell. He checked the calling number on his mobile. Siobhan, again. He angrily switched the phone off altogether and fired it on the couch beside him. She could rot in hell for all he cared. All those years together and they had never even been bothered with little white lies. And now this! Who was she? Certainly not the woman he thought she was. Having sex and pretending to want a baby as much as him and all the while swallowing her little yellow pill every night, trampling all over his dreams. Every time he thought about it and about her, he wanted to punch something. He ordered a Chinese takeaway and opened a bottle of expensive merlot instead.

Siobhan left yet another anxious message. 'Please Alex, answer the phone. I really need to explain it all to you. I want to make you understand. Please, I love you, I love you so much! Just talk to me, give me a chance to explain.' All her messages were along the same line. She had begged him all night, every hour on the hour, to pick up the phone. She had driven up to the house in Dalkey earlier that morning too but he wouldn't answer the door and she had no key. She waited outside in her car for a full hour, stubborn as hell. But to no avail. He didn't open the door. She then resorted to true psycho behaviour and sent him text after text after text but she never got a reply. She felt sick to her stomach. And to top it all off, the guilt over what she had said to Emma was killing her too. She'd tried ringing her a few times as well but Emma didn't answer either. She put the phone down on the coffee table and looked around, her huge sophisticatedly decorated and carefully furnished home was now like a lonely shell.

CHAPTER THIRTY

Almost two weeks had passed since Seamus had moved in, apparently temporarily. But there was no sign of his apartment being anywhere near sorted and Emma didn't see any sign of him trying to move things along. Her sympathy at the thought of poor old-fashioned Dad having to move into a hotel was wearing thin. God love him. He was trying to be so helpful around the house and he was so good to Amy but Emma couldn't wait to have her own space back. He loved being handed a cup of tea and the TV was on Sky News constantly. Amy was suffering from cartoon withdrawal!

Emma was just peeling spuds for the twelfth day in a row (Seamus didn't like all this new Eastern and Italian food ... meat and two veg was the only way to go) when she heard him come in through the front door.

'Don't bother with dinner for me love, I had a bite in your mother's,' he shouted cheerily as he went into the sitting room. 'Oh, but I'd love an auld cuppa if there's one going.'

Emma instantly threw down the potato peeler and went into him.

'What do you mean, you had dinner in Mam's?' she asked, annoyed that he was sprawled out in the infamously haunted chair. Without looking up from the TV, he said casually, 'Yeah, I had dinner with Joan.'

Feeling Emma's eyes on him, Seamus glanced over at her. 'There's nothing to it, love. I just went up to get my books and I ended up staying for dinner, that's all.'

'But I thought you two couldn't stand each other. You split up and, all of a sudden, you're having dinner together and it's no big deal?'

'Look, love, no-one ever said we couldn't stand each other. Well, at least I didn't anyway,' he laughed, 'just trying to keep a marriage working when we were so far apart was making things worse. Now, well, I suppose we don't have the pressure of having to be together, so we can actually relax around each other.'

'That's the most ridiculous thing I've ever heard, you both need your heads seen to,' Emma called out as she left the room. 'You're both too bloody old to be acting so bloody stupid!' she shouted out from the kitchen.

Seamus threw his eyes up to heaven as he shifted uncomfortably in the big armchair. Something was sticking into his leg. He dug down the side of the chair and pulled out a large dog bone. Digger jumped up and started barking excitedly. Emma ran back in to see what all the racket was all about.

'Where the hell did that come from? I haven't seen it in months.' She watched Digger throw the bone up in the air and catch it in his mouth, tail wagging at approximately one hundred miles an hour.

'It was down the side of this chair, I'm surprised he couldn't smell it. And by the looks of how much he loves it, I can't believe he hadn't ripped the chair apart to get at it already,' Seamus said, not noticing the blood draining from Emma's face. 'Though I guess he knew it was there alright, he was always keen to lie against this particular chair, I've noticed.' He chuckled, still oblivious to Emma's eyes welling up.

Siobhan called to the house again and was pleasantly surprised that Alex answered the door this time. Maybe his anger was thawing. But, he looked at her coldly and walked away from the door. There was no invite in. She could follow him or go home, he didn't seem too bothered either way.

'Alex, sweetheart, this is ridiculous, we have to talk about it. We're not going to solve anything when we're living in separate houses. You have to come back home so we can sort this out, it's been ages now. I've waited for you to call, but nothing. I wanted to give you some space but this is going on too long, honey, we need to sort this.'

He still said nothing. Siobhan was at a loss. She walked over to the bay window and gazed out over the sea. It was such a beautiful day, the sky was clear blue and the sea was like a lake. Dalkey Islands looked like they were alive, breathing in the nature around them and becoming even more beautiful with each breath.

But Siobhan didn't notice any of the beauty in front of her, all she could concentrate on was the ugliness she had created in her own life. All she could feel was apologetic, guilty and sad. The silence, coldness, and loathing radiating towards her from Alex was more than she could bear. In all their time together, all throughout their marriage, she had never known this side of him, never known how much hatred he could carry. 'Alex, I can't begin to tell you how sorry I am for what I did, but you have to understand.'

And with that, Alex stood up, came towards her with fury and anger spitting out of his mouth. 'Understand? Yeah, I understand alright, Siobhan. you're nothing but a devious, cold, calculating wagon who doesn't give a damn about anybody but yourself.'

She just stood still, shocked at his outburst. 'Alex, I know you're angry, but...'

Again, he was off. 'Angry? My so-called loving wife has been lying to me all this time, playing games behind my back...'

'I wasn't, Alex, I was trying to control my own life,' she butted in.

'Oh, for heaven's sake, woman, of course you were playing games. And all because you're a selfish brat who needs your career, your trips to the salon, your Prada bloody handbags, your massive house, and your fancy posh car.' Siobhan's heart began to pound harder and harder in her chest. Her apologies died away as her neck started to heat up and her breathing started to speed up. Anger began to rise from the depths of her stomach. She dashed past him and out the door before she said anything to make the situation any worse.

Back at work, her head felt like it was going to split in two any second. Usually her office was her solace but, today, work was the last place she wanted to be. She checked her watch, she had a meeting with a client in half-an-hour and she needed to sort herself out. She could feel the big black bags under her eyes and knew she looked washed out. It didn't exactly go a long way to instil confidence in a client when you appeared at a meeting looking like a piece of shite shat on by an even bigger piece of shite! She grabbed her make-up bag and slipped out to the loo.

As soon as she entered the ladies, she could hear a soft sobbing coming from one of the cubicles. She agonised for a moment over leaving whoever was having the meltdown alone, but she really needed to shovel some slap on her face. She tiptoed to the mirror and began to plaster her face with foundation when the cubicle door opened slowly. Julie walked out sniffling and stood alarmed when she spotted her boss at the sink overdosing on lipstick.

'Oh, Siobhan, I didn't hear anybody come in. Sorry, I was just, eh, blowing my nose, I've a dreadful head cold.'

'Yeah, right, and I'm the Queen of Sheba. Here, by the look of those puffy eyes, you could do with some war paint yourself,' Siobhan smiled as she handed Julie some foundation.

'Thanks. Declan and I broke up last night,' Julie sniffled.

'Oh, Julie, I'm sorry to hear that. It sucks, doesn't it?'

'What does?'

'Love.'

'Yeah, it does. I just hope to God that it's gonna get better, I feel like I'm going backwards now again. I really thought that Declan was the one, you know? God, all I want to do is meet someone nice, fall in love, settle down, and then someday think about having kids. Simple right?'

'Oh, believe me, Julie, it sounds simple but love can suck at any stage, even when you're married ... and happily married at that!'

Neither of them said anything for a moment and just when it began to feel really awkward, Siobhan broke the silence. 'Alex has decided to move out for a while, just until we sort out a few little problems, nothing too serious.'

Julie already knew. Alex had already called her a few times regarding client signatures and letters. He had told her where he was staying if she needed to get hold of him.

'I'm sure you two will sort out whatever it is very quickly,' she lied. She'd never heard Alex so determined to avoid Siobhan in all the time she'd known the couple. He seemed so moody, dark, and, well, not in the humour to sort out anything really.

'Actually, I know this isn't part of your job but I might need you to drop in some paperwork to him on Friday when you're going home this weekend. Would that be okay?' Siobhan knew that Julie still went home to her parents every weekend, to catch up with her friends mostly and to see Declan.

'Eh, yeah, sure.' Julie had planned on a quiet weekend to herself in her rented apartment but, sure, maybe a night out with her friends would do her some good.

CHAPTER THIRTY ONE

Jack was relieved to see the back of the lunch time rush. He hadn't slept great the past couple of weeks since seeing his brother and the extra few beers at night weren't even helping. He had spent yesterday evening listen to Alex whine about Siobhan and what she had done but, if he was being honest, it was all going in one ear and out the other. All he could really think about these days was his prodigal brother. The brother from the flames of hell, well, the brother that certainly used to be from down there anyway! He checked the time, Conor would be here in just under an hour now and Jack had to admit he was feeling anxious for the first time in a long time. His chest felt tight with anticipation and he had a heavy dark feeling in his stomach. Could they have a half decent brotherly relationship after the past? All these years apart! Jack didn't even know Conor anymore and he wasn't even sure he wanted to either.

Right on time, Conor walked through the bar door looking just as anxious as Jack was! Jack told Steve he was going on his break and nodded towards some seats to Conor. They were in the corner of the bar and fairly private. Conor had gone home to look after his rent and a few bits, so he was nervous now, meeting Jack again after the time lapse. They sat in awkward silence.

'Would you like a drink or something to eat?' asked Jack as if Conor was a new customer.

'Eh, no thanks, I'm fine,' replied Conor, sitting down. Jack took a deep breath as he sat down opposite.

'Thanks for meeting me again,' Conor said quietly, 'I know I don't exactly deserve a second chance.'

'What have you been doing since I saw you last?'

'I did a few bits at home, you know yourself, paid the rent, the bills and, eh, well, collect the job seekers' allowance.' His head hung as he spoke. Jack didn't know whether to laugh or cry. His big bully of a brother was a broken man in front of him. But you had to admire him, he was trying to make amends.

'Job seekers, eh?' asked Jack, 'and are you actively looking for a job at the moment or...'

'Yeah, but all I know is pub work, it was my life. I wasn't good at school like you were and I guess I didn't push myself either, not when I knew I was going to take over the pub one day.'

That stung Jack a little bit; he was never good enough to go into the family business! 'So I'm doing a free course in computers down in the library centre.'

'Oh right, do you like it?'

'Nah, can't stand computers!' laughed Conor, looking at Jack properly for the first time since he had walked in. Jack caught a glimpse of the brother he had once known, before he turned into a cruel bully. They stayed chatting for a while and were getting on okay when Michael came in and sat at the bar.

'I'm gonna get a coffee, do you want one or a beer even?' asked Jack.

'No, I'll stick to coffee, thanks, I'm off drink a long time now.'

'Of course, sorry. Good for you, a hard move to make but well done, right back in a second.' He crossed the bar and slapped Michael on the back as he passed. He made himself busy making the coffees.

'So, how's it going with the brother from hell then?' Michael whispered.

'Actually, yeah it's going okay, surprisingly enough.'

'That's great, I had a feeling it would be okay.'

'Yeah. I can hardly believe he's the same guy.'

'Look Jack, the teenager you remember was obviously immature, of course he's changed!'

Jack didn't respond but knew Michael was right. He had held Conor accountable all his life for how he acted as a teenager. Maybe he should try and grow up himself and bridge the gap. 'Come on over and join us,' he said, carrying the coffees back towards Conor.

Emma's mood slowly but surely began sinking into a dark place. Much to her amazement her Dad was actually proving to be a good help around the house. He insisted on babysitting Amy any time Emma wanted. He made Amy's lunch while Emma and Amy were eating the breakfast he had laid on the table every morning and then washed up. He read Amy a bedtime story every night and put her to bed while Emma relaxed in front of the soaps with a cuppa. If he'd made that kind of effort at home, Emma wondered if they would even have split up in the first place!

But ever since he found Digger's bone down the side of the armchair, Digger wasn't bothered with it any longer. He went back to lying in the kitchen beside the long radiator and all he did was chew on and play with the damn thing. So obviously it wasn't some spiritual connection to Aidan after all. This really pissed Emma off. She'd been in a mood ever since and couldn't shake the sad feelings stirring up inside her. She had drained her cup when Seamus came down the stairs with Amy following closely behind.

'Ah, there you are, love! Amy said you had lightning in your room,' he chuckled, 'so I checked it out and sure wasn't the light bulb a fraction loose in the socket!'

'What?' Emma said, stunned! Surely there wasn't an explanation for the flickering light as well; that was definitely Aidan. It didn't happen that often, so surely if it was a bulb it would be happening all the time.

'Yeah. Now, you'd have hardly noticed, it was a fraction of a bit out, you probably never noticed. Only Amy said it flashed on and off there one night. It's grand now anyway, so no more flashing, eh Amy. Aren't you a great girl helping out your auld granddad?'

Emma jumped up from the couch and ran upstairs. 'Please, please, please still flicker, please,' she prayed as she ran into the room and frantically switched on the light. 'Please Aidan, if you are here, do the light thing for me, please, please, please.

The three guys were getting on fairly well. Jack was back behind the bar pulling pints and pouring glasses of wine while Conor and Michael sat at the bar chatting to him.

'You've a great place here,' Conor said, looking around.

'Thanks, I thought I was going to have to sell not so long ago but Michael here helped me out on a few ideas and things turned around, thank God.'

'Oh, that's good, it would have been awful to have to give it up.'

Jack was toying with the idea of asking Conor if he'd like to help him out behind the bar. He was just about to ask when Michael's phone rang. Michael looked at it for far longer than normal then picked it up, answered, and walked away to the other side of the bar. Jack was curious. Why had Michael acted so weird about it?

'Cameron, huh?' Conor said, while throwing peanuts into his gob.

'What?' Jack was sure he misheard.

'Cameron. The call Michael got. The name Cameron came up.'

Jack looked over at Michael and he seemed to be having a pretty intensive talk.

'Oh.'

Conor wondered why Jack had gone all strange and dared to ask.

'Listen, it's none of my business but, eh ... is there something going on between you two?'

Jack slammed down a pint glass so fast Conor was surprised it didn't break and instantly he knew he should have kept his trap shut!

'You're right! It is none of your business and how dare you bring that up, never mind try to talk to me about it here. Michael is a good friend and is having some problems with an ex-girlfriend. Now, it's getting busy here so I suggest you go and lay around elsewhere.'

'I'm sorry, I'm sorry, I wasn't trying to ...'

'Just go, Conor. Please, just go.'

Conor put on his jacket without saying another word. He shouldn't have opened his big mouth and he wasn't going to make it any worse. He left, feeling like crap that he had managed to upset Jack again after spending a lovely few hours chatting and mending things!

'Where's Conor gone?' asked Michael as he returned to the bar.

'Ah, he had to go, so who was that? You seemed surprised by the call!'

'Actually, yeah, I was. I got an email from Cameron last week, seeing if we can meet up and talk about things, suggesting that maybe we ended things too soon!'

'Really, how do you feel about that?'

'I don't know. I emailed back saying we should just leave things and that it obviously wasn't meant to be, but now Cameron has booked a flight here.'

'You serious? She's not letting this go then, is she?'

'No, she wants to meet up next week to talk.'

'Wow, an expensive conversation!' Jack said and they both laughed but the smile faded off Jack's face fairly quickly.

Emma sat on the bed, staring at the light. Nothing. A full hour had passed. He's fixed it. He's bloody fixed it, she thought to herself. Then the tears started, softly at first and accompanied by a little laugh. 'A loose bulb,' she laughed and cried, 'a loose fecking bulb.'

A knock came to her door and her Dad popped his head in slightly, wondering what Emma was laughing for. She looked at him and laughed out again.

'A loose bulb.' She was overcome with laughter and fell back onto her bed roaring laughing.

Seamus just shut the door and went back downstairs to Amy. He'd definitely have to mention her reaction to Joan he thought to himself.

Emma's laughing faded as she felt her heart begin to pain her, like she was being stabbed with a jagged blade sword. The pain rose up her chest to her neck and within minutes her laughing had turned to bawling. Pure raw bawling. She tugged at her heart and brought her knees to her chest and just cried and cried and cried.

It was almost eight o'clock the next morning when she heard Seamus open his bedroom door and go into the bathroom. She hadn't slept well at all last night. She was afraid to fall into a deep sleep in case she would miss a flickering of the light. But nothing. She was miserable and tired. She hoped Amy would sleep on a bit this morning so she could stay in bed for longer. She was going to ring in sick, there was no way she could face work. She was sick to her stomach ever since Seamus had found that bloody bone. She really didn't want to allow it in but there was no point, the niggling little thoughts were slowing nagging away at her. Was Digger only ever interested in that damn chair because of that damn bone? She had watched him intently ever since and not once had he been bothered with it. And now, the light. The damn light! How many other things that had been happening had another explanation? She hated the way everything was now. Ever since that damn bone and those nagging niggling doubting thoughts, she could no longer feel anything around her. She couldn't sense anything, smell anything, feel anything, nothing, nothing at all except sadness. Lots of sadness. As the darkness of her heart filled her, she fell back into a restless sleep.

She could hear something. Ever so softly and ever so gently, but it was definitely there. She smiled. She knew it was all true, she knew it wasn't all in her head. 'Aidan,' she called, 'I knew you were here.' The knocking grew louder and her smile grew wider. She opened her eyes to the day desperately trying to brighten the room around the edges of her curtains. Confused as to where she was, she half-sat up, looking around. The knocking was still there, coming from her door. Then it opened and Siobhan peeped in at her.

'Hi, your Dad said it was alright for me to come up, I've been knocking for a while. Are you alright? I thought I heard you call Aidan…..'

'Eh yeah, come on in,' Emma replied, surprised to see Siobhan. Siobhan stepped into the room, staying close to the door in case a speedy exit was required. The sound of Seamus drudging up the stairs filled in the awkwardness for a moment. Then he popped his head in.

'How are you feeling love? Would you like a bowl of soup? Amy's after demolishing most of it, though. Right little eater, that one.'

'No thanks, Dad, I'm not hungry.'

'Not hungry at all, eh? You must have come down with something. Sure, I'd be famished if I missed my breakfast and lunch.'

Emma looked at the alarm clock. Two twenty! Wow, she didn't think she'd slept that long, it had only felt like a ten-second snooze!

'Alright, love,' he said quietly.

She noticed something blue in his hand through the gap in the door.

'What's that in your hand?'

'This?' he replied holding up Aidan's blue hoody that she had searched for the day she was going to the beach.

'Yes that, where did you get it?' she demanded, with anger soaring through her voice.

'It was at the bottom of the wash basket love, why?'

'I must have put it there myself,' she said, in a much softer voice now, all the anger gone. She didn't say anymore out loud, but she was thinking plenty to herself. Plenty of doubts and fears.

'Oh alright love, well I'm putting a wash on now anyway so I'll pop it in too,' he said while walking away from the door, 'oh and by the way, I fixed the mantle on the fire place for you,' he shouted back as he went down the stairs. 'It was tilted a bit there I noticed. Any bang off it at all and, sure, all the lovely stuff you have on top would've fallen off!'

Emma lay back down and the tears came full force again. 'What's happening to me?' she wailed, allowing all of her fears escape.

Siobhan rushed to her side, instantly forgetting their last harsh exchange of hurtful words.

'Sssshh now, it's alright, everything is going to be alright, sssshhhh.'

'No, it's not, how can it be? I don't know what's going on anymore, what's real and what's not! I'm so confused. If Aidan is *not* around, then it's definitely not going to be alright…*ever*!' she cried out between great big sobs.

Siobhan just held her, all the while thinking that the sooner Emma went back to the doctor the better.

CHAPTER THIRTY TWO

Alex sat at the dining table and pushed his takeaway dinner around the plate. Normally he loved Thai green prawn curry but tonight he wasn't in the mood. Eating a takeaway just didn't seem the same on your own. He knocked back his merlot and refilled the glass. He sighed deeply as he left the table and, with a heavy heart, walked across to the oversized window looking out over the sea. He watched the waves rolling towards the land and thought about how consistent they were. No matter what happened in the world, they kept on coming. He was really wallowing in self-pity. How could she have done that to me? he asked himself. Tricking me like an idiot. He couldn't imagine ever wanting to go back to her.

Just as his blood was verging on boiling point, the doorbell rang. He was really surprised to see Julie standing there on his door step when he answered it.

'Hi Alex. Sorry to bother you on a Friday evening. Did Siobhan text to say I was coming?' she asked shyly, feeling awkward.

'I don't know. I haven't checked my phone all day!'

'Well look, she just wanted to make sure you got these documents, they're from the Lacey file.'

'Come on in. Just leave them there, I'll look over them tomorrow.

'Would you like a glass of wine?' He had half the glass poured out before she even answered.

'Oh, I shouldn't really, I'm meeting friends later, so I want to get home, get a shower and changed. Besides, I'm driving.'

'Oh, Okay, well maybe just half a glass seeing as I've already poured it out now. I feel terrible knowing you came out of your way to give me these papers. I insist, really.'

'Alright, sure what the heck. I'll have half a glass, even though I shouldn't really. I haven't had anything to eat, so I'm sure I'll be half cut on that much as it is!'

She took the glass from Alex, thinking that she deserved some sort of a little reward for putting up with the two of them lately. Siobhan was all over the place all week again. She was hoping her name was not going to come up in conversation. The last thing she wanted was to get mixed up in the middle of their marital problems. Maybe having a drink wasn't such a good idea after all, so she decided she'd drink back the wine and get out of there as fast as possible.

Alex handed her the wine and walked over to the leather sofa and plonked his arse down. 'Sit down, it's only early. Sure, these days, the night only begins at all hours!'

She sat down opposite Alex and took a gulp of her drink, allowing the deep flavour of the rich wine slide down her throat. It felt good. She knew Alex fairly well professionally. A lot of the other girls in the office melted when he walked in and she wasn't blind either! If she didn't have total and utter respect for Siobhan, she would fancy him herself.

'So, tell me, Julie, how is Siobhan anyway?'

Ah crap, though Julie. How bloody awkward. She wondered how to answer exactly. Should she tell him Siobhan has been a walking demon all week, the wicked witch from the east with severe PMT, a nightmare to deal with that was snapping everybody's heads off?

'She's fine, you know, busy all week with meetings and all. You know Siobhan, she's all work,' she giggled nervously. She took another gulp and stared at the door, willing it to open and a big gush of wind to enter the room, swirl round a few times, grab her up, and just take her of the uncomfortable situation.

'Oh, but do I really know Siobhan, that's the question! I thought I did, but you know what, Julie, I didn't have the first clue about her. I devoted years of my life to that woman, that conniving liar.' He knocked back the rest of his wine in one go, got up and went over to replenish his glass. Finding the bottle empty, he went into the kitchen to open another bottle.

Julie couldn't believe what she had just heard. Years of working for Siobhan and Alex, it had been nothing but professional. This was way too strange. She wanted so badly to get the hell out of there. She looked over at the door longingly. Okay, Julie, she thought to herself. It's only a door, it's only over there, five maybe six feet away. All you have to do is walk over to it, open it and leave. Okay, I'm gonna do it, here I go, just leave the glass on the little table there, say thanks for the drink and go.'

She stood up confidently, ready to make her apologies to Alex, saying it was time for her to leave. He walked back in and, without asking, just refilled her glass, not noticing the look of absolute horror on her face.

'Siobhan's really let me down, she's taken it all from me, you know. I've put my entire life into my work and then my marriage and all I wanted to do was progress in life. To move forward. I can understand she wanted her career. I never for a minute disrespected that, did I?'

Julie sat there, wondering what the hell he was on about. Was Siobhan having an affair? She's hardly have time given the hours she dedicated to the firm. Did Alex want to come back to work full time? But he was never there and he seemed to have no interest in it. She was totally lost.

'Alex, look, I'm sorry, but I've no idea what you're going on about. Siobhan's always professional so you must know she'd never have told me whatever's going on between you. Honestly, maybe it's best to keep it between you guys. I mean, I work for you both and I'd like to keep things professional.'

Alex looked at her intently. She saw the moment of silence as her opportunity to leave. She'd endured enough awkwardness for one night. Relieved, she was just about to get up when Alex got up himself, got the wine bottle, and refilled her glass. 'You're right. I'm sorry. I shouldn't have said anything. Have another glass, sure I can call you a taxi in a few minutes. It's just nice to have a bit of company.'

She looked at the large glass of wine he had just poured out. Oh help, she thought, taking a fairly big gulp.

Siobhan sat curled up on her own cream leather couch with a cup of cocoa in her hand. It had been so long since she had had a cup of cocoa. It was a real comfort thing and right now she needed the comfort. Her emotions were running away with themselves constantly and she couldn't concentrate on anything. She knew she'd been acting weird all week. Poor Julie, she'd have to apologise to her on Monday. She wondered how she got on dropping the papers off at Alex's earlier. Would it be really unprofessional to ask after him on Monday morning? Involving Julie would be ridiculous. You never know, she said to herself, maybe he'll really miss me over the weekend and, on Monday morning, we'll try sorting out this mess. Yeah, he's probably lonely now, there, in that big old house thinking things through and hopefully calming down a bit. She hoped to God time alone would help Alex realise how much he loved her and that he would want to sort out things soon. In fact, she was sure that after Julie popped round with the papers he might even get in touch with her. It was a case they were working on together and that wasn't easy or professional when they weren't talking. So she was sure some element of maturity and sensibility would kick in and he'd at least want to phone her about business even. And, sure, that would be a start!

CHAPTER THIRTY THREE

Alex sat across from Julie on the three-seater leather couch and continued to rant and rave about Siobhan. 'You know, I still can't believe what she did! It's the lowest of the low, don't you think?'

Julie pondered this question. A few glasses of wine had taken the awkwardness out of the situation. She was feeling so tipsy at this stage, it all sounded so stupid to her. 'To be quite honest, Alex, I am bored rigid listening to all of this. I'm twenty-eight, I'm supposed to be in town enjoying my night out and trying to heal my own broken heart, not sitting here with an empty glass listening to your problems.' She stared over at him with one eyebrow raised.

Alex looked shocked for a moment before bursting out laughing.

'Well, madam, if it's fun and enjoyment you're after, let me provide that for you. And, as for your empty glass, give it here and I'll sort that out too. Sure, feck the wine, how about I bring out the vodka. Do you like cosmopolitans? I hear they're really good for a broken heart!'

'Cosmopolitans? How would an old guy like you know about cosmopolitans?'

'Less of the old, thank you. I know plenty about cosmos or any other cocktail you want. I'm a champion cocktail maker, I'll have you know. Now I'll just get my shaker, put some music on, and away we go.' Effortlessly, he set about making cosmos as he danced around the kitchen and made a point of getting across his Tom Cruise movements as he shook the cocktail shaker. He even had the proper glasses to serve them in.

Julie was a lot more relaxed with the help of many glasses of wine. She kicked off her shoes and strolled into the kitchen, sitting at the oak island in the kitchen, now cluttered with empty wine bottles, vodka bottles, cointreau, lime and cranberry juice. She was giggling at the fact he even had the cranberry juice. He handed her cocktail and they clinked glasses. He looked cute when he wasn't procrastinating and giving out. He was standing tall again. God, that smile would knock anyone to the floor, it was so amazing. He had a fit body and his hair was dark with gentle hints of grey subtly showing his age.

'Mmm, hats off to the bartender. This is pretty good, Alex, a talent you definitely get ten points for!'

'Mmm, you know what, Julie. You're dead right, this is pretty good! Come on, bottoms up!' They both knocked back the drink and Alex went about making more. Julie could feel her cheeks flush with the effects of the alcohol and her body was swaying to some sort of a rhythm as the music played in the background. The local radio station was pumping out all the Eighties' music. She knew a fair few songs but Alex was in his element singing along and moving his hips in a rather funny way. They knocked back another cosmo and this time Alex said he was going to experiment with a new cocktail. He was searching for the tequila.

'Oh no, not tequila! What are you trying to do, blow my head off completely?' she laughed.

'Ah, who's showing their age now?' he teased, wagging his finger at her, grinning cutely.

'Age? You really want to go there, old man?' she chuckled.

'Hey, I'll show you who's an old man,' he said, grabbing her off the stool and swinging her around into his arms. Duran Duran were playing in the background. He was singing and dancing along to Gold, swinging her back and forth. She was in hysterics laughing at him and his attempts at dancing. He was giving it his all, throwing his hips all over the place, twirling her under his arms and spinning her around. She was laughing so much that she couldn't dance properly and they were both going in different directions even though they were holding on to each other's hand. He twirled her around one last time but it was so fast and they were both so drunk at this stage that balance wasn't exactly a key strength, they both went tumbling onto the floor. Her first, then Alex crashing on top of her. They were both stunned by the fall for a spilt second but then started laughing hysterically. He stood up and put out his hands, she grabbed them and with ease he pulled her to her feet.

'Are you okay, any broken bones?' he looked at her, concerned.

'I think I'll have to let you know tomorrow. I'm a tad too tipsy now, I think to feel any pain!' She let go of his hand and walked towards the island.

'Okay, another drink and then another dance.' He refilled their glasses and handed Julie hers. She took the glass, smiling at him. He met her smile with his own and, for a moment, all they were doing was smiling at each other. He put his glass back down and took hers and placed it down on the counter also. He took a step over to her until they were now face to face. Suddenly the smiling stopped. He raised his right hand, trailed it through her long blond hair and brought it to rest on the back of her neck. His fingers gently caressing it.

She stood there, just looking into his eyes. He bent down and slightly touched her lips with his and moved his head back slightly so he could look into her eyes. She was full of desire for him now. She took a deep breath and tilted her head up in search of his lips again. He brushed his lips over hers and this time she thought she was going to burst if he didn't kiss her. His left hand found the small of her back and he pulled her to him masterfully. He gently kissed her shoulder and followed through with small little divine kisses all the way up her neck, heading back in the direction of her mouth. Julie closed her eyes and put her arms up to reach out for him. She put her hands on the back of his head and tilted her head to the side totally and utterly enjoying every second he was kissing her and caressing her neck with his hand. Even though she longed for his kisses to never end, she just wanted his mouth on hers. She wanted him so badly. His hands explored every inch of her back now and both hands came to rest on the back of her neck. He had kissed his way back to her mouth. He lifted his head again to look at her, questioning. At that point, she felt like she was going to die if he didn't continue. Siobhan was the last thing on her mind. Her body ached for him, tingled for him! His eyes were full of want also. He bent down and scooped her up. The manliness of the gesture took her breath away as he carried her up the impressive staircase and into his bedroom.

He sat down on the end of the bed with Julie sitting on his lap. Her arms were still around his neck and his arms were still around her. She released her grip and stood up in front of him. He gazed up at her with the same desire in his eyes. Facing him, she climbed onto his lap again, straddling him. He put his hands on the small of her back and pushed her in nearer to him till their bodies were crushed against each other, already almost as one. She ran her fingers through his hair and gazed into his eyes with anticipation, wanting him so much. He lifted his face up till he reached her mouth and gently kissed her, covering her lips with soft kisses. He looked at her again, both of them ready for what was coming. There was no turning back.

She lowered her head and kissed him wildly. Their hands were eagerly exploring each other's bodies, all over the place. The passion was wild, their breathing getting heavier and heavier. They were aching for each other now and their bodies were throbbing. He put his hands under her blouse in search of her breasts, cupped them with his hands and rubbed his thumb over her nipples, driving her wild. He took his hands away and removed her blouse altogether, unhooked her bra and threw it to the floor, revealing perfect breasts perking out to meet him. He held onto her, stood up, turned around and laid her on the bed. She reached up and unbuckled his belt. With his strong arms, he leaned down and the kissing, the passion, the arousal took on a whole new level.

Siobhan flicked around the channels, aimlessly looking for something to watch even though she wasn't actually concentrating on anything. She was deep in thought, curled up on the couch. What's Alex's doing right now? Was he too stubborn to contact her after Julie dropped in the papers? Should she ring him to ask if he got the papers; purely an excuse, of course.

Julie's so reliable there's not a chance she didn't give them to him. Maybe she should ring Julie, see what he said. How he seemed. Although, that's silly, she doesn't know him well enough to tell how he's holding up. Yeah, she'd text Julie anyway to see how things went. Or maybe not, she's out with her friends tonight, probably being chatted up by some young lad at this very moment. Poor thing, she deserves a good night out, she was fairly upset after her break-up with Declan.

She looked around the huge sitting room. It seemed too big all of a sudden! Too big, too cold and too....empty. Yes, that was it. It was empty. Everything seemed so empty now, her house, her work, her life! It was all so pointless, pointless without him. She was lonely, so lonely. She just wanted her husband back. She felt like nothing without him.

Suddenly seeing herself from Alex's perspective, she felt a sudden burst of anger towards herself! She'd been a total career freak with no time for a family or even time to consider his feelings on it all. All this time, she'd been going on about her precious career when, without Alex, she had nothing. 'I want him back,' she thought now. 'I want a family. I don't want to be alone. Yes, I want a family. Oh my God, I want a family, I want a family, I actually want a family......crap!'

She sat up and put the empty cocoa cup on the coffee table, shocked at her light bulb moment. All her worrying about getting pregnant, having a child, all her fighting with Alex over the past two weeks seemed so pointless now. It was like a switch had flicked on in her brain, her mind, and in her womb.

She stood up and said out loud, 'I want a baby, I want a child, children, a family.' She was smiling but the tears soon came. Then the smile faded and the tears came harder and quicker. She doubled over in pain. In emotional pain. After all this time of not wanting children, and putting her career first, what she wanted most was Alex and a family with Alex.

She lowered herself to the floor, holding onto her tummy, crying her heart out, louder and louder. The pain of the past two weeks, being without Alex, was too much for her. She wanted him back. Desperately.

Slowly, her crying turned into sobbing and then little sobs and, eventually, little sniffles. She sat up straight and wiped her eyes. 'Okay. I have to talk to Alex, I have to call him.' She grabbed her mobile off the coffee table and dialled his number. She was excited about what she wanted to tell him. She wanted a baby. They wanted the same thing now. She waited for him to answer. The phone was ringing out, no answer. She looked at the time, it twenty-past eleven. Not too late. Knowing him, he'd be sitting in front of the television with a glass of red wine, watching some political show or something. Still, no answer. She hung up the phone, disappointment inching its way into her heart. 'He's obviously intent on letting me stew. I know, I'll drive up to him. Yeah, I'll tell him face to face.'

She jumped up all excited again and went to get her car keys. But just as she reached the front door, she had second thoughts. Maybe it would be better to leave it until tomorrow morning. They could talk properly after a good night's sleep. It would be difficult to get Alex to forgive her betrayal. She didn't expect to walk up to him and say, 'Hey, by the way, I want a baby now,' and expect to fall back into his arms! Yes, she'd leave it until tomorrow. She prayed to God that he'd take her seriously!

Julie had been praying to God, too, but in a slightly different way! When she and Alex had both reached maximum levels of ecstasy and her calls for God couldn't have gotten any louder, she flopped down on the bed beside him. They were both shining with sweat and sprawled out in all directions, trying to cool down. Their chests were still rising up and down.

'Oh, that was, that was, incredible,' Alex sighted, looking over at her with a cheeky smile, 'and you calling me an old man. I think you should take that back. Three times.' His satisfied grin stretched from ear to ear.

'You are not an old man, you are not an old man, you are not an old man. There, now, I said it three times. You want to prove it just one more time?' She cuddled into his chest and kissed his neck.

'Again? Are you serious, Miss Julie? I know I'm a sex God but even sex God's need a rest!'

Julie smiled and threw her leg over his. With his free arm, he pulled her closer to him and gently rubbed her arm. They just lay there, their breathing slowly coming back to a regular rhythm. Closing their eyes, they were soon asleep.

CHAPTER THIRTY FOUR

Seamus drove up towards the house and the sight of Joan cleaning the windows immediately came into view. Good God, that woman is always working, he thought. She always has the house looking great. By the time he entered the back door, she had the kettle already on. He could immediately see the worry of the past few weeks etched on her face, although he had to admit it didn't take from her elegant beauty.

'Well, how are things now?' she asked with desperation in her voice.

'Yeah, you were right. I checked all the things in the house you told me about and, sure enough, there was a reasonable explanation for everything.'

'How's she taking that? She still won't answer my phone. Is she upset?'

'Yeah. She hasn't gone into work now for a couple of days and she's just lying in bed. Siobhan took her to the doctor and he put her back on antidepressants and prescribed something to calm her down and help her sleep.'

'God bless Siobhan. She sent me a text alright to say she was keeping an eye on her and to try not to worry but it's hard when she won't open up to me.' Tears began to fall.

Seamus put his arms around her and held her tight 'It's only because you're her mother and she is closest to you. She wanted you to say it was true, but you couldn't possibly do that. She has to face up to the truth now, maybe go to counselling, a bereavement counsellor even.'

'Maybe I should have handled it differently; I just want to be there for her.' Joan sniffed, wiping her tears away.

'At least she spoke to you about it. Sure, I'm not supposed to know anything about any of it. Do you know how hard it was to pretend that all the things I was fixing were just normal little jobs around the house. I knew I was upsetting her but I couldn't even comfort her.'

'I know you feel terrible but, at least this way, she won't kick you out for not believing her either. That way, you can keep an eye on her and Amy. How is Amy anyway, this must be affecting her!'

'No, she's okay. We're spending a lot of time together, going to the beach and the park, she hasn't really noticed Emma's mood too much. I just told her that Mammy has a bad cold and is in bed to keep warm. Sure, we're a great team at making the dinners now,' he laughed.

Joan pulled away and looked up into his face with shock. 'You … make dinner, did I hear that right?'

'Well, now, they're not as good as your dinners but, yes, we're managing to put something edible on the plate,' he chuckled.

'Well, I never thought I'd see the day,' she smiled.

'Yeah, last night I made a lovely curry. Now you sit down and I'll pour the tea.'

Joan looked amused. This was certainly not the same man who left just weeks before!

Siobhan was already on the road, in great form. She was going to get her man back and she wasn't going to take no for an answer. She decided to ring Emma and see how she was doing today.

'Hello,' came a croaky voice through Siobhan's earphones.

'Hey, how are you doing this morning, get any sleep?'

'Yeah, I took another tablet during the night and eventually drifted off.'

'At least you got a bit of sleep. How are you feeling?' Emma sounded awful in fact.

'Okay, just tired. I might try to go back to sleep. I'll talk to you later, okay?'

Emma certainly wasn't going to tell Siobhan or anyone else for that matter how bad she was feeling really. Her heart was aching. The darkness was unbearable, the emptiness. Life had lost all meaning all over again. She felt heavy and tired all the time. And guilty, oh so guilty. Amy, her sweet loving Amy. She couldn't even pull herself out of the black hole for Amy. Amy was so innocent and so amazing that she deserved to be happy. Happy with people who were better than she was, better able to look after her.

Her thoughts were tormenting her, swiping at her like an eagle playing with her soul. Teasing her, frightening her, never stopping, never relinquishing, just tormenting her on and on and on. The antidepressants certainly hadn't kicked in yet and, although the doctor said it would be about two weeks for them to start working, she wasn't so sure. How could anything take away this pain? He was trying his best to get her an appointment with the psychologist again, but there was a six-month waiting list. Emma wasn't fooled. They all thought she was psychotic and that's the reason she was going to a psychologist and not a bereavement councillor. She didn't care anymore. What did any of it matter? She turned over and closed her eyes and fell into another drug-induced sleep.

Jack yawned as he came down the stairs next door, completely unaware of Emma's mental torture. He was going through his own torture at the moment. He'd been so short with Conor, throwing him out of the bar like that, and he was feeling....he actually didn't know how he was feeling. There wasn't a word to describe it. Uncomfortable, maybe. Yes, uncomfortable. He felt uncomfortable. Things weren't sitting right with him. He felt like his world was upside down. Michael seemed very keen to patch up his relationship with Cameron and Jack knew that that meant he would probably move to the States. He'd become such a good dependable friend that Jack was sure he was really going to miss him.

And he worried also that Michael was doing the right thing. This Cameron one seemed to be calling all the shots as far as he could see. Yes, she was coming over from New York to see Michael especially but still, she shouldn't have walked away in the first place. Michael had settled down pretty well without her and now she was just going to waltz back into his life and expect him to drop everything and run back to her.

He had just poured out a coffee when the doorbell rang. Unusual to be getting callers at this time, he thought. When he opened the door, Conor was standing there with his back pack slung over his shoulder, fully loaded with all his gear. He was obviously leaving the village.

'Come on in,' Jack said, sighing. He made himself busy getting a mug and pouring another coffee. 'So, you're leaving, I see.'

'Yeah, I think it's for the best. All I seem to do is upset you and, believe me, that's the last thing I want to do. I've caused you enough hassle for a lifetime.'

'So you thought the best option was to run away like a coward?' Jack was getting the milk out of the fridge and had not yet faced Conor directly. Conor was taken back.

'I thought you'd prefer if I left. I, I'm at a loss as to how to … I don't know, how to be a good brother, I guess! I don't want to stay and wreck your head any more than I have done and, well, I can't stay and see you live a life that's all wrong and not say anything about it, so I have to go.'

'A life that's all wrong, eh?' Jack smirked but none too confidently.

'What would you know about my life and what's right for me?'

'Look, Jack, we both know who you are really. And I can see that I've been responsible for you trying to bury that part of you and that kills me! I made you ignore who you are for all this time.'

'You know nothing about me, so don't come in here and start…'

'Come on, Jack, you're gay. You know you are and it's not something you can run away from, not if you want to be happy in yourself.'

'Happy? How the hell could I ever be happy being such a 'faggot' as I recall you telling everyone. And when Dad treated me like I had some contagious skin-eating disease and you, well, you treated me like your personal jester.'

'I know how I treated you! You don't need to remind me and I'm appalled at myself. Look, if I'd realised how all that was going to affect you, I'd never have been so horrible.'

'Yeah right, Conor. You hated me.'

'I did not! You were my brother, of course I didn't hate you! Is that what you thought?'

'It's not what I thought, it's what I saw and felt and had to put up with.'

'Well then, I have to put this right, Jack. I have to see you happy if it's the last thing I do.'

'I am happy, well at least, I was happy before you turned up.'

'Happy living a lie?'

'It's better than being marginalised and judged.'

'Nobody's going to do that! Seriously, I was the immature and stupid one. Being gay is nothing to be ashamed of.'

'All I can see is the look of disgust on Dad's face how he blamed me for Mam's death,' Jack's voice shook.

Conor crossed the kitchen and put his hand on Jack's shoulder. 'I'm so sorry, I really am, and it's time to put it right.'

'No, leave it. I'm happy as I am, I just want a peaceful life, so just leave it.'

'No, Jack. I can't leave it. You *are* gay, and I want you to be gay and be happy.'

'I can't! What would they all think? I couldn't go through it again, I couldn't!' Jack yelled.

Conor turned Jack around and grabbed both his shoulders. 'You can and you will. No-one is going to even bat an eyelid, but if they do, they'll have me to answer to!' Then Conor hugged Jack for the first time since they were very young.

CHAPTER THIRTY FIVE

Siobhan was tearing up the motorway, full of anticipation at the thought of
seeing Alex. He wouldn't forgive her straight away and she was expecting
another two or three days where he'd let her stew, but then he'd come
home and they could get busy making a baby for real. She had already
stopped taking the pill, so she reckoned on a month or two, tops, and she
would be pregnant. She took the exit off the motorway and motored on
towards Alex's house.

Julie woke up to one hell of an almighty hangover. It hurt to open her
eyes and she was sure there was a rusty old hatchet embedded in her
forehead. Even worse than the hangover though was the dreadful feeling in
the pit of her stomach. She was nauseous with it and it was guilt and regret
more than tequila. How could she have done something so bloody stupid as
to sleep with Alex! How was she going to face him? How was she going to
face Siobhan with that stabbing feeling of guilt eating away at her? She
could feel it already storming around inside her.

Thankfully, Alex was already up and gone out of the room. She had to
get up and go hunting around the room stark naked for her clothes. Well, at
least her knickers weren't too hard to find. They were hanging naughtily
from the lamp shade. She grabbed her stuff quickly and ran into the
en-suite, locking the door behind her in case he came up to the room. She
had no idea where he was but she sure as hell didn't want him to see her
naked. Although that was pretty pointless seeing as he'd been doing
unspeakable things to her naked body just hours before. All she wanted to
do now was have a quick shower and get out of there.

Downstairs, Alex loaded the dishwasher carefully, trying not to make
too much noise. Julie was fast asleep when he woke up and he didn't want
to wake her. He had no idea what on earth he was going to say to the girl.
What had come over him to jump on her the way he did? And the way she
responded to him drove him more insane. She certainly wasn't the same
Julie that worked for Siobhan anyway. What an absolute mess! He was
furious with Siobhan over everything but now he felt desperate. Desperate
for her not to find out. What if she did find out? Then that would be it. The
marriage would definitely be over. As soon as he opened his eyes and saw
another woman in his bed this morning, he knew he didn't want to end his
marriage. He loved Siobhan and he wanted to be with her, surely they could
work it out. Sleeping with Julie was something that they would never patch

up but maybe they could get over the baby business. He'd just finished cleaning down the counter tops when Julie came creeping shyly into the kitchen.

'Morning,' she said, clearly dying with mortification.

'Hi,' he coughed, 'coffee?'

'Yeah, I think I better. I'm still well over the limit to drive.'

He smiled bashfully. 'Crazy night,' he said, testing the waters, hoping she wasn't going to make a big deal of it.

'Yeah, it really was. Look, to be honest, I feel really awkward about the whole thing!' Relief set in and Alex felt himself breathe for the first time since awakening! 'Yeah, I have to admit, I feel a bit weird about it myself. I mean, don't get me wrong, I had a great night and you're such an amazing girl but…'

'Siobhan!!'

'Yes, Siobhan.'

'Last night was great but it was a mistake on both our parts. I'm sick over the fact that I slept with Siobhan's husband and if she ever found out…'

'She won't … Okay? Listen, we're the only two people who know and we both agree that it was a mistake, yeah?'

'Yeah.'

'Then let's forget it. Let's pretend it never happened and move on. She doesn't have to know anything about it.'

'Okay, yeah, great!' Julie agreed, downing the last of her coffee.

Siobhan pulled into the petrol station near Alex's house. She got two luxurious lattes and two freshly made fruit scones and picked up a plastic knife, some napkins and a small portion of jam just in case he wasn't going to let her through the door. At least she could eat it in the car.

Julie searched for her shoes and coat and went about putting them on while Alex threw the mugs into the dishwasher. He filled a glass of water then and offered her two tablets for her thumping headache.

'Oh, just what I need! How did you know?'

'I needed them myself,' he laughed.

'Oh yeah, I'm sure you did! Well look I better get on my way,' she said rather shyly.

He walked her to the door and they stood there feeling awkward and embarrassed. Do I kiss him, hug him or shake his hand, wondered Julie, not exactly sure how you say goodbye to a man she had just spent the night with.

'Right, well, I better go, thanks for … eh … well …' she spluttered self-consciously.

'Yeah, you too,' he said following it with another suspiciously needless cough.

Julie opted to give him a split-second look that said all that she needed to say. Thanks for the mind blowing orgasms and let's never speak of them again! She started the car and made her way to the electronic gate. She'd never noticed before how long it took to open, it seemed to take forever.

'Come on, come on, come on,' she called out, itching to get away. Finally, the gate was fully opened and she made her escape, but there was no escaping the guilty feelings.

The gate had just closed when Siobhan pulled up and buzzed them open again from her phone. The aroma of the lattes was wafting up her nostrils and teasing her taste buds. She really hoped Alex would at least let her in but patience was going to be a key player here in getting him back.

She had no sooner rang the doorbell when he answered it, looking like shite. He looked totally shell-shocked to see her at the door holding breakfast.

'Well, can I come in? I'd really like to talk to you!' To her utter surprise, without any more persuading, he stood aside and let her in!

CHAPTER THIRTY SIX

She felt encouraged by the lack of aggro on his face. The time apart had obviously made him realise how much he loved her still and how they truly belonged together. Not wanting to come across too sure of herself, she stopped just inside front door and held up the scones. 'Fresh from the oven or so I believe.'

It was as if Alex hadn't even heard her. 'Go on into the kitchen. I'll put the kettle on.'

She held up the cardboard holder with the two cups. 'No need, I brought lattes.'

He walked past her again as if he hadn't heard her. Clearly, he wasn't interested in anything she brought.

She threw them on the counter, suddenly forgetting any hunger pangs. 'How are you?' she asked cautiously.

He looked suddenly upset. 'Alright, missing you, I guess!'

'Really?' She couldn't believe he had come out with it so readily. 'Me too, I've been doing a lot of thinking ...'

'Me too,' he said. And he had! All morning, ever since he woke up beside Julie. He wondered how stupid he could have been to cheat on Siobhan. She didn't deserve that. Yeah, he was angry with her but he still loved the bones of her. He always had, ever since she first walked into his dad's firm all those years ago. She was the love of his life and he knew the minute he woke up beside another woman that Siobhan would always be the love of his life. If the price he would have to pay for spending the rest of his days with her was to do it childless, then that's what he would do. He owed her that much now.

'Let me go first, please,' she butted in, fearing that he was going to tell her he was going to start divorce proceedings. 'I want you to come home, I want us to be a family, I mean, a real family. Let's have a baby!'

'What are you saying?'

'I'm saying, let's do it, let's have a baby. I'm sorry I put you through everything and I know I should have talked to you properly about how I feel but the thought of losing you has definitely introduced me to my biological clock!'

Alex listened, looking at her in disbelief. She walked over and took his hand in hers, squeezing it gently. 'Let's go home and make a baby!'
He wasn't sure if he had heard her right. All he could see in front of him were images of Julie's naked body. They were by no means repulsive but

the thoughts of cheating on Siobhan were. He tried to choke them back as he hugged her. What had she said? Make a baby? He had just spent the night having sex, amazing sex as it happens, but with Julie! And now Siobhan was telling him she was ready to have children, despite all her reservations and fears and uncertainty! All for him! He suddenly felt like the biggest creep walking the earth.

He took her gently by the shoulders and looked her in the eyes.

'Are you sure about this?'

'Yes, I am, I've done so much thinking about it and I'm so ashamed of myself for how I treated you and lied to you. I just felt that I couldn't be the mother type. But now I know that, without you, I'm no type at all. I'm nothing without you, nothing!'

'Look, I know I was really angry and harsh and I said some horrible things but the last thing I want is to force you to make this decision.'

'But you're not, I really want to do this,' she smiled up at him.

'I don't know. I think we should sit down and talk it through though.'

'Okay,' she answered and sat down, 'admittedly, I'd be doing this mostly for you because I want you to be happy, to feel that you have fulfilled your life to the last. But the real reason I want to do this is because you make me so happy, you always have done. Throughout our entire marriage. You've put me first. You have made me so happy, secure and loved. I've never had to worry about bullshit like you going off and having affairs or other women turning your head. I was always enough for you. And, now, I want to give you what you want.'

'Are you sure?' he asked, feeling awful.

'Yes, but I want to get pregnant as soon as possible, no flaffing about, and I'll want to get back to work as soon as possible after the birth also!'

He couldn't help but laugh. 'Typical you, I'll schedule in my pregnancy for nine months' time and expect to be back at work a week after.'

'Well, I'm not the stay at home type; I think I'd rather ten jobs than stay at home with a crying baby all day!'

'What makes you think it would be crying all day?'

'Eh, because I wouldn't have a clue what to do with it, I'd probably feed it coffee for breakfast or something! And I know I'd go shopping and leave it behind me or something stupid like that!'

'No you wouldn't, you'd be a great mother.'

'No I wouldn't, but it doesn't matter because you'd make up for the two of us.'

'Sure I wouldn't have a clue what I'd be doing, I've been a suit and tie man my entire life!' he joked.

'Yes but your enthusiasm alone will rear this child!' she giggled.

'So I'm going all daddy day care and you're gonna be bread winner.'

'Exactly,' she said, 'you can be the yummy mummy.' They smiled at each other excitedly.

'Right, so as I said, I don't want to be messing about with this, I want to get moving as soon as possible, so I suggest we go to see a fertility expert as soon as I can get an appointment.'

'You're really not messing about, are you?'

'Nope,' she giggled again, 'project baby is on!'

CHAPTER THIRTY SEVEN

Emma carried her weary body up the stairs as soon as she got in from work. Seamus and Amy were gone to see Joan for the afternoon which suited her fine. All she wanted to do was climb back into the same bed she dragged herself out of that morning. It had become her only sanctuary. She had done well today, all things considered. She'd remained calm and patient with all her innocent little students. God love them. Sure, they had no idea what a cruel world they were forced to grow up in.

She had just flung off her shoes and crawled into bed when the doorbell rang. Go away, she thought. But the doorbell kept ringing.

Jack stood at the door wondering what to do. He had seen Emma drive in and knew she was home. He was so busy sorting his own head out, he had totally neglected her. Siobhan had told him she was in a bad way, mourning Aidan all over again now that she had finally come to realise he wasn't haunting her. He rang Emma's bell again and waited. Still no answer. Obviously she wasn't going to answer, so he left, feeling even shittier. He felt like such a crappy friend. But he just had so much going on himself. For years, he had buried the real Jack and now Conor had gone and resurrected him. Yes, it was damn hard, living a life of lies. Living a life that was unnatural to him but natural to everyone else around him. He didn't want to risk ever having to go through the ordeal of being bullied for his homosexuality. So he just buried that part of himself. Only thing is, he buried it alive. It still had a pulse and no matter how far he buried it, that flipping pulse just wouldn't go away!

As much as Conor tried to convince him it was no big deal any more, Jack felt it was a huge risk coming out. In certain countries, he'd have been 'hunted' for his 'illness'. As much as society had changed, it was still pretty unaccepting of homosexuality in reality. No, as far as he could see, homosexuality was still a challenge for the wider society.

And, then, there was Michael to consider. How would he feel about it? He would be really pissed that Jack had never told him the truth. He'd be disgusted that he was sharing a house, nights out and nights in and such a close friendship with a gay man! He couldn't do it. He couldn't come out.

He was only in the door when Michael arrived home.

'Well, any craic?' Michael asked, seeing Jack in the kitchen.

'Nah, I was just over at Emma's there!'

'Oh, how is she?'

'Dunno, she wouldn't answer the door.'

'Oh really? She's really going through it. Was it like this the last time as well?'

'Yeah, only this is worse because it seemed natural the last time!'

'Ah Jack, what's natural in this world, eh?'

Jack looked at him.

'Anyway, I've a bit of news!' Michael said. 'I'm moving out!'

'Oh!' was all Jack could say.

'Yeah. Well, as you know, Cameron has been calling and, well, we've been talking things over and decided to give things another go,' he waited to hear Jack's response but Jack stayed silent. Michael was surprised, he thought Jack would have been happy for him! 'Anyway, Cameron thinks we'd have a better shot at it if I move to the States!'

'Do you want to move?' Jack finally asked.

'Well, I guess I gotta give this a shot.'

'Why?' he asked.

'Why?' Michael repeated, surprised.

'Yes, why? Why do you have to give it another shot?'

'Because I have to, I can't let the relationship die when I could have done more. I mean, how many times do we get a chance to be loved and be happy?'

'I see!' But clearly Jack didn't. He was full sure that Michael wasn't going to get the happy ending he was seeking. If they couldn't make a go of it here, why should America be any different? Anyway it was his life, far be it from him to be worrying about it all. He had enough on his mind!

'Anyway,' Michael laughed, 'at least you get your house back now, you can start up your womanising again!' Michael winked.

'Womanising?'

'Yeah, I know you've been conscious of me here and I've seriously dampened your Romeo style with the ladies so you can revert back to your good old life now.'

'Right!' muttered Jack unenthusiastically.

'And now that Conor's back, I guess you could do with the space here to get to know him again. You know, he doesn't seem all that bad now, despite what he was like years ago. And he really does seem to care about you!'

'Yeah. I was thinking of offering him a job at the bar. He was actually a great manager. Now that he's got himself together, he could do with a second chance at things. He could move in here too, I suppose.'

'Wow, from zero to ninety, eh?'

'No. I've been thinking of going travelling myself a bit anyway.

Just to get away.'

'What? No way! I thought you were happy out here, I thought things were going well.'

'Ah, I think Conor has stirred up a lot of crap and I need to go sort my head out. Get away from it all.'

'Sounds like you're running from something, Jack, but you gotta remember that whatever it is you're running from is just gonna run right behind you.'

'Well maybe if I run fast enough and far enough, it may never catch up with me!' The conversation was brought to a halt by the sound of the doorbell.

'Oh I wonder if that's Emma? Maybe she saw me earlier and is ready to talk now!' A second later, he opened the door to find a stranger looking at him. He was as tall as Jack and, although he wasn't bursting out of his Armani shirt, he looked like a man who frequented the gym pretty regularly. His eyes were beyond brown, they were like looking into a lake of dark chocolate and they complemented his dark skin perfectly. He obviously preferred to keep his head shaved which really suited him. 'Can I help you?' Jack asked.

'Yeah, I believe Michael Lawson lives here?'

'Yeah, he does. Michael!' Jack shouted at Michael to come to the door.

'Yeah?' Michael said, walking out of the kitchen. When he saw who was at the door, he nearly dropped.

'Cameron!' he spluttered.

'Surprise!' Cameron grinned.

'Cameron!' Jack repeated. 'You're Cameron ... you're damn right, it's a surprise!' Cameron ignored Jack and went straight towards Michael, enveloping him in an intimate embrace. Michael's face was ashen as he stared at Jack. Jack was staring back at them, in total shock. Cameron was a ... man! He shook his head and looked again but, yep, Cameron was still a man!.

'Cameron, what are you doing here?' Michael exclaimed.

'As soon as you agreed to get back with me, I had to come and see you!'

Well, why the hell didn't you tell me?'

'Because I wanted to surprise you.'

'Well, you certainly did that!' Jack butted in, grabbing his keys off the hall table. 'I'll leave you to it.' With that, he left as fast as he could!

'No, Jack, wait, please!' Michael shouted after him but it was no use.

'What's going on, Michael? Why are you so pissed at me and who the hell is this Jack guy? Why are you so worried about him? I thought you said he was straight and you were just mates?'

'Yeah, but he's a good guy and he has seriously helped me so much.'

'So, what, you have feelings for him now...?'

'Don't be stupid, he doesn't even know I'm gay. Well, he does now! But he has serious issues with the whole thing, so I'd say he's pretty freaked out right about now!'

'Right, so you go and move in with a homophobic ... clown ... smart move!'

'I wasn't expecting you to show up on my doorstep and announce to the whole town that I'm gay!'

'You sound like you're ashamed of it, all of a sudden.'

'Of course I'm not, don't be silly.'

'Well, at least I know you haven't been with anyone else! You've been too busy pretending to be straight!' Cameron laughed.

Michael didn't see the funny side at all. He was mortified that his secret was out, to Jack of all people. They were good friends, never an easy thing for Michael. As soon as his mates realised he was gay, they instantly changed around him. How the hell was Jack going to react to this? By the look of horror on his face when Cameron arrived, not good would be a fairly good bet! Cameron was so camp that he would surely rub Jack up the wrong way, pardon the pun! Best thing to do was to pack up and just leave as soon as possible. He could stay at a friend's in Dublin till the day he was to leave. And leave for good!

CHAPTER THIRTY EIGHT

A couple of months went by and Emma was still struggling. She couldn't cope with it all any more. Although she was seeing a psychologist and on some pretty strong antidepressants, she still couldn't shift the sadness of Aidan's loss. He was gone, truly gone!

She was lying on the sofa, thinking about how much things had changed lately and how it was all going over her head. Conor had moved in next door and was managing the bar. He had popped in and out to say hello but had backed off asking her out completely. Better for him to stay away from a fruit cake, she had thought to herself many times.

Jack was like a lost puppy without his best friend and was planning on doing some travelling himself soon. Siobhan and Alex were trying for a baby for real this time and were already impatient about not conceiving! Emma had warned her to give it time. But to hell with that! Siobhan wasn't going to wait around. She had a schedule to keep and wanted the baby born as soon as possible, so she could get back to work. Surely now that she had actually made the decision to have a baby that was the hard part over and done with! She imagined getting pregnant was a doddle! She had swung an appointment with Dr Long on account of Alex already having his fertility test done there. They were just waiting for the result now.

Seamus and Joan had taken Amy to Dublin Zoo again. Amy loved all the attention and outings so much that she hadn't really noticed her mother's depressed mood and behaviour. Emma was thankful to her parents for that, even if she was frustrated with them for their stupidity on breaking up. One minute, they were breaking up and, the next, they were spending all their time together. Emma couldn't understand it. It pissed her off actually. Why split up and then spend time together? She'd never have split from Aidan in a million years, and she was the one left grieving for her husband.

Just as her mind was becoming increasingly unsettled, the front door opened and Jack waltzed in. Damn Seamus for giving him a bloody key. They all had a fecking key it seemed and were in no fear of using it! It was driving her even crazier than she felt she already was!

'Well, how's the form today?' he asked, throwing himself into a chair.

'It'd be better if you and Siobhan didn't feel free to waltz in every two minutes to check up on me!'

'We're not checking up on you, we just want to see how you're doing, that's all! We care about you ... is that a crime?' he retorted.

'What's got you all fecking snappy?'

'Nothing.'

'Yeah, right! If you're gonna intrude on me and my woes, then you better spill'

'I found out that Michael is flying out tomorrow.'

'Oh!'

'He's worked his notice and organised everything and is flying off tomorrow to start a new life.'

'You're gonna miss him, aren't you?'

'Ah, a bit, I suppose. He was a good friend!'

'Mmmm. I just don't understand why he never told me he was ... you know ...'

'Gay?'

'Yeah!'

'For feck's sake, do you really have to wonder that? Sure, you can't even say the flippin word'

'Of course I can'

'No you can't. You've such a phobia of homosexuality it's ridiculous. The poor guy was obviously afraid to tell you in case you'd throw him out and turn your back on one of the best friendships either of you have ever known!'

'Emma, I'm not homobloodyphobic!'

'Yes, you are, big time.'

'No I'm not and I'd have never have thrown him out'

'Yes you are, I've never met anybody as fecking homophobic as you.'

'To hell with this, I only came round to see how you are!' he grunted as he stood up and turned towards the door, all set for a rapid exit.

'Then, why are you so bloody scared of yourself then, tell me that!'

'What did you just say?' Jack said, turning to look at her.

'I said, why are you so scared of yourself, of who you are, who you really are?'

'What do you mean?'

'Gay! That's what I mean? You're so homophobic you're even homophobic towards yourself!'

'That little...... He had no right to tell you.'

'Who?'

'Conor.'

'Conor never said a word.'

'Then how did you ...?'

'Oh come on Jack, I've known that for months now! It was fairly obvious you weren't comfortable with it, which was what I couldn't figure out but I just let you live your life the way you saw fit! But seeing as you're constantly butting into my life lately, I think I've every right now to say what I think. Don't you?'

Jack fell back into the chair, dumbfounded. All this time Emma had known. Who else knew?

As if reading his mind, Emma answered. 'Siobhan knows too but Alex is pretty clueless. And, as far as I know, that's it. Your silly secret hasn't gone too far.'

'Silly secret?'

'Yeah. Newsflash, Jack, no one really gives a damn.'

'Well, if that's the case, then why are people being tortured for being gay in….'

'Bloody hell Jack, it's Kilfarrig we're living in you know!' she butted in.

'I've experienced my fair share of bullying.'

'Conor told me all about that alright.'

'I thought you said …'

'I brought it up one day myself, he tried to deny it but I wasn't having any of it. I already knew you were gay, but I'd no idea why you were so dead against it! So I asked Conor.'

'And he told you all, did he?'

'Yep, all about how he treated you and made your life hell. All about your dad and how you left.'

'Then surely you can understand why I don't want to be this way.'

'No, I don't.'

Jack looked confused. If it was sympathy he was expecting, he was gonna be sorry.

Emma's voice was clipped with impatience. 'I don't understand it at all actually. The way I see it is, you're gay, you found someone you really cared about, possibly even fell in love with, and you let him go. Just because you had a hard time when you were a flipping teenager.'

'Wait, you think I love Michael?'

'I'm not finished, thanks … so while you piss your life away, I'm here one hundred percent in love with my man and he's dead! So as much as I want to be with him, I can't. And there you are, letting that one special person walk out of your life for good. You're a complete idiot! Oh, and by the way, Conor is in knots over how he treated you! He blames himself entirely for the way you are today! Maybe if you let yourself be you, then he can forgive himself. Now, get out of my house before I get up and throw something at you.'

Without uttering another sound, Jack slowly got up and left. He was in shock. Emma really was crazy! In love with Michael! "In love." No way! Michael was his friend, that's all. Someone he had a laugh with, able to have intelligent conversations with, be comfortable around, almost like a comfort blanket. He was more like a friendly soul mate … he certainly wasn't in love with him. Was he? Well … maybe just a little bit!

CHAPTER THIRTY NINE

Alex was very pleased with himself. It was the third time this week he had won the round of golf and each time against one of the club's better players. He accredited his improved golf swing to everything else in his life going well. Siobhan was eager to get pregnant soon and they were trying plenty. His fling with Julie was long forgotten and his marriage was better than ever. He was feeling so positive about it all. He pulled up outside the house and was surprised to see her car at home; she wasn't due to be home for hours yet. Maybe she was ovulating and didn't want to waste any time. He smiled to himself, just the thoughts of making love to her was enough to bring on an erection! But as soon as he opened the door, all he could hear was great big hefty sobs coming from the living room. Sure enough, there she was blowing her nose into a tissue.

'What's wrong?' he asked, rushing to her side.

'I can't … we can't, the results, I can't … I … the doctor … he said' she sobbed in hysterics.

'Sssssshh, slow down, slow down, I can't understand a word you're saying.'

She took a deep breath and turned to face him. Her eyes were red and blotchy and her nose looked almost swollen. 'Dr Long rang me this morning and wanted us to go in and see him. I had that Cleary case meeting today, so I told him to just tell me over the phone.

'Okaay, and what did he say?'

'I can't have children, Alex, not now, not ever!' she began spluttering again.

'What?'

'I'm so sorry.' She began to sob again.

'I don't understand. Why?'

'I'm in the early stages of premature menopause?' she cried.

'I have something called Primary Ovarian Failure, seemingly my follicle stimulating hormones are not functioning the way it should be.'

'I don't understand, how come you've been having your period all this time, surely they'd have disappeared by now? Maybe there's still a chance?'

'I thought the same thing,' she sobbed, 'but seemingly I still have the follicles but they're not working properly, so I still get my period but it's too late for me to get pregnant. Look I don't really understand it, I just heard that I can't get pregnant and zoned out for the rest. I'm so sorry.'

'I can't believe it!' His heart was somewhere on the floor in front of him and yet he could still feel it shattering into a million little pieces.

Siobhan continued to sob her heart out beside him, uncontrollably inconsolable that she couldn't give him a child. A few seconds passed before he turned to her and grabbed her hands. 'Don't!' she cried, pulling her hands away. 'I've let you down.'

'No, you haven't!' He grabbed her hands again more tightly this time, 'you hear me? You *have not* let me down.'

'I have. Of course I have.' she exclaimed, her nose running, and not all that attractively either! 'I'm never going to be able to give you what you want!'

'But you do, every day. If we can't have children, then so be it, but at least we have us. Me and you.'

'You're not angry?'

'Angry? How could I be angry with you?' he said, trying to swallow the anger of the situation amidst the heartbreak he felt. 'I have you! So, no, I'm not angry.'

'But that's not enough!'

'It is, of course it is.'

'But you left because …'

'I left because you lied to me not because you didn't want kids. You tried, Siobhan, you were willing to do it for me and that's all I could ever ask.'

'So you're not going to leave?'

'Ssshhh,' he said softly, pulling her close to his chest. He stroked her hair and kissed her head softly. 'No, I'm never going to leave you, not again. I love you and that's all that matters.'

'I was so afraid I lost you.'

'Well, that's never going to happen.' They held each other tight for what seems like an eternity.

'You know what the worst part is?' she eventually asked, breaking the sombre silence.

'What's that?' he asked.

'Julie,' she sobbed.

'What about her?' he asked, puzzled and uncomfortable that Julie's name should come up now of all times.

'She's pregnant! She's only about two months gone but there's no mistaking the round little bump on her usually flat tummy!'

A quick calculation nearly caused Alex to have a secondary coronary! There was no mistaking it! He had to be the dad! 'Are you sure? How do you know?' he gulped.

'Of course I'm sure. I suspected it for a while and she has an obvious bump but she confirmed it today. She's been sneaking out to the toilets these past couple of weeks now to puke her guts up. So I asked her straight out today and she told me.'

His heart was pounding, his voice was gone, his legs were shaky and his palms were wet.

'She handed in her notice. She's moving to Liverpool, her sister lives there apparently.'

'What? She's moving away?'

'She acted really strangely when I asked her about it. I guess she was trying to keep it a secret for as long as she could. I think maybe the father might be a one-night stand or something. She doesn't seem too happy about it anyway, and she mentioned something about her father skinning her alive when he finds out! I feel sorry for her in a way but I'm glad she handed in her notice, because I don't want her bump in my face! Not now when I know I can't ever have one.'

'But I thought you didn't want kids, so why would it even bother you?'

'Because I feel like a failure, don't I?' She stood up abruptly and started to sob again.

'Ssshhh,' he pulled her back down, 'you're not, you're not.'

Her sobbing ceased immediately as she nestled into him. She couldn't hear his heart pounding and she couldn't see his face either which had the words "Oh crap" written all over it!

Alex sat at the kitchen table, staring at his mobile phone. Siobhan had gone for a run. He ran his hand through his fine head of peppered grey hair for the hundredth time trying to figure out this whole mess. If Julie was already a couple of months pregnant, then she clearly wasn't going to look for any involvement from his part. Maybe it wasn't his, he thought. No, who was he kidding; he just knew it was his! But why hasn't she contacted him? What should we do now? Say nothing and let it go? Face her? Tell Siobhan?

A million thoughts raced through his head. He couldn't lose Siobhan. But could he ignore the fact he was going to be a dad? And Julie was leaving, soon, all he had was her number, no address, though that wouldn't be hard to find. He needed to figure out what he was going to do and fast. He picked up his phone and searched his contacts list for her name and number so quickly that he couldn't find it, he kept going past it. He was afraid if he went any slower, he wouldn't be able to go through with it. Within a couple of seconds, Julie's voice floated into his ear. 'Hi Alex,' she said, 'I was expecting you to call.'

And there it was, without saying a word or even hearing word about any babies, it was one hundred percent confirmed that he was going to be a father after all.

CHAPTER FORTY

Jack hadn't slept a fecking wink. He checked the time, it was just gone seven and immediately his thoughts went to Michael's flight, which was scheduled to depart Terminal 2 in less than two hours. He'd gone over it and over it and over it all night. How would it work? How *could* it work? He had only just allowed the lid of that box to open ever so slightly. But to admit feelings for another man, even if it was only to himself, was a huge step for him. He couldn't even let himself think beyond the emotional attachment to Michael. He dared not even go there with the physical attraction. He couldn't even remember feeling anything sexual towards him. He couldn't even imagine a sexual relationship with another man. He was so confused! The thoughts of it terrified him. But the thoughts of Michael getting on that plane and never seeing him or hearing from him again terrified him even more!

Suddenly, a moment of clarity hit him and he jumped out of the bed and threw on his clothes. Even as he was zipping up his jeans, he wondered what the feck he was doing. Even if he was going to chance telling Michael how he felt, the fact of the matter was that Michael was going to be boarding the plane to start a new life with Cameron! Jack could be chasing after a man, risking his safety net, his secret, and opening a can of worms for nothing. But he had to do it! He couldn't let Michael go without at least talking to him. He knew Michael had left as soon as possible because he thought Jack was angry with him. He mistook Jack's silence and avoidance for anger and disgust. The day Michael left the village, Jack had worked a double shift and barely grunted goodbye when Michael came to say farewell to him and Conor at the bar. He regretted it now though. And he hoped he wasn't too late or he'd regret it for the rest of his life.

Michael had just got off the phone from Cameron for the fifth time that morning. He was beginning to drive him a little crazy. Cameron was so excited that the time had come for Michael to join him in the States and could barely contain himself on the phone. Michael was tiring of it already and he hadn't even left Ireland yet! He turned his phone off in an effort to avoid any more calls from him! The taxi pulled up outside Terminal 2 and the driver helped Michael with his cases.

He looked around and took a deep breath. 'Going to miss you, Ireland,' he said out loud. Then he headed indoors towards the check-in desk.

Traffic on the M50 was crawling at a decrepit snail's pace.

'Come on!' shouted Jack. He'd never make it at this rate. Michael would be boarding the plane within half an hour and he was flipping stuck in traffic! He had no idea how he was going to get to Michael once he got to the airport. He hadn't even thought that far ahead. His focus at the minute was getting to the feckin' airport. He could just about make out flashing lights ahead of him. Must be a crash, he thought. Great! He banged the steering wheel with his fist. I'll ring him, he thought, and started searching for his phone frantically.

'Hey, Michael here, leave a message and I'll get back to you.'

'Shite, bloody answer your phone, for feck sake! Michael, it's Jack. I'm on the M50, stuck behind a crash I want to talk. Ring me!!'

Michael checked his watch, thirty minutes to go. He decided to just head towards the gate and wait. He took out his phone as he walked along and toyed with the idea of ringing Jack. A simple call to say goodbye again. Sorry for keeping him in the dark about his sexuality. He couldn't get the look of disgust on Jack's face out of his head. No, he thought again, better not ring him. I'm the last person he wants to hear from. He put his phone back and walked on.

Jack finally got past the crash which turned out to be something small, thank God. It was all the bloody rubberneckers trying to get a look that caused the traffic tailback. Who'd have thought that a little old lady rear-ending a middle-aged bald man could be so interesting! He put his foot to the floor and prayed hard that he could make it in time. He guessed he was going to have to buy a ticket or something to even get to the gates. He clicked redial again …

'Hey, it's Michael here, leave a message and I'll get back to you.'

'Michael, hang on. I'm nearly there, we have to talk. Don't board the plane yet…' He drove like a Formula One racer, overtaking cars on their right and their left and flashing anyone in his way. Praying the whole time. 'Please God, let me make it.' The more he felt that he wasn't going to make it, the more he knew he had to.

Michael sat, looking out at the planes taking off. His plane was parking and fuelling. Right on time. He took out his phone again and switched it on. Maybe he'd send Jack a text. While he was waiting for it to boot up, he threw a few words around in his head. 'Jack, sorry I never told you that I'm actually gay …' No, that wouldn't do. 'Just a quick text to say goodbye … sorry …' No, that wouldn't do, either. 'Hey there, sorry for…' Arrgghh, he just couldn't think of what to say. Frustrated, he switched the phone off again without bothering to look at it.

At last, Jack roared into a taxi rank right outside the building, not caring about parking tickets or clamps! 'Please God, please God, please God,' was all he could mutter.

He made his way up to the information board and searched eagerly for the 8:55 flight to New York. His adrenalin was pumping and his heart felt as though it was going to jump out of his chest!

NEW YORK   AMERICAN AIRLINES   AA291   8:55 DEPARTED 9.03

Regret slammed into him. He was too late! He walked back to the car feeling completely lost, dragging his broken heart behind him. He pinched the tears out of his eyes and sniffed the water that was running down his nostrils. Two taxi drivers stood at his car, giving out stink. He knew they were gunning for him, but he didn't care! Right now, he didn't care about anything!

Michael sat in and made himself comfortable. He buckled up while he waited. He wasn't sure what the delay was but he hoped they'd get going soon. All he could hear were voices arguing. Getting louder and louder.

'I don't bloody believe this,' he said to himself, 'trust me to get into a taxi where the driver's too busy arguing to actually drive.' He got out to see what all the commotion was all about.

'I'm going, will you calm down. I didn't fecking commit a bloody murder!' Jack shouted. He jumped into his car and was about to pull off when he saw a familiar face get out of the taxi in front of him.

Michael saw him at that exact moment too and the two of them just stared at each other in disbelief. Ignoring the two angry taxi men, Jack got back out again.

'I thought your plane had departed ...'

'It has!'

'I don't understand then, why are you still here?'

'I don't understand either ... I just couldn't get on it! And why are you here?'

'To talk to you.'

'Come on, get out of here, go and have your weird talk someplace else,' shouted one of the taxi guys.

'Get in, before I'm killed here,' Jack said, pissed off at the red-faced taxi man. Michael hopped in without hesitation.

'Let's go grab a coffee, we need to talk.' Jack said.

'Think I'm going to need more than a coffee.' replied Michael. What the hell was Cameron going to say! He was going to have to make that really really awkward phone call soon! He wasn't looking forward to it. On top of all that, what was Jack playing at?

Jack ordered a coffee and a tea while Michael got a private spot away from nosy ears. He was still wondering what he had just done by walking away from the gate when Jack sat down beside him.

'So, how come you didn't board the plane?'

'I don't know! I just couldn't, just couldn't imagine a life for me out there.'

'What about Cameron? Does he know yet?'

'No!' Michael said, guilty and elated at the same time.

'Do you think he'll move back here then?'

'I don't know, I don't think I want him to.'

Jack's eyebrows shot up, surprised.

'I guess I just don't love him enough to create a life with him!' Michael said, with a clear head for the first time in a while.

Jack's heart started a slow beat of delight, but he was still nervous about opening up.

'How could I be so cruel to him?' Michael asked.

'Look, it's better you realise this now and not in a few months' time when you guys had already moved in together and settled.'

'I suppose.'

'Do you want to ring him? I can wait at the bar and give you some privacy.'

'Yeah, I will in a bit but I want to know why you're here. What did you want to talk about so badly?'

Jack suddenly got really nervous again.

'What is it, what's wrong? Are you still angry with me? I'm so sorry, Jack, I couldn't tell you because I didn't want to ruin our friendship. Look, I don't make friends easily and I couldn't bring myself to risk it!'

'Why did you think you'd be risking it?'

'Because any time I've made a male friend, they get really awkward when they find out I'm gay. Plus, I felt you were really uncomfortable with the whole gay thing too. Then when you were telling me about Conor and all that happened in your past, I knew I couldn't tell you. I thought you'd hate me!'

'I'd never hate you, Michael, and especially for something like that. You've become a great friend to me too, you know.'

'Well look, I'm really sorry I wasn't honest with you. I just hope we can be friends.'

'Well, the thing is, I haven't exactly been too honest with you either!' Michael stayed silent, confused now.

'I'm, I'm actually, kind of, well, I'm …' he spluttered.

'What? Come on, spit it out, what is it?' Michael urged.

'Okay,' Jack sighed heavily, 'I'm actually gay too.'

'Oh, Okay. I wasn't expecting that! So, are you bisexual then?'

'No, I'm just gay …'

'But you're an infamous womaniser…no?' Michael was really confused now.

'No, I'm not! But I have spent a long time trying to act …. normal!'

'Normal?'

'Well I mean, sorry, I'm not good at this.'

'At what? Coming out?' Michael joked, but his voice had a definite tone of seriousness.

'Yes, but it wasn't or isn't just a closet, Michael. It's a dark, lonely and absolutely terrifying coffin. I've been stuck in it for years, unable to breathe. I don't know how to be me now! How to be comfortable in my own skin even.'

'Well, all I can say is that you should stop trying to be someone or something you're not, forget about labelling yourself as straight or gay. It doesn't matter either way. Just think of yourself as the wonderful person that you are and think about all that love that you have to give to another person, be it a woman or a man, who cares! Enjoy being free! Just be you! And then, one of these days, when you're comfortable with that much, you'll meet someone really great who'll make you feel one hundred percent comfortable and happy, someone who'll make you good about yourself.'

'If you really think that way, then how come you didn't come out to me?'

'Because I was afraid you'd go all weird on me and we'd end up drifting apart,' Michael said, earnestly, 'I honestly thought you were dead against homosexuality, I was afraid to tell you.'

'Sorry I made you feel that way.' Jack said. They both shared a smile.

Michael stood up and took the phone out of his pocket. 'Wish me luck with Cameron.' he shouted back to Jack as walked away.

Jack sat at the table and began to make shreds of a beer mat. He looked over at Michael, who was walking up and down the foyer talking into his phone. It looked like a tense conversation! Within minutes, Michael was on his way back looking very stressed out.

'He's not taking it very well! He hung up on me and has turned his phone off now. I'll give him a few hours to calm down!' Michael said, taking a massive slug of his beer as if his life depended on it.

Jack knew he had to tell Michael why he had really gone to the airport or he'd seriously chicken out. 'Do you want another pint' he asked.

'No, actually I better get going. I should sort out accommodation again and all that,' he laughed.

'Actually, before we go, I need to talk to you about something else,' Jack said, trying to ignore the nerves creeping up to a high level again.

'Oh yeah?' Michael looked intrigued.

'Remember you were talking about meeting a good guy…'

'Yeah?' Michael butted in.

'Well, I think I already have!' Jack said and then waited for Michael's reaction.

'That's great, Jack. Life's too short to be afraid to be happy.'

'It's awkward, though,' Jack continued, 'because I'm only starting to come to terms with all this myself. I couldn't imagine a physical relationship with someone. I do feel an emotional connection to this person but I feel like…well, I guess I feel like, you know …'

'What?'

'I've never been with a man!' Jack said embarrassed.

'Oohh, so you feel like a virgin again.'

'SSShhhh, will you!' Jack said, looking around to see if anyone had heard.

'Boy, this is really getting to you, isn't it?' Michael laughed. 'Look, a physical relationship isn't the be all and end all. If you've found someone worthy of you, then that's great and I'm sure he'll take things as slowly as you want! He'd be a lucky guy so he better treat you well anyway or he'd have me to answer to.'

'Do you really think so?'

'What?'

'That he'd be a lucky guy?'

'Sure do.'

'Really?'

'Yes I do. You're an amazing person and I wish I'd been honest with you from the very beginning. Maybe things could've turned out differently, maybe…oh nothing. I'm just glad you've met someone.'

'Yeah, well look, it's you. You're the person I'm talking about! You're the person I've met!' Jack thought he was going to vomit. Talking to a woman never gave him the same feelings of sheer anxiety!

'Are you being serious?' Michael asked, not believing what he was hearing.

'Yeah, I'm hardly messing. It was hard enough to get the words out!'

'I, I'm shocked! Are you sh sh sure you feel that way?' Michael spluttered.

'Well, I didn't chase after anybody else like a bloody lunatic this morning!' he laughed, nervously.

'You mean, you want to give *us* a go?'

'I'm saying I want us to remain friends, I want you to come back with me, move back in, well into your old room and let's see what happens. I don't know, how do you feel about that?'

'That sounds really great,' Michael said, smiling.

Jack sighed with relief for the first time in a long time. And for the first time in years, decades even, he felt genuinely happy.

CHAPTER FORTY ONE

Seamus held the door open for Joan and Amy as they ventured into Lily's for a cuppa and a cake. Amy ran straight up to the counter to show Lily the new furry toy Seamus had just bought her.

'Oh my, now isn't he adorable!' Lily said sweetly.

'Lily, it's a girrrrlllll doggy! He has no long stick, see?' Amy corrected Lily while showing her the anatomy of the teddy.

'Oh right, silly me.' Lily said seriously.

'Yeah, silly Lily, my friend Tom has a stick. He squeezes his wee out of it like the way you have to milk a cow.' Amy informed her while Lily done her best not to giggle.

'It's fairly cold out there today, Lily,' Joan said, pulling her coat tight around her, desperately diverting the conversation away from sticks!

'I know, there's a right nip in the air. Sure, go on and grab that table beside the stove there now and I'll bring ye over your favourites or do you want something different?'

'No, no, that's perfect, Lily, thanks.' Seamus said, directing Amy to the table. They were just settled when Lily arrived over with a tray of coffees, apple juice, and three calorific-looking cupcakes.

'How's Emma doing, I've not laid eyes on the girl now in a good while!' Lily enquired as she laid the goodies out on the table.

'Oh, she's busy out these days, you know yourself how the time just flies by too.' Joan smiled.

'She's not really busy though, Nana, she just stays in bed or lies on the couch all the time,' Amy said as she licked the topping off the top of her cupcake.

Lily knew Emma's tendencies towards episodes of depression and had suspected as much herself. Amy, God love her, had really let the cat out of the bag. She felt bad for asking now and rushed off to clean some imaginary dirt off the counter.

Joan and Seamus were grateful for Lily's exit. Seamus looked lovingly at Amy and spoke very gently and softly. 'You know, honey, that your Mam is okay, she's just tired from work, that's all,' Seamus said softly.

'No, she's sad.' Amy replied, in a very matter of fact manner.

'Oh honey, everyone gets sad sometimes, but she loves you very much. You know that, don't you?' Joan butted in, her heart aching.

'Yeah, like my fwend Sally, she cried for ten whole days when her pet hamter went to up to Evenses!' Amy said sadly.

'Heaven?' Joan asked, confused.

'Yeah, Evenses, that's what I said! Gran!' Amy replied, not at all impressed with Joan for not listening properly! Seamus smiled at his granddaughter, all the while realising just how much this was actually beginning to affect her. Who'd have thought that at her age she'd pick up on it so sharply. Joan looked out the window, trying to blink away fresh tears from her eyes. This was getting so serious now that it was beginning to affect little Amy too. She was going to have to tell Emma and together they would have to try to come up with solutions to shield Amy as much as they possibly could.

Alex anxiously walked up Julie's driveway and knocked on the door. His life changed forever as she opened the door and, sure enough, there it was, a small but undeniable baby bump.

'Come on in, I don't want my neighbours to see you hanging around out here!' she said anxiously.

'How are you?' he asked.

'I'm fine,' she replied, 'well, apart from the morning sickness which comes on pretty bad at night.'

'Oh, you'd wonder why it's called 'morning' sickness, wouldn't you?' he joked nervously, 'it should just be "any time" sickness!'

'Yeah, well, whatever, it's not exactly fun at whatever time of the day or night!'

'Sorry.' Alex could see she obviously wasn't in good form so he cut straight to the chase. 'Why didn't you tell me?'

Julie didn't answer.

'It's mine, isn't it?' he asked but immediately wished he hadn't.

She shot him a look that could kill. 'Don't insult me! Do you think I would pass this child off as yours if it wasn't? Believe me the father of this baby being a married man is not exactly an ideal situation for me!'

'Sorry sorry sorry! I just don't understand why you didn't tell me when you found out; you knew how much this would mean to me!'

'Whoa, slow down there. The reason I didn't tell you is because of that shiny gold band on your left hand there!'

Alex looked at wedding ring on his finger but his wife was far from his mind right now. 'Didn't you think I'd a right to know?'

'It doesn't really matter!'

'Of course it matters! It's *my* baby, for God's sake! And you were planning on just moving away with it.'

'I knew I should have just moved away as soon as I found out!'

'What? Why? Why would you do that?'

'Because you're married! And I don't want this baby tainted by my…' her voice started wobbling.

'Your what?'

'My mistake, my drunken mistake, of sleeping with a married man, and not just any married man but a married man who is married to my boss, sorry my ex-boss, who is such a lovely woman and doesn't deserve this.' she broke down, weeping.

'Julie, it doesn't matter how this happened, this baby is a blessing!' he urged.

'No, it's a big mess Alex! My parents are so disappointed.' she cried.

'Seriously Julie? We're not living in the dark ages anymore, you know. It's hardly the end of the world.'

'I know that but getting pregnant is just about bearable to them but telling them the dad is a married man would kill them! I had to tell them I was seeing the father but he left me when he found out I was pregnant! My father went crazy and has just about stopped asking for his name and address so he could go and kill him!'

'Well, they're gonna find out eventually.'

'Oh no, they're not! I've handed in my notice and I'm going to stay in Liverpool with my sister for a while. I need to get away from here.

'That's ridiculous,' he scoffed, 'how am I supposed to be part of my child's life then?'

'Simple, you're not.' she retorted coldly.

'Excuse me?'

'You have your wife, Alex, so just go back home to your cosy little life and forget about all of this!'

'Don't be stupid! How can I forget about the fact that I am going to have a son or a daughter out there?'

'You have to! Besides, I can't see Siobhan being overly happy about it all either, can you?' It was more of a rhetorical question really as both of them already knew the obvious answer to that.

'Let me worry about that! I know it could really come between us but we're strong and I'd hope we could figure something out.'

'Come on Alex, she'll leave you for sure once you tell her! Do you really want to risk that?'

'Of course not but, like I said, we're strong and I'm sure we'll work through it.'

'Well you don't have to work through anything out because I don't want you involved in any of this!' she said defiantly.

'It's a bit late for that now, isn't it! So, I'm sorry Julie, but there's no way I'm turning my back on this baby!'

They'd both been facing one another in a standoff but she walked away from him and looked out the kitchen window. A few silent seconds slipped away before she spoke again.

'Alex, I'm leaving and I want to start again in Liverpool, I can't bear what I've done to Siobhan and I do not want to spent the rest of my life parading it around in front of her.

'I'm not saying any of this will be easy but Julie I can't let you leave with my baby, please, it may be my only chance to be a father.'

Julie could see the desperation in his eyes, but it wasn't enough to make her want to stay. 'I'm sorry Alex, I really am, but as soon as I can I'm going. I'm not staying here. If you really want to be part of the child's life you can come to Liverpool whenever you want, but I don't want it known you're married! So Siobhan can't ever come, I'm sorry but that's the way it has to be. Whatever you choose however I am going and I doubt I will ever come home again. I want to make a life for me and this child away from my disapproving parents and away from..'

'Me?'

'Well, not you, but the fact the dad is married yes…'

'Don't you think you're being really irrational about all of this and a bit overboard? Your parents will love this baby as soon as they lay eyes on it.'

'Maybe, but I'm better off away from it all, to give myself and this kid the best chance to make a go of things. Besides, I really miss my sister and moving over to be near her will be great.'

'So, there's nothing I can say?'

'No, nothing.'

Alex drove home, a nervous wreck! When he got there, Siobhan's car was in the driveway, which was highly unusual. He let himself in and prepared himself to act normal but as soon as he saw her lying on the sofa, his nerves kicked up a notch.

'What are you doing home?' he asked.

'I decided to have a sick day myself. I went in and Julie had phoned in sick, so I said what a good idea! If Julie can pull a sickie just because she's pregnant, then why can't I? Just because I'm not pregnant doesn't mean I wouldn't like a duvet day!' she said, feeling very sorry for herself.

'Now that's not the Siobhan I know,' he frowned. Even when she was genuinely sick, it was hard to keep her home.

'Ah I'll be grand, just drained from all this baby stuff, you know. I'll take a day out and get back into it all tomorrow,' she said, sitting up.

He sat down beside her before he fainted.

She noticed his anxiety and began rubbing his back. 'God, you're so tense! Please don't be worrying about me, Alex. It's you I feel bad for, I've really let you down.'

'No you haven't, stop saying that!'

'What's wrong with you, then? You have rocks in your shoulders!

Come on, talk to me.' she urged.

'I'm gonna go for a walk or a run or something,' he said standing up.

She grabbed his hand and stood up too. 'Tell me please! We need to be honest about how we feel or we may never get past this.'

'Please, Siobhan, just leave it!' He pushed past her and went to leave.

'No, now talk, Alex. What is it?' she demanded.

He turned to face her, defeated. 'I'm so sorry.'

'Sorry about what? What are you talking about?' she asked, confused.

'The baby, Julie's baby!' he said, very quietly, almost hoping she wouldn't hear him.

Her face paled. 'What about her baby?' she asked, saying every word very clearly and slowly.

'It's mine.' He put his hands to his face, not able to face the devastation in her eyes.

Her stomach plummeted and tears stung her eyes. 'Tell me you're joking!'

'I'm so sorry, it happened once when we separated that time. I was so angry with you over everything and got really drunk one night!' 'Oh, so let me see if I have got this right, you go and have sex with my secretary and get her pregnant and it's all my fault?' she cried out.

'No, God no! It's all my wrong doing. I know that and I can't tell you how sorry I am!'

She brushed past him to leave the room and he grabbed her arm to stop her.

'Please, Siobhan, wait, let's talk about ….' He never saw the slap coming as her hand came flying up to meet his cheek full force! He nearly fell over and the sting of it brought water to his eyes! The last thing he saw was Siobhan glaring at him wildly before she left the room and the last thing he heard was her slamming the front door!

CHAPTER FORTY TWO

Emma heard the banging on the door and decided to actually answer it this time. But not quickly enough for Siobhan's liking as she let herself in with her own key.

'Oh yeah, I forgot everyone seems to have a key to my house!' Emma complained but Siobhan just sat down and started bawling.

'Oh, what's wrong?' Emma said, concerned.

'He's only gone and got Julie of *all* people up the bloody pole, that's what!'

'Say that again!' Emma wasn't quite sure she had heard her properly.

'Alex, my husband, has gone and got Julie, the two-faced tramp of a secretary of mine, pregnant! Bloody fertile slapper wagon!' she spat out.

'Oh my!,' was all Emma could think of to say, 'what are you going to do?'

'Throw him out, I guess.'

'How far gone is she? What's he saying about it all?'

'Oh, he's soooooooo sorrrrrrrrrry! Pathetic, isn't it. Sorry. Sorry is for something like "sorry I ate the last bar of chocolate, not oh I'm terribly sorry there darling, but I managed to get another girl pregnant!" Makes me sick, she's young enough to be his daughter herself!! Supposedly it happened once, while we were apart that time.'

'Ah now, she's not that young and he's not that old.'

'Who cares about the ages anyway, Emma? All I care about is that the man I love and trusted with my life cheated on me with a good-for-nothing tramp and she's giving him the one thing I can't. Never mind the fact that he did the dirt on me.'

'He was very pissed off at you then.'

'This is about Alex cheating on me, Emma, not about anything else.'

'Yeah, but if you really want to get into it, you cheated on him too in a way.' Emma was in no mood to rub Siobhan's back and sympathise with her.

'I can't believe this; you're actually taking his side!' Siobhan said, outraged.

'I'm not taking anyone's side. I'm just saying that you should think back and remember how upset he was and how much you hurt him. So, no matter how hurt you are now, you have some part to play in all this!'

'That's hardly an excuse to jump into bed with the next trollop that walks past!'

'No it's not, I know that.'

'I just can't believe this is happening.'

'Yeah. Alex and Julie! I thought you said she was really shy and she seemed to be from a really strict background?'

'Yeah, but I guess they're the ones you want to watch out for,' replied Siobhan scornfully. 'And I was so happy when he said he'd forgiven me and he was willing to come home. Now look at us!'

They were interrupted by Joan and Seamus arriving back. 'Oh hello, love,' Joan said, noticing the state of Siobhan, 'we didn't mean to come back in on you so soon, Emma love.' Maybe now wasn't a good time to talk about Amy.

'No, not at all, Joan. Actually I'll leave you to it,' Siobhan said, standing up.

'Actually,' Seamus said, 'it's a blessing you're here really. Would you mind taking Amy for a bit?'

'Dad, no, Siobhan's really busy.' Emma protested.

'You know what? That sounds like a good plan actually. A big bowl of yummy chocolate ice cream with extra chocolate sauce for good measure?' Siobhan asked Amy.

'Oh Lord, we've just come from Lily's, Amy has had a cupcake already.' Joan giggled.

'Oh, the bowl of ice cream is for me, Joan!' Siobhan said as she held out her hand for Amy to take it, 'even big girls need ice cream sometimes too, don't we, Amy?'

'Yeah, Sivvy, but I'm still hungry, the cupcake was too small!' Amy said, looking like a little puppy begging for leftovers! They all laughed. As soon as Siobhan and Amy were gone out the door, Seamus turned to Emma.

'Right now, we have to talk!' he said, seriously.

Jack was delighted to see Amy and Siobhan.

'Hey there, my favourite little lady, what are you doing here?' Jack said, as Amy ran up to him in The Cellar.

'Sivvy is getting me ice cream even though I had a big cupcake!' she informed him, beaming mischievously.

'Hey you, I thought you said it was only a small cupcake?!' Siobhan said, pretending to be angry.

'Oh yeah, it was really small. But can I still get ice cream?'

'Of course you can, honey,' Siobhan sniggered, 'as long as I don't have to clean up the crap overload puke later on!' she whispered to Jack.

'So two bowls of your finest chocolate ice cream with extra chocolate sauce, please.'

'Hmm, now I know there's something going on,' he eyed her suspiciously.

'Sit down there and I'll be back to you with as much chocolate as I can get, alright?'

'Yay!' shouted Amy.

'I've news for you anyway,' he called back to Siobhan as he strode off towards the kitchen.

'Oh!' she replied, wondering why he had such a smirk on his face. He was back within minutes to dish out two oversized bowls of seriously chocolatey ice cream swimming in chocolate sauce.

'Yummmmmy!' screamed Amy at the sight of all the vomit-inducing chocolate sauce.

'Okay, Jack, expect a bill for car valeting tomorrow.' she laughed.

'Fair enough,' he laughed too. 'Now spill, why the chocolate?'

'Dunno, Joan and Seamus asked me to take Amy for a bit so I'm guessing they want a talk with Emma.'

'Oh, wonder what that's about? But I was actually referring to you, what's going on? Why the need for chocolate?'

'Oh nothing really, I just found out that my husband is going to be a dad to my secretary's baby!' she exhaled loudly.

'Alex?' he asked, flabbergasted.

'Yep that's the one. Seemingly our time apart wasn't all that bad for him.'

'What???? I just can't believe it!'

'You're not the only one.' she said, spooning a massive helping of ice cream into her mouth.

'How do you feel?'

'Numb.'

'Wow, it's a lot to process alright, what are you gonna do?'

'I've no idea! Marriage is over, I guess! I mean the fact he slept with Julie is bad enough. I don't even want to think about it. But the fact that she's carrying his child is really awful. She can give him something I can't. How am I supposed to get past that?'

'I don't know, you are going to have to talk that one through.'

'Emma thinks it's partly my fault' she claimed, feeling pretty sorry for herself.

'What? Did she actually say that?' he looked surprised.

'More or less!'

'No, I'm sure she didn't mean it that way.'

'Yeah, she reckons that what he's done is no worse than my lying to him about the pill that time.'

'Look, she's all over the place at the moment, so try not to take anything she says to heart.'

'No,' she sighed, 'she probably speaks more truth now than anyone else! Maybe her depressed state of mind just knocked the sugar coating of it!'

'So you think you're to blame?'

'I honestly don't know what to think! I guess if I hadn't driven him away, he wouldn't have done it! I know him and I know that he must have been in some awful state to do something like this to me.'

There's no excuse for having sex … oh sorry, I mean having a "playdate" with someone else though, is there?' he said, using finger quotations to fool Amy.

'I know that.' she replied, 'it hurts to think that he could just go and jump into bed with someone else.'

'My mammy jumps into bed all the time!' Amy revealed harmlessly, 'well, she doesn't really jump in; I think she gets in really slowly, like a snail.'

'Oh!' Siobhan and Jack said together.

'It's complicated,' Siobhan said, getting back to the topic of Alex, 'anyway, I'm so fed up thinking about it right now. You said you have news?'

'Yeah I do, but it's nothing really.' He was living on cloud nine right now and he didn't want to rub his happiness into Siobhan's face.

'Oh come on, just tell me! It's obviously good news and, believe me, I could do with hearing some good news.'

'Ok then. You know Michael?'

'Yes?' she said slowly, raising her eyebrows.

'Well, we've decided to be friends.'

'Okaaaay. So …?' She raised her eyebrows again, wondering what the fuss was all about.

'No, I mean, *really* good friends.'

'Rigggggghhhht.'

'As in, *very* good friends.'

'Yeeessssss!'

'Oh, for God's sake, woman. I mean as in a couple!' he whispered.

'A couple of what? Idiots?' she laughed, but when she realised just exactly what he was telling her she flung her hand to her mouth. 'What? You and Michael? You? Michael? You? Are you for real? You and Michael are…?'

'Yes!'

'Oh wow, I always knew it, I knew there was something about you.'

'No, you didn't.'

'Okay look. I did cop on to it a while ago, I never dreamed that you and Michael would get together though! I thought you were just friends…are you happy?'

'Yeah, but I'm kind of just getting used to coming out as they say, so

I'm really nervous of people's reactions. But apart from that, I'm ecstatic! We're taking it really slowly though.'

'Ah that's great. And, sure, who gives a shit what anyone else thinks? As long as you're happy, that's all that counts.'

'I don't give a shit anyway!' Amy said. Jack and Siobhan burst out laughing. Jack headed down the bar to serve another customer.

'This is yummy, Sivvy,' Amy said between spoonful's.

'Maybe we should bring some back to Mammy. She misses my daddy, you know!' she said, her forehead wrinkling with sadness.

'Yes, pet, he was so good to your mammy and they loved each other very much.'

'Yeah, and he looks after me too.'

'Does he?' she asked, baffled.

'Oh yeah, Mammy said he looks down at us from Evenses.'

'Heaven?'

'Yeah, that's what I said. You're like Granny, you don't listen too good!'

'Oh, I'm very sorry, pet.' Siobhan said, struggling to hide a smile.

'My friend Holly has a dad.' Amy revealed cheerfully.

'Does she?' Siobhan asked, her heart breaking.

'Yeah, she's really lucky.' Amy insisted.

And with that, Siobhan's heart shattered completely. Not only for Amy but also for herself. There was no denying it, a dad was a pretty important thing and how could she live with herself if she deprived Alex of that.

CHAPTER FORTY THREE

'So, what's all this about? Is something wrong with Amy?' Emma asked, looking from Joan to Seamus and back to Joan again.

'I'll put the kettle on and then we can have a chat, okay?' said Joan.

'No, just tell me, what's going on with Amy.' she asked again, becoming more irritated and agitated.

'She knows you're … well, that you're depressed. It's starting to impact on her now too,' Seamus said gently.

'She's only a child, Dad, and I'm not exactly falling to pieces in front of her now, am I?' she argued defensively.

'No, you do that up in your bedroom, but she's not stupid, Emma. She notices that you spend a lot of your time in bed now and you don't seem to want to be around her as much anymore. She's fairly smart to cop on to it all, you know.' he replied, beginning to feel pretty agitated himself.

'Look, love,' interrupted Joan, 'we know you're going through a really tough time at the moment and we are here for you a hundred percent but we just feel you should know that Amy *is* starting to notice and be affected by it.'

Emma burst into tears instantly. Holding her head in her hands and supporting her elbows on her knees, she allowed great big tears to erupt from her eyes and fall onto the floor.

'My poor baby,' she cried out, 'what am I doing to my poor little baby. I'm no good for her.'

Joan and Seamus both rushed to her, each sitting either side, hugging her and holding her.

'Oh Emma, don't say that, don't ever say that!' Joan cried helplessly, tears falling from her own eyes.

'You're her mother, she needs you. She needs you more than anybody else in her life.' Seamus said croakily, tears threatening to fall too.

'She'd be better off if I was up with her daddy, I'm only damaging her too!' she continued to cry.

'No, no, Emma,' Joan said desperately, grabbing her hands. 'Now, you listen to me! That child needs you, so you have to stop thinking this way and, as hard as it is, you have to put Amy first here, and that means being here for her.'

'But that's what I am doing, I am putting her first.'

'What, by leaving her with no mother or father? Leaving her to grow up an orphan?' Seamus scolded, despite holding back his tears.

She stopped crying and looked up at him as if he had just slapped her.

'Oh my God, an orphan, poor little Amy an orphan! What am I doing?' Emma asked, bewildered.

'We need to get you back on your feet, love,' Joan said gently, 'if not for your own sake, for…'

'Amy's!' Emma sniffed, finishing her mother's sentence for her.

'Yes, and a good way to start is to let go of those thoughts. Amy needs you, we need you.'

'I just want her to be happy.' Emma cried again.

'And that's what she wants, for you to be happy.' Seamus said eventually giving into his chocking throat. His tears fell slow and steady. Joan reached out to him and rubbed his hand.

'I don't want to feel like this all the time, you know.' Emma wept.

'Ssshhh,' Joan said, stroking her hair, 'we know you don't love, we know.'

'I loved him so much!'

'We know, love, we know.'

'I just don't know how to let go.' she blubbered.

'You don't have to let go, love, you just have to learn to live without him being here beside you, but you can always carry him in your heart.' Joan spoke slowly and sympathetically.

'I just miss him so much!'

'We know, love.' Seamus said, drying his tears. 'He's still here in Amy, you know.' Emma looked at him and smiled, a beautiful genuine smile, the first one in months.

'I'd never do anything to hurt her, you know!'

'God, love, we know that, sure you're a terrific mother. Just look at what a great child she is. You did that.' Joan offered.

'Yes, but now I'm messing it all up.' Emma stated despairingly.

'No, you're not.' Seamus said.

'But you both said so.' she maintained.

'No, love, we just thought that you needed to know that she's beginning to pick up on what you're going through.' Joan spoke gently again.

'Yeah, my poor Amy.' Emma cried. And cried. And cried. Her parents sat and held her while she cried a river of emotions.

'Are you alright? Seamus asked softly once the tears died down a little.

'Yeah, I am. There's something I need to do. Can you wait here for Amy?' she asked.

'Yes, of course love,' Joan said. 'Sure your dad can wait here and I can keep you company, what do you say?'

'No, Mam, this is something I need to do on my own, don't worry I'll be back shortly,' she said, trying to relieve her mother's anxiety as she hugged her tightly at the same time.

Emma knelt down at Aidan's grave and wiped away yet more tears. 'Sorry I haven't been here in a while. I've been a bit pissed off at you! I really thought you were still around me in a spirit form; kind of crazy alright, isn't it, when you hear it out loud! Although everybody was telling me for weeks that I was driving myself insane, I just wouldn't listen. I guess deep down I knew they were right. I just didn't want to say goodbye. But Mam said something that made so much sense. She said I don't have to let go, that I don't have to say goodbye because you'll always be with me, in my heart. And even Dad made so much sense when he said that you live on in Amy. So I won't be able to touch your skin, or hear your voice, but I'll have it all with me, every bit of it, every memory we shared, every kiss, every touch, laugh, everything. My heart is overflowing with you, darling, overflowing in every part, every single cell in my body. And although I'm going to pull myself up and out of this black hole and invest all of my energy into getting better for our little girl, it doesn't mean that I'm not totally gutted that you're not here with me. I just need to live for Amy now! I'll be around every Sunday to say hello but I know you won't be following me back home again. So, sweetheart, I love you and I hope you get to rest in peace.' she kissed her finger and placed it lovingly on his headstone.

CHAPTER FORTY FOUR

Siobhan threw the keys on the hall table and went looking for Alex. He was in the sitting room nursing a brandy. All the fire had left her after her time with Amy. 'Listen, Alex, I've been thinking. A dad is a pretty important person to have in a child's life and it would be heart-breaking to know you have a child out there and you're not part of their life. It's not fair on the child. So, do what you have to, you won't get a big fuss from me.'

Alex sat up straight, new hope crossing his face.

'But I can't be part of it, so if you want to be a father, I won't stand in your way but you do it without me. I don't want any fighting or legal battles. All I want is this house and I think that's fair. You won't need to support me or divide up your investments and pension.'

His face fell but he said nothing.

'Anyway, think about what it is you want. I'm going up to my room, I hope you don't mind sleeping in the spare room tonight.' She turned and walked away, cool as a cucumber.

The next morning, she woke up to the sound of Alex opening the door. He handed her a coffee while sitting on the bed beside her. She graciously took it as she sat up, surprised at how much sleep she had actually gotten.

'I need you, Siobhan, and if I don't have you, then I'm nothing. So I need us to stay together and I need you to forgive me. I'll have to support the child financially, how could I not? But that will be it, I promise. Please, forgive me, I can't lose you!'

She put the coffee down and reached out to him. 'Are you sure about this, I mean absolutely sure, now?'

'Yes, I am. I can't be without you, so if being in this child's life means I have to sacrifice you then I can't do it. You're my world!'

She threw her arms around his neck. 'Oh, Alex, I'm sorry I had to make you make that choice. I just couldn't live with it but I know I've made mistakes here too, let's start afresh and put them behind us.'

'Yes, that sounds like one hell of a deal to me.' He grabbed her and hugged her tightly, 'I love you so much.'

'I love you too.' She beamed.

As soon as he got into the shower, Siobhan got her mobile and punched in Julie's number. When Julie answered, her stomach jumped a little. She told Julie that she didn't need her to work out her notice at the firm and that she would be paid up to the end of her time as per her contract anyway. She could pick up her things from the office the following day and to be in and gone by twelve. A reference would not be provided by Siobhan, although Julie was welcome to go crawling to one of the other solicitors for one, knowing full well Julie would be way too embarrassed to ask for one. Their conversation was short and to the point, even if Siobhan found it difficult to remain calm and professional.

That afternoon, Alex went to speak to Julie. He had knots in his stomach at the thoughts of what he was about to do.

Julie answered the door looking like death warmed up. 'I didn't expect to see you again, thought you would realise what a mess this all is.' she exclaimed, walking back into the kitchen.

'It's one big mess alright.' he muttered.

'Didn't take long to make you call it that too did it?'

'I don't mean the baby, obviously! I just mean the situation!' he sighed, 'Look, there's no easy way to say this, but Siobhan doesn't want me to be involved...'

'I can't believe you actually told her! She would never have needed to know.' she interrupted.

'I had to, I needed to be honest with her if we were to have any chance of surviving this...but unfortunately it meant I lose out on the chance to be a dad to this little one.' he said sadly while looking down at her tummy.

'I'm sorry Alex.' Julie said genuinely, seeing the look of loss on his face.'

'But I will look after you and this baby financially. You'll never need to worry about that. We'll set up a bank account so I can transfer money and when you get to Liverpool, go find a nice apartment or house you like and I'll lease it for you or even buy it if you want.'

'How's all that going to pan out with Siobhan?'

'Once we get set up and running, I'll take a step back, okay?'

'Okay, I'm leaving on Friday so....say farewell to the bump.' She laughed unconvincingly.

'Friday? But I thought you were going to stay around for a while until you had everything sorted?'

'It was really only work I had to sort out and well....that's sorted now.'

'Oh.' He didn't know what to say. He just felt numb.

'Okay well I have loads of packing to do so....'

'Oh okay, yeah I'll.....I'll let you get sorted,' he said, yet he didn't move a muscle.

She walked passed him and to the front door, he followed her feeling like he was losing a part of his world before he even met it. He stood at the door, reluctant to leave.

'Thanks for calling over, Good bye Alex.'

He didn't even say goodbye, he just walked out the door and towards his car, with tears in his eyes.

CHAPTER FORTY FIVE

Michael couldn't help but notice Jack's puzzled face as he got off the phone.

'We've been invited to dinner in Emma's on Saturday night!' he said, shocked.

'Oh really? Wow, she really must be trying her best to get back to her old self, good for her.' Michael smiled.

'Oh wait, is she cooking?' he asked, looking worried.

'Yeah,' Jack laughed, 'but don't worry, she's an awesome cook, it's just the baking she's a bit crappy at.'

'Hey, guess what?' asked Michael, grinning from ear to ear.

'What?'

'This will be our first outing, pardon the pun, as a couple! How do you feel about that?'

'Oh, well, actually, do I really have to be seen in public with you?' laughed Jack, feeling happier than ever before. Michael threw the tea towel at him and laughed.

Alex was elated that Siobhan was giving him another chance but he was devastated about losing access to the baby. Everything was set for Julie's money transfer and there was no other reason for him now to be in contact. Siobhan seemed to be taking it all fairly well in her stride. They were getting on better than ever, with no problems or glitches. Emma's dinner was giving them both something to look forward to as well. Siobhan had relayed the whole story of Emma's breakthrough and they were both intent on supporting her. It seemed that neither of them wanted to dwell on the past any more.

Seamus's apartment was finally ready and Emma was relieved to see him pack up his belongings. Now that he was moving out, she knew she would have to get back on top of her game completely. Especially where Amy was concerned. In a way, Seamus living there enabled her to stay buried in her deep dark hole. He took over everything so there was no need for her to worry about any of it. She had to admit that he was beginning to make some seriously nice dinners and he had become accustomed to keeping the house organised and clean. However, as much as she loved him and was grateful to him, she was glad to see him get packed and set to leave.

Conor had put a deposit on a lovely cottage just on the outskirts of the village. He felt for the first time in a long time that his life was starting to piece back together again, even though one vital piece would always be missing. His feelings for Emma were strong enough for him to give her enough space and time before he asked her out again. But he held out hope that at some time in the future she would surrender to his charm. He was deeply suspicious, however, that she was attempting to set him up with her crazy friend, Tracy. She had dropped her name too many times while inviting him to dinner Saturday night for it to be anything other than a set up. But what Emma didn't know was the fact that if he couldn't date Emma he wasn't interested in anyone else. Nope, he was gonna hold out in the hope that just maybe, someday, she would look his way. And hope was a pretty powerful thing!

CHAPTER FORTY SIX

Emma took the cake out of the oven and quickly opened the windows to let the smoke out. It was totally obliterated on the top but she didn't have the time to do another, so she hacked off the really charcoaled bits and smothered the rest in butter icing. 'There,' she said to herself, 'delicious!' She went on to prepare the roast, peel the potatoes, chop the carrots and mix the Yorkshire pudding mix, humming away to herself. Amy was busy drawing pictures and everything seemed so normal. She was happy to be feeling so normal, normal was good! She had such a determination to get back on her feet fully over the next few weeks. Although she couldn't ignore the 'empty' niggling feeling in the pit of her stomach. But she shrugged it off and got off with her dinner.

Joan and Seamus came back from the shops fully loaded down with bottles of wine, fruit of all kinds and a seriously chocolatey chocolate cake from Lily's. 'What did you get a cake for, Mam, sure I told you I was baking one!'

'Oh yeah, I must have forgot love.' Joan said, trying to ignore Seamus grinning widely at her.

'Okay. Anyway, I'm going upstairs for a shower now, so can you set the table, Mam, no one can set a table quite like you!' she called after her while running up the stairs.

'I knew I shouldn't have let your dad talk me into coming over early,' Joan shouted back. 'Great to see her doing so well,' she commented to Seamus when Emma was out of earshot.

'Yeah, it really is, but don't forget it may still take a while, she's been through so much.'

'Yeah. You know, Seamus, part of me actually really wanted for it all to be true.'

'You're still an auld romantic, Joan.' he smiled.

'Ah, you know what I mean.' replied Joan smiling.

'Yeah, but it's better for Amy to have this business laid to rest as well. Poor kid, she never even met Aidan, so could you imagine how confused she could have become from it all?' he asked.

'She does know Aidan, of course she does!' Joan half argued.

'All she really knows is that he was her dad and what he looks like from his photographs around the place, but that's it. She didn't meet him or get to know him so it would be so hard for her to understand, not to mention the fact she's only a child. Sure isn't it hard enough for an adult to understand these things!' he replied.

'Wouldn't it be great if there was an off switch to our feelings.' Joan said, with wishful thinking.

'God now Joan, if you could invent such a thing now, we'd be millionaires!'

'What's this "we" business?' she scolded playfully.

He went over to her, smiling, and kissed her lovingly and tenderly on the lips.

'Ohhh, *that* we!' she laughed.

'Yes, you cheeky woman. When will we tell Emma about us getting back together, over dinner maybe?'

'Yes that's a great idea.' she agreed, kissing him again.

Emma had just come down the stairs when Siobhan and Alex arrived with a cake from Lily's.

'What's this?' she asked, looking at the white cake box.

'Oh, just a little something.' Siobhan said quickly as she walked in past her, trying to hide her guilt. Tracy was next to arrive and she carried in a homemade chocolate cake.

'What is it with you guys? I said I was baking and not to bring anything!'

'Oh did you?' Tracy said innocently, 'I mustn't have heard you properly,' then she caught sight of the rock formation on the counter, 'anyway, it's just in case….well you know yourself.'

'No, I don't know Tracy! Just because my Christmas cakes may have turned out a bit dodgy doesn't mean the rest of my baking is too. Ask Siobhan, she thinks all my cakes are delicious, don't you Siobhan?' she rapidly turned towards Siobhan for back up.

'Ehh yeah,' was all Siobhan could commit to as she suspiciously eyed up the rock formation masquerading as a cake also.

'See!' she turned back to Tracy with a triumphant look.

'Yes of course they're great, I didn't mean anything bad Emma.' She smiled sweetly at Emma and quickly gave Siobhan daggers. Out of ear shot she informed Siobhan that seen as she liked Emma's baking so much, she could also have her piece also!

Conor arrived next with double chocolate ice cream and some sweets for Amy. Jack and Michael followed closely behind with another white box from Lily's!

'I give up! I tell you all to just bring yourself but yet again you show up with more food than I know what to do with! So ye can bring them home with you later again.'

'Yes Conor,' scolded Tracy, 'Emma's been slaving over the oven all day baking a delightful cake for us all so you can forget about that tub of cookies and cream ice cream…' her sentence seemed to taper off as she began to drool at the sight of the ice cream tub in Conor's hands.

Two empty bottles of wine later, they were all sitting around the long wooden table in her dining room enjoying the food and the banter. Jack and Michael were completely at ease being side by side and nobody made any comment about the new dynamics of their friendship. This began to annoy Jack a little until, finally, after everyone had mopped up the last of their roast dinner, he tapped his glass to make a little speech. Everyone fell silent instantly except for Amy.

'Mammy, Jack is trying to break his glass!'

Everyone laughed heartily except a very confused Amy.

'I have something I'd like to say, if I may?' he said bravely.

'Of course.' Emma cheered, knowing what he was going to say.

'I just want to say that this has been a fantastic night …'

'Hey, it's not over yet,' jeered Seamus giddily.

'Ha ha ha, Seamus, no it's not, we still have the sponge cake to come…' he said laughing. Everyone joined in, even Emma who had no idea she was the butt of the joke.

'Anyway,' he continued, 'what better way than to spend an evening with good friends,' he lifted his glass to Emma, 'family,' he tilted his glass to Conor, 'and last but not least to the people who make our lives extra special!' finally tilting his glass to Michael.

'Hear, hear.' They all lifted their glasses.

Seamus piped up a bit confused, 'So are you two queer now?'

'Dad!' Emma scolded severely.

'Yes, we are 'queer', Seamus.' Jack said, happily.

'Well, isn't that a good one and you the gigolo of the village,' he laughed.

'Anyway,' Joan interrupted, 'we can do better than that, can't we, Seamus?'

'Huh, oh yeah,' he said lifting his glass again, 'to second chances …'

'Come again?' Emma asked.

'I'm moving back to where I belong!' he smiled.

'But what about you two being separated?' Emma quizzed.

'Like he said, love,' Joan said, putting her hand on Seamus', 'he's coming home to where he belongs.'

'Oh, that's great, you guys!' Siobhan cheered and the others all joined in.

Emma got up and hugged them both tightly. She had tears in her eyes but they were more from the empty pit inside. It was all working out for everyone around her. Not that she begrudged them one little bit though, she was genuinely delighted that her parents had sorted themselves out!

Now that everyone was sharing their news, she felt it was as good a time as any to say a few words herself.

'Amy, sweetheart, why don't you go up to your room and get the picture you were drawing today?' Amy got down off the chair and ran off.

'I want to say something myself actually. I know I've been hard to live with the past few months. And I'm sorry, I guess I couldn't let go, it was so incredible to feel that I didn't have to. You know, thinking that he was around me was so comforting, so amazing, even a slight flicker from a bulb made my day! But I know you've all been worried about me and I'm really sorry for putting you all through that. I know you all thought I was going crazy but it just felt so, so real I guess! But I accept that I needed help and I needed to let go. So, I'm no longer mad!' she laughed, raising her wine glass.

'Ah love, nobody thought you were gone mad!' they all muttered, embarrassed.

'Yes, you did,' Emma jokingly accused, 'and let's face it, I was acting pretty crazy so I don't blame you. But how and ever, it's good to have you all here around me and even though I may not have appreciated it at the time, I do really appreciate how much you all care about me!'

'Even if you are stone flipping mad!' joked Tracy.

They giggled and clinked glasses again. Amy came running back into the room all excited to showcase her artwork. She handed it over to Emma proudly.

'Ah thanks, honey. I've been so looking forward to seeing this masterpiece all day. You were you up in your room for ages drawing this, weren't you?' Emma kindly said.

'Yeah,' Amy grinned proudly as everyone around the table made the appropriate noises over it to satisfy her creative ego!
Emma's smile faded as she examined the picture more closely.

'Honey, who is that in the picture?'

'Silly Mammy!' Amy tittered. She climbed onto her mother's lap and began to explain her drawings. Everyone turned serious at the sight of Emma's face visibly turning pale, 'that's you, that's me, and that's daddy!'

Everyone made the appropriate noises again.

'Oh, that's lovely Amy, that's fabulous. Did you draw that all by yourself?' They all looked at each other, clueless as to why Emma had become frozen.

'But Daddy has black hair, darling,' Emma said, pointing to the matchstick man in the drawing with lots of silver hair.

'Oh, Mammy, you're so silly,' Amy giggled, 'Daddy has silver hair, he only coloured it black with markers but it's silver again now!'

Everyone went dead silent. Everyone knew that Aidan's hair was as grey as a badger but he was so self-conscious about he used to dye it jet black. They all glanced at the pictures around the room. Yep, all the pictures were of Aidan with black hair!

'How do you know that darling?' Emma whispered, her heart in her mouth.

'Because it's always silver when he talks to me.'

Everyone gasped!

'Daddy talks to you?' Emma asked, tears in her eyes.

'Yeah, Mammy, he comes down from Evenses and says he loves me.'

Emma flung her hand to her mouth and started crying little but definite sobs.

'He loves Evenses too though, I think.'

'Really?'

'Yeah, but I think he has to come all the way back here to check on you all the time! Why do you need him to check on you, Mammy?'

'I just miss him, I guess.'

'Yeah, he misses you too but I think he wants to stay in Evenses now, Mammy, because you said bye bye so he can rest now! It must be a long way from Evenses to our house, Mammy! He must not really get much sleep when he is travelling through the sky all the time.'

Emma's tears were falling as Amy spoke so candidly.

'He said he loves Mammy and he said he loves me too, all the way to the moon and back. He's happy that you can say goodbye now and he's going to have a big rest. Is that alright with you, Mammy? Sure, can't you see him when you go on to Evenses?'

'Yes, yes, I will, please God!' Emma laughed then cried even more.

'Ah, Mammy, don't be sad, please. I don't want you to be sad anymore, that's why I drawed you the picture!' she claimed profusely.

'I'm not sad, honey,' Emma whispered through soft falling tears, holding onto Amy tightly, squeezing her, 'I'm happy, I'm so happy!'

Nobody knew what to say. Tracy began to slyly look around the room, half expecting to see an apparition. Siobhan and Jack just looked at one another, completely dumfounded. Joan and Seamus clutched hands but had no clue what to say and Michael sat uncomfortably as shivers ran down his back. Conor looked on as Emma cried into Amy's hair, still holding onto her daughter closely. He knew she was not only crying because Amy had seen Aidan too but also because she was vindicated. No more claims of madness. That in itself was a colossal reprieve for Emma! He was sure the picture was no coincidence. Aidan had reached out to Emma, to uphold her sanity when everyone around her doubted it.

Joan began to weep silently. 'I'm sorry, I'm so sorry!' she wept, 'I'm so sorry, love, I've let you down. You must've been so hurt and disappointed in me.'

Siobhan opened her mouth to apologise when Emma eventually

looked up from her embrace with Amy, her face all blotchy.

'Ssshhh, don't be sorry, anybody. I know you all had my best interests at heart. You helped me let go, he can rest easy now, and so can I, we can both be at peace now.' She moved back her chair, lifted Amy under her arms and stood up. Amy proudly clung onto her neck and wore a bright smile across her face. Emma picked up her glass and toasted. 'To miracles!'

Everybody immediately stood and grabbed their glasses 'To miracles!' they echoed. Emma felt a heavy weight being lifted from her and it felt almost spiritual. 'Thank you, Aidan,' she said under her breath, 'thank you!'

CHAPTER FORTY SEVEN

The night passed in a warm wonderful atmosphere. At least until Emma brought out her cake. All of a sudden, there were panic stricken faces all around.

'Now everyone, a nice slice of homemade sponge cake with butter icing and cream on the way. Just the thing to finish off a lovely meal, eh.' she delighted in saying as she sawed through the rock on the table.

'Oh, I'm stuffed, seriously love!' Joan was quick to get in with her excuses but they were just as quickly disputed.

'Nonsense, Ma, sure you have to have a bit, this is one of your recipes!' Joan looked at it, stunned, 'really?'

'Yeah, now it might not taste as nice as yours but it's your recipe, so I'm sure it's lovely.' Emma grinned, sawing out pieces for everyone. The slices landed on the plates with a thud.

Tracy and Siobhan looked at each other, trying not to laugh. But they looked grateful when handed their piece.

'Now, I do admit I was a bit all over the place today when I was baking it, so it may be a little overdone but I'm sure it's grand.' Emma explained quiet calmly.

'Mmmm, it's delicious!' commented Conor as he crunched through his mouthful. Michael busied himself checking one of his back teeth, he was sure he had broken a bit when he bit down on the sponge.

'Can I have some more cream, please?' asked Seamus, thinking that if he absolutely drowned his piece in cream, it would have to soak into it a little and make it a small bit more edible.

'Of course, Dad.' Emma went into the kitchen to fetch the cream. Everyone started looking around frantically for places to hide their cake. Jack crumbled his into smaller pieces and flung them onto Michael and Alex's plate to their dismay. It was too late for them to fling it back as Emma came waltzing back in with a bowl full of cream.

'Oh, Jack, you're finished already. Here, I'll cut you another slice!' she said, delighted to see his empty plate. They all burst out laughing at Jack but Emma was too busy carving to notice what they were laughing at.

'Oh, this bit might have got a little bit more overdone than the last piece, Jack, but it's still nice anyway. Here, I'll give you a nice big slice seeing as you liked it so much.'

Tracy pointed at him with her fork and laughed out loud. Emma stopped what she was doing and gave her daggers. Ooops, thought Tracy, before she decided it would be very clever to change the subject before she had the monstrosity of the rock cake thrown at her.

'So, Alex, were you away during the week?' she asked casually.

'No, why?' he replied.

'Oh, no reason, I just thought I saw you at the airport, that's all!' she replied innocently.

Siobhan nearly choked on the charcoal sponge in her mouth. 'What did you say?!' she asked Tracy with furrowed brows.

'Oh I thought I saw Alex at the airport yesterday, but obviously I was mistaken. I was dropping my....'

'Were you at the airport yesterday?' Siobhan cut Tracy off, clearly not interested in who she was dropping off. Even Emma, who wasn't even sitting beside Alex, could sense him seize up. The look of dread on his face was enough to tell that Tracy hadn't been mistaken.

'Were you at the airport yesterday?' she asked him again, more forcefully this time. Her whole world hung on his answer.

'Let's talk about this when we go home, We don't want to ruin Emma's night.' he said politically, trying to minimise damage control before it even happened. He was relieved when she didn't seem to argue with him but his mind was doing somersaults as to how to get out of this one.

'Anyway, I was dropping off my little sister, Lucy. Emma, you've met Lucy, haven't you?' she asked, completely unaware of the tension building between Alex and Siobhan.

'Oh, yeah, she's lovely. Where's she jetting off to this time?'

The sound of Siobhan stabbing her piece of cake and smashing the fork against the plate made everyone slightly nervous. Amy laughed as a piece went flying off the plate and bounced across the table.

Siobhan was doing her best to simmer her boiling blood. Her colleagues had told her that Julie was back home visiting her parents last week for a few days. She hadn't told Alex that Julie was around because she thought it would be really hard on him. But now, it seems he already knew!

'Thailand,' answered Tracy, trying desperately to ignore the tumbling food and the sour look on Siobhan's face.

'Oh, lucky thing, I'd love to go to Thailand!' chorused Jack and Michael at the very same time. Then they looked at each other in awe of their perfectly synchronised statements.

Siobhan put her fork down on her plate with a clatter. Oh crap, thought Emma.

'No, actually, Alex, let's talk about this now! Did you go to the airport yesterday?' she scowled.

'Siobhan, come on, let's talk about this at home.'

'Answer the question, did you go to the airport?' she demanded.

'Yes,' he muttered finally, 'but you have to understand …'

'Were you with her?' she demanded again, as everyone fell silent with their eyes down on their plates.

'Siobhan, please, not here.'

'Why? Are you afraid they'll find out that you got another woman half your age pregnant? And that I offered you an easy way out of this marriage, to walk away with all your stashed-away cash, free to play mammies and daddies with your little trollop. But, no, you fell at my knees and begged forgiveness and swore to me that I was all you wanted?'

Alex stared at her, mortified.

'How long have you been in contact?' Siobhan continued.

He didn't answer. He didn't know what to say.

'Tell me, tell me now Alex or I swear I'll...?' she spat out.

'A while?' he eventually shouted back under the pressure.

Siobhan sat, stony faced for another few seconds. Everybody was still busy examining the charcoal crumbs on their plates. She stood up eventually and asked Alex to follow her into the kitchen.

As soon as they were gone, everyone let out their breaths.

'Holy cow!' whispered Tracy, 'why didn't someone kick me or something!'

'I'm sure they'll sort it out,' Emma reassured her, 'they're a strong couple.'

'Heavy stuff though!' Conor joined in and they all nodded in agreement.

In Emma's kitchen, Alex and Siobhan faced off across all the dirty dishes.

'So I'm not enough for you?'

'I'm so sorry, I really am, but I had to be part of my son's life!'

'Son?'

'Yeah, it's a boy. But I swear to you it's nothing to do with Julie, I just need to be able to...'

'Were you going to tell me?' she cut across him sharply.

He said nothing. And that in itself that said it all.

'You looked me in the eye, Alex! You looked me in the eye and you told me I was what you wanted, that I was enough for you! I thought our marriage meant something! But you chased after her and your....your son, also to add insult to injury, you did it behind my back!'

'Let's not get into the whole issue of doing things behind each other's back, shall we not, Siobhan, because you're not exactly the innocent party there either, are you?'

'Well, at least I didn't go and have sex with the next person I laid my eyes on!'

They glared furiously at each other.

'Oh Alex,' Siobhan said, as if she had just discovered something new, 'we're never going to get past all this, are we?'

'No.' He looked at her sadly, tears filling his eyes, 'I need to go to Liverpool, I need to know my child!'

They stood for what seemed like forever, starring at one another. No fight left, no energy left.

'I'll move out first thing in the morning,' he eventually said, breaking the silence.

'I'll stay here tonight,' she replied woefully.

He crossed the short distance between them and kissed her on the forehead. Tears fell simultaneously from their eyes, drenching their cheeks. He walked away from her for one last and final time. He passed the beautifully lit dining room and just walked out the front door. Too upset to face the others.

Emma heard the front door close and knew it was the sound of a door closing on Siobhan and Alex's marriage for good.

Siobhan was sobbing her heart out when Emma and Jack rushed into the kitchen. Without saying a word, they both wrapped their arms around her and held her tightly. Eventually they untangled and smiled at each other lovingly.

'Could be worse!' Emma announced.

'Yeah? How?' quizzed Siobhan, intrigued despite her heartbreak.

'Yeah, there could be no cake left but, luckily enough, there's quite a lot left. And I think we could do with some more, eh.'

Jack looked at Siobhan, distress written all over his face. 'Oh no,' he said, 'she's right, there is!'

Emma placed her hands on her hips and frowned with a mix of confusion and anger but Siobhan just burst out laughing. Which set Emma off laughing too. 'Okay, it was a bit of a disaster this time, I suppose.' she reluctantly agreed.

'This time?' Jack and Siobhan said in unison, before breaking into a fit of hearty laughter. Jack grabbed the two of them again and kissed both their foreheads.

'Come on women,' he said, 'if we can get through everything that life has thrown at us in the last year even, then I'm sure we can get through anything. So let's go tackle this flipping cake.'

THE END

ABOUT THE AUTHOR

Carina McEvoy lives in the South East of Ireland with her husband and two daughters. Thinking life as a stay at home mother would be pure luxury, she took a career break from teaching. However her bubble soon burst when she became a full time taxi, chef, environmental hygienist, medical practitioner, counsellor, peace negotiator, dietician and general slave to her extremely busy seven and four year old! But she wouldn't have it any other way.

She is also extremely passionate about promoting positive mental health and dreams of a society where the stigma of mental health is extinct. She writes for an honest, open yet sometimes quite humourous blog *The Anxious Banana*.

In between her jobs listed above, she can found either writing or stuck in a good book! She is currently working on her second novel.

Lightning Source UK Ltd.
Milton Keynes UK
UKOW01f1106280816

281552UK00002B/42/P